Head tucked do
eye contact with anyc
and crashed headlong into someone who shouldn't have been there. The impact was so unexpected and so solid, I lost my balance and would've fallen if the obstacle hadn't reached out a strong hand and grabbed my arm.

"Are you okay?" the low, anxious voice asked.

No! I'm mortified! I wanted to scream. "Yes, yes. I'm fine. So sorry." I brushed away his concern and his hand, too embarrassed to actually look at him as I hurried away. My cheeks were on fire. I prayed for the ground to open up and swallow me, but it didn't.

When I'd put enough distance between us, I chanced a look over my shoulder, and groaned when I saw him still staring after me. "Of course, he's Adonis personified. Just my luck." I was too far away to read his expression. Probably wondering how I'd escaped from my straight jacket. Finally, he reached down and picked up the notebook he'd dropped when I crashed into him, and turned back to the cluster of students standing beside a bike rack. Hopefully, I'd never see him again.

Red Curtains

by

Leanna Sain

A G.R.I.T.S. Novel

Enjoy your GRITS
(and tell your friends)
Leanna Sain

This is a work of fiction. Names, characters, places, and incidents are either the product of the author's imagination or are used fictitiously, and any resemblance to actual persons living or dead, business establishments, events, or locales, is entirely coincidental.

Red Curtains

COPYRIGHT © 2016 by Leanna Sain

Contact Information: info@thewildrosepress.com

Cover Art by *RJ Morris*

The Wild Rose Press, Inc.
PO Box 708
Adams Basin, NY 14410-0708
Visit us at www.thewildrosepress.com

Publishing History
First Mainstream Mystery Edition, 2016
Print ISBN 978-1-5092-1010-7
Digital ISBN 978-1-5092-1011-4

A G.R.I.T.S. Novel
Published in the United States of America

Dedication

This book is dedicated to my writing group,
Weavers of Words (aka—WOW):
Ann, Carol, Karin and Judy.
I love you all.

Acknowledgments

I'd like to thank my husband for his support and encouragement in my writing. If it weren't for him this book probably wouldn't have ever been written. It was his brilliant suggestion that landed us in Savannah, GA (one of my new favorite places) for our 26th anniversary, which is where I saw "Lily" and the seed of this story sprouted.

Thanks to my readers for their patience in waiting for my books (sorry it takes so long) and their enthusiastic response when each one is finally released.

Thanks to the great folks at TWRP, and my wonderful editor, Ally. It was worth the wait to have finally found you. Here's hoping it's a "happily ever after" situation.

Most importantly, I thank God for giving me another story to tell and the words to tell it.

Dear Readers,

Get ready to enjoy your first "bowl" of GRITS. Confused? Let me explain. I'm not talking about "stone-ground dried hominy, slow-cooked in water or milk and served piping hot with a pat or two of butter." No, in this case I'm referring to the acronym for: *Girls-Raised-In-The-South.* As is the case with each of my novels (except *WISH*), I create main characters who are strong, creative, successful Southern women—GRITS, if you will. No, they're not perfect, but they grow and overcome some pretty big obstacles, coming out stronger and more confident at the end. I didn't really *plan* a series; it sort of just happened that way. Personally, I think the *characters* wanted the series even more than I did. I had no choice but to give in and let them have their way.

In this book, I'll take you to my new favorite place…Savannah, Georgia. I discovered this wonderful historically rich city a few years ago when my husband and I celebrated our anniversary there, and I fell in love with it. Researching this novel was pure joy. I love history, and that's something Savannah practically oozes.

Unfortunately, Savannah is plagued with the same problem facing so many cities today: homelessness. Researching those kinds of statistics was heartbreaking and made me wonder what I could do to help. One thing is to make people more aware of the problem by writing about it, but even more than that, I've decided to donate a percentage of *Red Curtains*' sales to the *Stand Down* program that I mention in the story. It may just be a drop in the bucket of what's needed, but I'm sure every little bit will help. Who knows, maybe reading about it will encourage others to help in some small way, too.

I alternate points of view between Cleo, Jonas, and Lily. Each chapter will tell you from whose eyes we're viewing the story.

So here's your "bowl" of GRITS. Pull up a chair, dig in and enjoy!

Blessings,
Leanna

Chapter One

Cleo

RRRRIINNGGG.

The jangling bell sent a jolt of adrenalin through the entire classroom, turning glazed-over zombies into explosions of energy.

"Happy holidays," Dr. Hudson shouted over the sudden melee.

Laptops snapped closed, backpacks zipped, and bits of conversation and laughter fluttered around me like confetti.

"Who you gonna use for the project?"

"Oh, I've had that lined up since he first assigned—"

"—easy "A." Using my sister's kid. Hey, hand me that paper, will you? They're getting her a puppy for Christmas. I'll get extra points for sheer cuteness."

"—got it covered. Don't forget. Moon River tonight."

"Right. See you there."

"—no, the parents have booked another cruise. Jamaica, this time. I'll use someone on the ship for a model."

"Lucky dog! We never go anywhere."

"Gotta jet. One more exam—"

"D'you see it?" The gruff, male voice asked right

behind me.

"You mean the sweater?"

My ears perked up. Sweater? Were they talking about—?

A low growl of laughter followed. "Did I? What do you think has kept me awake for the last hour?"

"Yeah…Santa's little helper." Another suggestive laugh. "She can sit it my lap anytime she wants."

Yep. That's who I *thought* they were talking about. Ellie Hampton…my nemesis. From the time she strutted into class wearing four-inch heels, a tiny leather skirt, and a skin-tight crimson sweater edged with fake white fur and a neckline cut clear down to *there*, the Y-chromosomal half of class had spent the entire hour gawking at that indecent amount of flesh she was exposing. How very Christmas-y. Like the guy said, she was a regular "Santa's little helper." The Playboy bunny version, that is.

As if she could hear my thoughts, she turned, gave me a wink, and blew a mocking kiss in my general direction before surging forward, elbowing her way through the crowd to reach her latest conquest. With a sick feeling, I watched her link her arm through his and press against him, an action that sent twin mounds of flesh oozing up, and nearly overflowing her neckline. The guy's tongue was practically hanging out of his mouth. I was afraid he'd trip on it.

Stupid, stupid, stupid. I shook my head in disgust. No time to worry about him, though. The last student just exited the classroom.

I grabbed my backpack, and stumbled toward my teacher with what I hoped was a confident demeanor. I also hoped he couldn't hear my heart banging noisily in

2

my chest. "Dr. Hudson?"

He glanced up from his computer looking very "professor-ish" with his reading glasses perched on the end of his nose. I could see the blue light from the screen reflecting in them. "What can I do for you, Miss Davis?"

"Um…" *Don't say "um." It doesn't exude confidence, and you need to appear confident.* "It's about the assignment…the one you assigned for Christmas break?"

His eyes invited me to continue.

"Um," I croaked, fighting the urge to smack my forehead. "I'm afraid it's going to be a bit of a problem for me."

His bushy eyebrows looked like fat gray caterpillars when they rose in silent question.

"Not the paintings, themselves, sir. It's finding the model that's going to be the challenge."

The caterpillars drew together, a crease forming between them. "That shouldn't be an issue. As I told the class, you're welcome to use a friend as a model for the assignment."

I tried not to wince. "I don't have many friends, sir."

That wasn't entirely accurate. I didn't have *any* friends.

The crease deepened. "I'm sure that's not the case, but family members are also potential candidates. It doesn't matter as long as your work fits the parameters. You'll need to do four to six paintings for me using the same model for each one, and they need to tell a story. The class is Advanced Illustration, after all. I should be able to "read" your story by looking at your paintings."

3

"I know all that, but—"

"Miss Davis." His voice was suddenly stern. "You *do* realize the importance of this assignment, don't you?"

"Yes, sir."

"Tell me. I want to hear you say it."

I sighed. "The project counts fifty percent of my grade. If I fail it, I fail the course. If I fail the course, I won't graduate in May."

He nodded. "Right. Now listen to me. I've been teaching here at the Savannah College of Art and Design for thirty years, and you are one of the most talented students I've ever had. I'm expecting you to excel at this. Not just complete the assignment; *excel*. Don't let me down."

"Yes, sir," I mumbled in defeat. I'm sure he meant his words to be encouraging, but I was having a hard time seeing them that way. I turned to leave, shrugging the straps of my backpack onto my shoulders. It felt like it was filled with fifty pounds of rocks.

"Miss Davis!" Dr. Hudson called just before I reached the door.

I paused and glanced over my shoulder.

"Have a good Christmas!"

My smile felt stiff, but it was the best I could do. "You too, sir." I answered in a tone that belied the words, but he didn't seem to notice. His eyes had already returned to his computer screen. "Christmas, shmistmas," I muttered to myself as I trudged out into the hall. "I'm doomed."

I had to make a detour to the women's restroom before leaving the building. A quick glance under each stall let me know I had the place to myself. Good. I

4

wasn't up to small talk or the uncomfortable silence of ignoring someone standing at the next sink while I washed my hands. Just as I slid the latch, though, I heard the door *swish* open, and my heart sank. I wasn't alone after all. I barely stifled a disappointed groan. That would've been embarrassing. A groan wasn't a sound one wanted to hear in a public restroom.

I waited an inordinately long time, hoping whoever it was would do her thing and leave. No such luck. What the heck was she doing? Okay. No way to avoid it. I couldn't hide in the stall any longer. I'd give my hands a quick wash and make my escape.

My spirits plummeted the instant I saw who it was. Ellie. Just my luck. I should've stayed in the stall. I briefly considered stepping back and re-latching the door, but she'd already seen me. No choice now. I stepped up to the sink, and eyed the counter. It looked like an Avon lady's bag had exploded. Mascara, eyeliner, lipstick, foundation, eye-shadow…you name it, she had it piled up in front of her. My eyes met hers in the mirror. It took conscience effort to keep my eyes from drifting downward. I was afraid I'd have a front row seat to a wardrobe malfunction. Sort of like NASCAR fans waiting for a wreck to happen in a big race. Don't kid yourself. That's why they're there. Why else watch a bunch of cars circle endlessly for hours?

The amount of makeup Ellie was wearing would've lasted me a year. If she were a guy, I'd say she was readying herself for a drag queen competition. I almost offered to let her use my palette knife, but wasn't sure she'd get the jibe.

"Hi, Cleo," she chirped.

"Ellie." I hoped she'd just let me wash my hands

and go, but of course this was Ellie. There was no way that would happen.

"How many times do I have to remind you? It's *Elle*, not *Ellie*." Her eyes flashed daggers at me. "*Elle*…like the magazine."

"—like the magazine," my voice blended with hers. "Sorry, I keep forgetting," I lied, not sorry at all, and I hadn't forgotten. She'd been "Ellie" when I met her my first day at my new school, eleven years ago when I'd moved to Savannah. We'd been friends then—something I had sorely needed. Her mother was nearly as hateful as my aunt, and that made us kindred spirits…until middle school, right after her parents' divorce. That's when she'd changed, and it was more than just her name. I still remember the way she'd said it. It should've given me a clue. "Elle," she'd whispered seductively, hand on her hip. "…like the magazine, like the supermodel." Then she swept her head around so her hair cascaded over her shoulder in slow motion. True story. That's when she'd turned into a man-eating monster, someone girls avoided when possible and endured when they couldn't. I never stopped calling her Ellie, though, because I knew it made her mad. "Do you have your model lined up for Dr. Hudson's assignment?" I asked, just for something to say.

"Oh, yeah," she answered with a wicked gleam in her eyes. "Bob," she sighed. "*This* is going to be a fun project."

"Uh," I winced. "I'm not sure nude paintings are exactly what the teacher had in mind, Ellie."

"Elle!" she corrected, her voice clearly irritated. "And I didn't see that as one of the stipulations on the list he gave us, so don't worry about it."

"Whatever." Figured. Ellie went after anything male. It didn't matter the color; it didn't matter the age. Heck, it probably didn't even matter the species.

"Just making a few touch-ups before my date with Adam."

"You mean, Bob, right?"

She laughed like I'd just told the funniest joke ever. "No. Bob's my model for the assignment. My *date* is with Adam."

I clamped my lips together. *Let it go, Cleo. Just let it go.*

"Don't you just love the color of this eyeshadow?" she quipped, changing the subject. She needed to work on her segue. "This one's Frappuccino Mist, and this is Coffee Bean," she pointed at each in turn with the applicator. "I watched a YouTube video that shows exactly how to get this sultry effect. I think I've nailed it, don't you? You know Adam, right? Oh…maybe you don't. I'd introduce you, but you're not his type. He's more into the "bend and snap" kind of girl."

Good to know. I was back to trying to ignore her, hoping she'd take the hint and leave me alone. I scrubbed my hands, hurriedly rinsing them off.

She didn't. Take the hint, I mean.

"You know…"bend and snap?" from the movie, 'Legally Blonde'?"

Please don't demonstrate it…please don't…*please.*

"Like this." She bent over from the waist, bringing the tiny leather skirt dangerously close to revealing that which shouldn't be revealed, then she whipped back into an upright position, thrusting her Dolly Parton-like breasts forward with her hands up on either side of them, framing them, like they needed any other attention-getting device.

Then she did it again, just to make doubly sure I got it. Once she was upright, her eyes rested on my chest with a pitying expression. "I don't think that technique would work with you, though. You have to have *something* to "snap." Jeez, Cleo…I've seen adolescent *boys* who have more up top than you do," she laughed. "Have you grown *any* since we met? Maybe that's why Darren…oh, what was his last name?"

My cheeks burned. I snatched a handful of paper towels. "Townsend," I ground out through clenched teeth.

"Oh, yeah. That's right. Maybe that's why he dumped you."

Darren Townsend. Remembering the name made my blood boil. The one and only time I'd outwardly shown any interest in a guy had been during my senior year in high school. In spite of my nearly debilitating shyness, I'd worked up my courage, practicing in front of a mirror until I was finally ready to talk to him. But just as I was about to take the plunge, Hurricane Ellie swept in and poured on her charm.

"I did you a favor, you know. You should thank me." She smirked. "The guy was a loser. Did you know he dropped out of school? I heard he's living in his parents' basement, now. He's got a job sweeping floors at the Piggly-Wiggly. Squanders all he makes on lottery tickets."

"Thank you?" I choked out, outraged at her suggestion. Because of her, I'd sort of given up on the idea of dating, allowing my shyness to take control of my life. The whole ordeal might not have been so bad, but she'd dumped Darren within days. She hadn't really wanted him. She just didn't want anybody else to have him, namely me. I decided to sit back and watch her after that, observe her in action. I even kept a notebook for a while, which in retrospect sounds pathetic, but I had documented proof that she systematically pulled the same routine with every guy in school…including teachers *and* the assistant principal. She was a black widow with an insatiable appetite.

"You're welcome."

It felt like a slap. She actually thought I'd thanked her. My hand fisted around the paper towels, itching to commit bodily harm.

"You have a cute face," she went on as if nothing was wrong, studying me like a specimen under a microscope. "Nice, thick brown hair. I like the cut; bobbed off chin-level like that and pulled back with that pretty clip. The fringe of bangs. You don't wear much make-up, but with your skin and those eyes, you don't have to. Of course, that's not your real eye color. No one has turquoise eyes. Where'd you find them? The contacts, I mean."

She didn't give me a chance to answer; just kept serving a barrage of backhanded compliments. "You have a flair with clothes. Fluttery and feminine in layers. That helps hide things…or lack of things, I should say. Smart move." She winked and began gathering up her war paint, dropping the items into a zippered cosmetic bag and then tossing it into her large red leather purse.

Finally, she fluffed her hair, unloaded half a can of hairspray on it, then did that duck-lip thing that girls mistakenly think is sexy. "Adam's waiting for me.

Toodles." Flouncing out the door, she left me gasping for breath in a wake of hair product and strong perfume; her mocking laughter echoed off the tiled walls.

I unclenched my fist and threw the paper towels in the trash, then glared at my reflection. A relatively attractive, dark-haired girl glared right back at me. Mom's face; Dad's eyes…a constant reminder of parents I'd never see again. They died in a car accident when I was nine. That's when I first came to Savannah to live. Eleven years ago.

I stopped glaring and studied myself, starting with my eyes. They were my best feature. Unique…sky blue with green flecks around the pupil, giving them the turquoise appearance Ellie had mentioned. They weren't contacts and she knew it.

"What's wrong with you?" I whispered. "You're reasonably attractive. You're not weird. No dreadlocks. You're not covered with tattoos or multiple piercings like so many of your classmates. Yes, you're a "brainiac," but is getting "A's" bad? It doesn't mean there's something wrong with you, does it? Besides, with no friends, what else are you supposed to do with your time?

"You're shy…*too* shy. Of course, with "friends" like Ellie and a name like Cleo, what do you expect? Why couldn't your mother have named you something normal, like Ann or Beth or Melissa? Why did she have to be all into ancient Egyptian history and name you after Queen Cleopatra? Who *does* that to a baby? A normal name would've saved you a lot of teasing growing up." A deep sigh fogged the mirror and my reflection shrugged. "It could've been worse. She could've been into Greek mythology and named you after one of the nine muses. Just think…you could've been Erato, or Calliope, or even Urania. Cleo isn't the worst she could've picked. Besides, you've gotten past the issue with your name, mostly—"

The bathroom door *swished* open, and I jumped so hard, I think my feet actually left the tiled floor. I whirled away from the mirror and slid past the two chattering girls so I wouldn't have to speak to them.

Head tucked down so I wouldn't have to make eye contact with anyone, I barreled out of the building and crashed headlong into someone who shouldn't have been there. The impact was so unexpected and so solid, I lost my balance and would've fallen if the obstacle hadn't reached out a strong hand and grabbed my arm.

"Are you okay?" the low, anxious voice asked.

No! I'm mortified! I wanted to scream. "Yes, yes. I'm fine. So sorry." I brushed away his concern and his hand, too embarrassed to actually look at him as I hurried away. My cheeks were on fire. I prayed for the ground to open up and swallow me, but it didn't.

When I'd put enough distance between us, I chanced a look over my shoulder, and groaned when I saw him still staring after me. "Of course, he's Adonis personified. Just my luck." I was too far away to read his expression. Probably wondering how I'd escaped from my straight jacket. Finally, he reached down and picked up the notebook he'd dropped when I crashed into him, and turned back to the cluster of students standing beside a bike rack. Hopefully, I'd never see him again.

Once my cheeks cooled, I drew a deep breath, forcing myself to exhale the tension from both the Ellie encounter and the collision. The crisp December air felt just about perfect. It was the only time of year I really liked it here. Savannah doesn't have four seasons like the mountains of North Carolina, where I lived before my parents died. It's more like three…or maybe even two and a half. There are a couple of months of what *they* call winter, *I* call it fall. A *very* short spring follows, which you better enjoy because it doesn't last long. I generally used it to prepare myself for what was coming next. Summer in Savannah is hotter than Hades. If you don't drown in the humidity, you'll get eaten alive by all the insects. The only way to survive it is by staying inside or heading out to Tybee. The beach breeze makes the heat semi-tolerable and keeps the insects mostly blown away.

It was too early to head home, so which way should I go? Toward the river or toward the park? River Street would be a congested mess. Too many tourists. I needed peace and quiet if I was to figure out what to do about a model for my assignment…or lack thereof.

Right. Forsyth Park, then.

Whoops! Two old, blue-haired women, bearing fistfuls of shopping bags exited the Gryphon Tea Room right in front of me. Barely avoiding a collision, I managed to zigzag around them and keep going.

"Cleo? Is that you, dear?"

Oh, no! I recognized that warbling, sugar-sweet drawl. Myra Davis…and Nanette Holcomb was sure to be with her. I winced, then pasted on a smile and turned to face them. Yep. I was right. There they stood, looking like they'd just stepped away from a photo shoot for some fashion designer's holiday collection. The amount of gold and diamonds glittering from their ears, necks, and hands made me squint. It rivaled a jewelry store display window. They were widowed friends of my aunt. Old money. Their husbands had died in a boating accident a few years back. Rumors had flown like a swarm of bees for a while after that, especially when it was discovered that the husbands had just increased their already-huge life insurance policies. There'd been an in-depth investigation for insurance fraud, but I guess they never uncovered any wrong-doing on the women's part. I remembered overhearing my aunt telling someone they'd received boatloads of insurance money and were running around, spending it like "drunken sailors."

"Afternoon, ladies," I said, hoping I didn't have to endure them for long. "Beautiful day, isn't it?"

"My, my, my," Nanette drawled, wearing her normal sour expression. "We were just talking about you. Weren't we, Myra?"

Myra set her shopping bags on a nearby bench and tugged her bright red beret to just the right angle before answering. "Yes, we were. Not five minutes ago. I just asked Nan if she'd heard how you were getting along since Patricia passed, God rest her soul. You must be practically rattling around in that big, ol' place by yourself. Is Patricia's house-help still with you?"

"You mean Minnie and Tobias?" I gritted my teeth behind my smile. It made my blood boil when anyone referred to them as "house-help." They were all the family I had left. I doubt I would've made it this far without them "Of course, they're still there. It's their home too."

"We haven't seen you at church since your aunt's funeral, dear," Nanette deftly changed the subject.

The accusation was there…just under the surface.

These ladies were members of the same church my aunt was. The same church I vowed I'd never set foot in again.

Myra's syrupy drawl poured right over the uncomfortable moment. "You're lucky, you know."

"Lucky?" My pasted-on smile wouldn't last much longer. "How do you mean?"

"She means," Nanette interrupted. "...you're lucky you didn't end up in an orphanage, dear; lucky your aunt came to the rescue and took you in after your parents died. A lesser person might not have done the same."

I almost choked. Lucky? Lesser person? The only reason my aunt "came to the rescue," was because she was my only living relative. Both sets of my grandparents were deceased, and neither of my parents had siblings. *Ahnt* Patricia was my mother's spinster aunt, and she took me in to save face. She didn't want Savannah tongues wagging about the fact that she'd turned a blind eye toward her niece's orphaned child, but when I say she wasn't "happy" about the situation, that's very likely the biggest understatement in the history of mankind. And yes, she required me to call her "ahnt" rather than "ant," like we said in the North Carolina Mountains. The only time I ever used the pretentious word was within her earshot. I didn't have to worry about that now, though.

The fact that my mother had never wanted to visit her aunt should've been a clue to me. Shoot, Mom had never even *talked* about her, other than to briefly mention that Aunt Patricia had been her guardian. It hadn't taken me long to figure out why.

Aunt Patricia was a tyrant, pure and simple.

Silence finally penetrated my thoughts, and I panicked. How long had my sidewalk companions been quiet? Two sets of eyes stared at me; one curious, one judging. Oops. I'd obviously missed something. "Forgive me, ladies. I'm afraid I'm preoccupied with an important assignment for one of my classes. What did you say?"

Myra patted my arm. "That's fine, dear. We understand, don't we Nan?"

Nan just sniffed; obviously offended that I hadn't been hanging on her every word.

"You want to do your best in school," Myra continued. "Why, it's only natural. It's the perfect way to show your gratitude to your aunt for all she's done; you know...taking you in, raising you, paying for your college... MmMm. She's a saint, all right. You can ask anyone. They'll say the same. I know you miss her," she wagged her head back and forth wearing a mournful Bassett hound expression. "We surely do. Don't we, Nan, dear?"

"Patricia was an invaluable asset to the community," Nan intoned, sounding like a funeral director. "Every committee on which she served bears an empty hole that can never be filled half as well."

"A-men" Myra chimed in. "I still can't believe she's gone, and to be taken like that..."

"It *was* very sudden," I agreed.

"To think something as simple as the stomach flu could come in and steal her away like that...just dreadful."

It *had* been dreadful. That bug had hit half the town's population last summer, but it really did a number on Aunt Patricia. At her plumpest, she could pass for an anorexic, so the non-stop vomiting and diarrhea quickly took its toll. By the time she finally relented and let Tobias take her to the hospital, she was severely dehydrated, to the point that her body systems were actually shutting down. They tried to get fluids into her with IV's, but it was a case of "too little, too late." She slipped into a coma and never woke up.

"I heard tell they might have been able to save her if she'd just come in earlier," Myra lamented.

I nodded, not trusting myself to speak.

Her head did another Bassett hound shake. "Just dreadful."

I hoped my expression was an appropriate mask of sadness, and didn't give away how I was really feeling. My aunt's aversion to doctors and her stubbornness is what killed her, and I didn't miss her one bit. I needed to leave before they started pushing me to join some of their stupid committees. They'd already dropped several not-so-subtle hints by way of phone calls and cards. Well, Myra had. Nanette was too busy looking down her nose, finding fault with one thing or another. Right now she was eyeballing my worn jeans and scuffed cowboy boots. I wasn't interested in their committees or their opinions. *At. All.* "Well. I'm sorry to have to cut our visit short, but I have an appointment, and I really need to run. It was nice seeing you ladies again." I took a couple of backward steps away from them, planning to bolt if necessary.

Nan nodded and gave me her usual stiff, judgmental smile.

"Delighted," Myra drawled. "Do let's get together for tea, soon."

"I'll check my calendar," I lied. "Bye, now."

I turned and speed-walked as fast as my boots would take me, my mind churning. Was it wrong for me to be glad Aunt Patricia was dead? My life was certainly less stressful. That was for sure. My aunt had hated me, and no, it wasn't my imagination. She hid her true feelings from everyone else under a mask of gracious gentility, portraying herself as the perfect Southern belle, but with me, the mask came off. The Jekyll and Hyde routine had made it impossible for me to explain my situation to an outsider. I'd tried...believe me. My teachers, guidance counselor, and pastor all thought I was crazy. Especially Pastor Maitland. He thought Aunt Patricia walked on water, but he *would*. Look at how much she gave to the church.

It wasn't just him, though. Every single person with whom my aunt came in contact thought she was the greatest thing since sliced bread; that the Savannah city planners needed to put their heads together and figure out how to add a twenty-third square so the great Patricia Davenport could have a larger-than-life sized statue put up in her honor.

So what was wrong with me? Why was it me she hated? I'd done nothing. She had treated me that way from the moment we met. *Something* made Aunt Patricia look at me through glasses tinted with a secret sin from the past. It colored her opinion of me and painted a big red letter across my chest. At least poor Hester Prynne knew what her letter stood for. Something I couldn't say for myself.

I paused in front of a shop window, glancing over my shoulder to make sure the women weren't watching me, and turned back to study my reflection, almost expecting to see a red graffiti-like image scrawled across my torso, but there was nothing.

I repeat...*nothing*.

"Ellie is right," I whispered. "You *do* look more like a boy. All the fluttery layers of lace and femininity in the world can't hide what isn't there. Even a Wonder Bra has to have something to work with, right?"

Poor body image...that's what the experts call it. That's the biggest reason I was so shy. Of course, losing everything familiar as a young girl in one fell swoop—parents, home, and friends—didn't help, but people get over stuff like that. However, when you're a girl, but you look more like your Dad than your Mom in the boob department, it isn't something easily gotten over.

I turned away from my reflection in disgust and headed for the corner of Gaston and Bull Streets. At the other end of the crosswalk was an entrance to the park. I could just catch glimpses of the Fountain through the trees. There was nothing I could do about some of my problems, but maybe, just maybe I'd find a model for my project. I was due some luck

This was probably my millionth time visiting Forsyth Park. From the very start, it was my favorite place in Savannah—an escape of sorts—ever since I first moved here. Sometimes I brought my painting paraphernalia, sometimes I didn't. This was a "without" day.

Once I reached the Fountain, I closed my eyes and drew a deep breath, hoping to exhale the stress that had my shoulders as taut as a piano string. Pine tingled my nose and my eyes popped open to discover the source since I knew there weren't any pine trees in the park. It was the garland. Someone had trimmed the wrought iron railing that circled the fountain with the real deal, not the usual plastic stuff. Real evergreen and red velvet bows. It not only *looked* like Christmas, it *smelled* like it too. Holiday music wafted in the same breeze that misted my skin from the fountain's spray. Afternoon sunshine tinseled everything it touched. The fountain's tritons and swans fluted arcs of molten gold into the December air.

Ahhh. I could feel myself relax. Watching moving water always did that to me, same as watching flames in a fireplace. It was more than just seeing it, though. Sound played almost as big a role as sight, providing a steady white noise that guaranteed a coma-like condition.

"Mommy, look at that lady!"

The shrill cry of a young child broke through my hypnotic state, and I turned in curiosity.

Her long, dark overcoat nearly dragged the ground, hanging open in the front, revealing multiple layers of faded clothing in various plaids, stripes, and florals. Her feet scuffed along in men's work boots several sizes too large. Their long laces had been pulled extra tight, cinching the tops of her boots, and looked cutting-off-circulation painful. It was probably the only way she could keep them on.

She pushed along a squeaky two-wheeled metal cart, mounded with plastic bags that probably held all her worldly possessions. She was one of Savannah's homeless. Not a good thing to be in any situation, and especially not *now*, with how they kept finding them in the river. Unfortunately, they were a common sight and mostly overlooked, but no one could overlook this person…not wearing that hat.

I'd seen hats similar to this before…on a court jester in a medieval play, on clowns, in pictures of the Mardi Gras parade in New Orleans, but never those colors. Think vivid. Vibrant. Think eye-poppingly, heart-stoppingly bright! Think of the boldest pink you can imagine paired up with a neon green so blinding that it makes you squint. Add little silver bells on each dangly tail, and you'd have to agree that this woman would *never* blend into a crowd.

I couldn't help it. I gawked, but I wasn't alone. I tore my eyes away just so I could glance around for a second, and felt a grin spread across my face. There wasn't a single person in the vicinity who wasn't staring right along with me.

"What's she doing, Mommy?"

The child was asking the same question the rest of us were.

The old woman shuffled up to a huge sycamore tree whose gnarled roots were trying to push through the sidewalk's edge and leaned forward until her nose pressed against its mottled, peeling surface, eyes closed, lips moving. Was she praying? Communing with nature? Casting a spell? I was too far away to hear. I needed to get closer.

Hurrying forward a few steps, I maneuvered through the crowd of people who had paused to enjoy the spectacle. Just as I got a good position, she reached inside her overcoat and pulled out a black, sequined drawstring bag. It looked like it was attached to the belt at her waist. She slowly opened it, reached in, and then made a big production of pulling her hand out, elaborately sprinkling some of the contents at the base of the tree.

"Is that magic dust, Mommy? Is she a witch?"

"Shut up, kid," someone other than the child's mother urged, garnering an outraged look from Mommy, but nothing else. We were all waiting for what would come next.

When the sprinkling ceremony was done, the old lady simply drew the bag closed, dropped it back under her coat, and shuffled on down the sidewalk as if nothing unusual had happened. The squeaking wheels of her metal cart faded as she moved farther away.

The crowd dispersed with quite a bit of murmuring, going back to whatever they'd been doing before the woman's performance. There's one thing you can say for Savannahians...it's easy to *grab* their attention, but difficult to *keep* it.

But this, even I was curious about. I had to see what she sprinkled around that tree.

There—glistening in the afternoon sun like a galaxy of tiny stars dusted over the tree's mammoth roots—was glitter.

I stared at it for a long moment before glancing up, searching through the crowd for that hat. I caught a flash of pink and green just as she was exiting the park and breathed a sigh of relief.

The weight that I'd carried on my shoulder into the park was suddenly floating away. I'd found my model.

Now all I had to do was convince her.

Chapter Two

Jonas

"I'm fine, Mom." I tried to stifle my exasperation while my hand clutched the phone receiver a little tighter. I flung my head against the back of the couch, and rolled my eyes so far back I could practically see the occipital lobe of my brain. "You've got to stop worrying so much."

"I know, Jonas, but you're the only one of my kids not living a block or so away from me and I want to make sure you're okay. Especially today since—"

"Yes, I'm well aware of the significance of the day," I cut her off. I didn't need to rehash this with her. "It was three years ago, Mom. I'm over it." I tried switching subjects. "And it's not like I'm living on the other side of the world. Savannah *isn't* that far from Charleston, you know."

"But honey, if you're over it, then why—"

"Mom!" She was like a dog gnawing a bone. Once she got her teeth into something, it was almost impossible to get it away from her.

"Okay, okay. I'll stop. I just wish you'd find someone special, someone to help you forget about Jill. It's too bad it didn't work out with your sister's friend, Maggie."

"The timing was all wrong. I was a mess, and so

was she…still hung up on some guy named Thomas. Besides, I thought you said her dad was too weird."

"He *is* weird. Both of her parents are. Don't get me wrong, I'm all for being proud of your heritage, but they take it past the healthy stage. It's more of an obsession, I think. Your sister idolizes him, though. I'm glad Samantha got the job as his grad assistant, but I'm afraid the man's going to turn her into as much of a Civil War junkie as he is."

"Sam loves her job, Mom, and Dr. Poinsett is lucky to have her."

"Stop trying to change the subject."

"What do you mean?" I hedged. I *was* trying to change the subject. "By the way, why don't you interfere in Sam's love life? She's just as single as I am."

"What makes you think I don't?" she laughed. "But to answer your question…you're a man, and every man needs a good woman to keep him in line."

"And *that* wasn't a sexist comment at all."

She ignored me. "All your brothers have good wives and—"

"—and successful jobs," I interrupted. "That's what you were going to say, isn't it?"

"Now honey, I'm not saying journalism isn't a good job. I just wish they were paying you what you're worth. At least enough so that you could live somewhere besides—"

"Please don't start on my apartment again. I know it's not great, but I'm not here that much, so it doesn't even matter."

"I know, but if you'd just let your father and me help you a little—"

"No, Mom. Dad understands. I think he's proud of me for what I'm doing too; standing on my own two feet like this. My apartment's not a mansion, but it's something I can afford...*without* your help. I actually kind of like it. It's so small, it's a cinch to keep clean, and with only one room, I don't have to walk far. Three steps in any direction and *boom*...I'm there."

Her sigh was audible over the phone. "I just want you to be happy, and if writing for that newspaper does that, then I guess I'm happy for you. But back to Maggie—"

I was glad she couldn't see me roll my eyes. She hated it when I did that. "Mom—"

"Hear me out. Don't you think it's worth trying again? Maybe you guys were just having a bad night that night."

"Sorry to dash your hopes, Mom, but there won't be another date. Not with her. You can officially take her off your list of "possibilities." She got married not too long after our disastrous evening together. Didn't Sam tell you? I know it surprised her too. It was kind of unexpected. His name's Jake and they're blissfully happy. In fact, when I was up there last week for Dad's birthday party, I ran into her at Target's. She's pregnant. *Very* pregnant. Looks like at least ten and a half months worth. All belly. If she doesn't have that baby soon, she'll burst!"

"Right. I get it," she laughed. "But I need more grandkids!"

I snorted before replying. "I think my virile brothers and their very fertile wives have taken up every bit of my slack. The whole lot of them are worse than a bunch of rabbits. They're doing such a good job of filling Charleston with a new generation of Holmes kids, I won't even need to contribute. Maybe I'll just stay single," I teased. "Jonas Holmes…career bachelor. One of those crusty old curmudgeon journalists. What d'ya think?"

"I think I'll pretend I didn't hear you say that," she laughed again. "Gotta run. Your father is giving me his "quit your meddling" look. Love you sweetheart."

"You too, Mom. Bye."

I shook my head and smiled in spite of my exasperation as I hung up the phone, and took the three steps it took to get me to my closet-sized bathroom. Mom was great. Very "mom-ish" at times, but great. She was like a mother hen, wanting all her chicks near enough so that she could gather them up underneath her wings whenever she sensed danger—which was often. I lived too far away for her to do that with me and I knew it was hard on her, so I tried to cut her some slack.

I reached into the tiny shower stall that was barely wide enough to fit my shoulders, and turned on the tap, waiting for the water to get hot before stepping in. *Ahhhh…*just the way I liked it. Almost blistering. Veils of steam swirled around me, smoking the glass door. Water pelted against my scalp and shoulders, thawing away the tension that always occurred whenever I heard Jill's name. It wasn't as bad as it used to be, but it's taken three years to get this far.

I grabbed the soap and starting scrubbing, but my mind was far away. Why was I so different from everyone else in my family? My five older brothers had followed Dad's footsteps and gone into the medical field. Each one had their own successful practices now, living the American dream with loving wives and quickly growing families, only blocks away from each other and my parents. My little sister had an apartment near her job at the College of Charleston. My mother had balked over that at first, but finally let it go because Sam threatened to move to England. Everyone knew she was joking, but it got Mom off her back. I was the only one who lived more than ten minutes away.

Had I always been different? Pretty much. At least as far back as I could remember. My brothers even jokingly referred to me as the "black sheep" of the family, not because I'd chosen an evil path, but because I'd chosen differently. While they'd all been active members of the debate team and chess club, I'd opted for sports: football, basketball, baseball, and track. As long as it pushed me, made me sweat, that's what I wanted to do.

Being in a family with seven kids wasn't the norm when I was growing up, and though it had its good points, there was a negative side too. I'd always felt like a number—the sixth Holmes boy—which was probably why I tried to be different, why I chose "arts" instead of "sciences," writing over being a doctor, and also why I jumped at the chance to work at the Savannah Tribune in an entry level position when the opportunity presented itself. Yes, my mother's friend was the editor, and yes, I shamelessly used that connection when I found out about it, but I wanted to get out of Charleston—away from being asked, "Now, which one are you?" And of course, away from the Jill debacle. It'd been a chance I couldn't pass up.

I did anything they asked at the Tribune, from fetching coffee to sorting mail. Eventually, I got a chance to show them I could write, but so far it'd been the boring stuff: car accident reports, house fires, new business openings, obituaries, or an article about the rash of bicycle thefts at SCAD; what I'd been working on today. What I really wanted—what I dreamt about—was a regular feature position, something that might even be syndicated. Due to recent events, I had an idea for a series, but I needed to get it okayed by my boss. Until then, I had to live on a pretty tight budget; something I'd become a pro at doing. Something Jill had been unwilling—

Uh-oh. The hot water was cooling. My cue to hurry. Pretty sure my water heater was about the size of a goldfish bowl. I only had seconds to finish up. I grabbed the shampoo, squirted some in my palm and quickly lathered my hair. I'd learned the hard way with this shower. When I felt that temp change, I needed to get rinsed, and out as quickly as possible. The water would go from hot to freezing in an instant.

Hah! Made it! I turned off the water, and grabbed a towel, briskly drying, before wrapping it around my waist and stepping out onto the rug. I used the hand towel to dry off the steamy mirror, and stared at my reflection. The man in the mirror gave me a wry smile, then sternly ordered, "Count your blessings, man, and don't even think about going into a funk if anyone else mentions Jill's name today. You're over it. It could have been worse, you know...you could've *married* her, had kids...*then* found out all she was after was the money."

I pulled my electric razor from the drawer, plugged it in and switched it on, buzzing my face smooth while continuing the conversation with my reflection, which took some weird mouth maneuvers and some garbled speech. "This is where you're supposed to be, buddy. Right here in Savannah. Away from Charleston. Away from your family. You need to make it on your own merit, not just the Holmes name. It's the best way."

I turned on the tap, grimacing when it coughed out rusty water. Once it ran clear, I rinsed out my razor, splashed on some aftershave, brushed my teeth. After rinsing my mouth, I made a face before gulping a big swig of the brackish liquid, then gazed at my reflection once more. "Your wisecrack to your mom about staying a bachelor was just that. You know you want to find someone. Maybe even someone like that girl who ran into you today…or *not*, but the only way you can be sure she loves you and not your family's money is by not letting her know you have it. If it takes living in this dump to pull that off, it's a good trade-off. Now, get dressed. You've got an idea to pitch to your boss."

****

My hand was poised to the right of the engraved nameplate on my boss' closed door—*Joel McMillan—Managing Editor*. I took a deep breath and rapped a knuckle against the wood. It sounded loud in the hallway.

"Come in," the gruff voice answered.

I stuck my head in. "Do you have a minute, sir?"

"Oh…sure, Holmes. Have a seat." He waved vaguely toward the only other chair in the room. "Be with you in a sec."

The man was a grizzly bear; tall and beefy, barrel chest, salt and pepper crew cut, growly voice. He made me nervous, but I've heard some of my female workmates talk about how "hot" he is. Go figure.

Seeking something to distract myself, I eyed what I

could see of the chair he'd indicated. It was buried under a small mountain of files and papers. The towering stack looked in danger of toppling with the slightest breeze or bump. I'd have to move it or else remain standing since there was nowhere else to sit. Praying the stack wouldn't collapse in a heap, I eased my fingers under the bottom, lifted it as if it were a landmine ready to detonate, and carefully placed it on the floor, making sure it was leaning slightly against one of the chair's legs for support before taking my seat.

He sat opposite me, his desk cluttered, his attention focused on whatever it was he was reading. Haphazard piles of old newspapers, binders, and post-it notes joined a half-eaten bacon, egg, and cheese biscuit from McDonalds and a nearly empty salad container from Wendy's. A couple of leaves of lettuce and a soggy crouton foundered in a puddle of dressing. Nearly every inch of the desktop was covered. Certainly no Zen-theme here. McMillan grunted, slashing a red line through a large section of copy on the paper he was reading. He was old school; clinging to the days of pen and ink while the industry rushed into cyber-space.

Finally he peered at me over the top of a pair of bifocals. "What can I do for you, Holmes?" he growled.

Here goes nothing... "Well, sir...I've been following the news lately."

One bushy eyebrow cocked up at the same time his mouth turned down on one side. "Glad to hear it, son."

I mentally knocked my head against the desk. *Gah! You're an idiot. Next time, try engaging your brain before opening your mouth.* Nervously clearing my throat, I tried again. "Yes sir. Anyway, I noticed that they just found another body in the river yesterday. Another *homeless* man," I emphasized the word, hoping to see a spark of interest in the man's eyes, but he just glanced at his watch. *Get to the point. You're losing him.* "Well, I think the paper should do an article about it...some investigative reporting on that situation, sir. This *is* the third body. I think there might be a connection between the deaths."

His eyes narrowed and he studied me carefully. "A connection?"

My heartbeat sped up. He was interested. "Yes, sir. I believe so."

"And you think this is something our readers would want to know about? Homeless men ending up in the river?"

"Yes, sir," I repeated. "Something's not...well, something's just not right. I can't really explain it. Just a feeling, I guess, but I think we should pursue it...see what comes up. What do you say?"

"Gut feeling, huh?"

"Yeah...I mean, yes, sir."

McMillan rubbed his bristly chin, reached for a coffee mug that said, "Neat people are just too lazy to look for stuff" on its side, took a sip, and made a face as he *thunked* it back down on the desk, sloshing some of the liquid on a "while you were out" memo, which he ignored. "Okay, Holmes. I had a teacher in college who told me to never ignore gut feelings. Thanks. I'll get Davidson right on it."

My heart plummeted. "D-davidson, sir?"

"Yes." His eyebrows lowered. "Something wrong?"

"No, I guess not."

"Good," he gave me a perfunctory smile, his eyes dropping back to the papers on his desk. "I need your piece on the fatal accident out on I-16—the one with the five nursing students—on my desk by noon."

I remained fidgeting in my seat. What just happened? He was giving my idea to Davidson? *Taylor Davidson?* The guy who'd been making my life hell ever since I'd started working here? No! I was *not* letting that creep have my story! Time to stand up and fight.

"Uh, sir?"

He seemed surprised I was still there. "Something else on your mind, Holmes?"

"Yeah...yes, sir." Sweat beaded on my forehead. I gripped the arms of the chair so I wouldn't wipe it off. "I was sort of hoping *I* could do it...the story, I mean. I could even do it on spec on my own time if I had to. That way you wouldn't have to pay me for it unless you like it."

He studied me for a long moment while I slowly stewed in my sweat. I'd hate to play poker with this guy. His expression gave nothing away.

Finally, his lips twitched in the barest hint of a smile. "Okay. You got the green light, son. On the clock. Show me what you can do."

I did it! Snaked it right out of Davidson's hands, too. This must be what Superman feels like. Invincible. Able to leap tall buildings in a single bound. My boss had just handed me the world's greatest gift: a chance. It was up to me to shine, to show him and my family that I was a real writer, not just some hack, typing out boring drivel that no one even read.

The exhilaration was a lot to absorb. I floated down

the hall to my cubicle and sank into my desk chair—a supposedly ergonomically correct one, according to the memo they'd sent out. It didn't feel any different than any other chair to me, though. I tilted back in it and stared at my silent computer screen saver; a cartoon little man aimlessly wandered around his tiny cartoon island. It usually had sound, but I'd had to mute the volume several weeks back because of dumb ol' Davidson, in the next cubicle over. Seems Mr. High-and-Mighty complained about the character's whistling. Claimed he couldn't write because it "broke his concentration." Yeah, right. I'd like to break more than his concentration. Always on my case about something. If he couldn't find anything legitimate to complain about, he'd send me for coffee and then gripe about it.

"How many times do I have to tell you? *Three* creams, *two* sugars, Holmes," he'd say. "I could train a monkey to get it right!"

I wanted to yell, *Get your own coffee. Then, if it's wrong, you have no one to blame but yourself.* If he'd drink it black—like a man—instead of all girly with all the creams and sugars, it wouldn't be a big deal. I couldn't say anything, though. He claimed to be buddy-buddy with the boss. I couldn't take that chance, but it was hard. I had to bite my tongue sometimes. Hmmm. Maybe they weren't as "tight" as he claimed. I was able to change McMillan's mind, wasn't I? He'd given *me* the go-ahead, not Davidson. The thought made me smile. Even so, it was probably in my best interest to try to stay on Davidson's good side. There was a reason for the adage, "last one hired; first one fired."

"Holmes!"

Speak of the devil. "Yes?"

Silence.

Ha! I'd surprised him. I usually jumped when he called. "You're late," he complained, his voice sounding disgruntled. "Guess I'm gonna have to mention this to Joel."

"Oh, don't bother. He knows," I replied, making my voice sound light and airy. "That's who I was with. We had a meeting this morning."

Silence, again. Two in a row. I grinned, checking the childish desire to peek over the wall that separated our desks. I wished I could see his face.

A whisper of sound came, then Taylor strolled around the partition and leaned against the doorjamb, studying his cuticles. "Meeting, huh. What about?"

"Pitched him an idea for a story."

He looked up, and gave me a pitying smile. "Aww...shot you down, didn't he? Don't feel bad, Holmes. Happens to the best of us."

Acting as if I were hard at work on something that needed to be done yesterday, I started typing the lyrics to "The Battle Hymn of the Republic" at hyper-drive speed. My fingers flew over the keyboard. Han Solo's Millennium Falcon couldn't have kept up. I paused at the end of the second stanza and glanced up. "What d'ya mean, bad? He gave me the green light. I'm doing the story."

I'd have given a million bucks for a photo of the look on his face.

"Oh." For someone who made his living with words, he seemed woefully at a loss. After several seconds, he finally added, "Well, you seem busy. I'll leave you with it." Without another sound, he spun around and headed back to his office.

I bit my lip to keep from laughing out loud. Suddenly, all the weeks of verbal abuse I had endured since being there floated away.

I kept my fingers tappity-tapping, but my mind outpaced them. This story was going to open doors for me, take me to heights I could only dream about. Maybe I'd even write a book…sign with one of the big publishers. My name would be as commonplace as John Grisham, Tom Clancy, Stephen King. First the book, then Hollywood would be clamoring to turn it into a movie.

But how? A little voice inside me whispered, and my speeding fingers faltered. Although my gut was telling me that the three homeless men found floating in the river were connected, it was being very silent about where to start. Did I go to the police? Ask them? Would they even tell me anything?

Doubtful. The police tended to get their nose out of joint when they felt like the press was horning in on their investigation. I'd probably just get the run-around. They'd pass on the least possible information they could get away with, pat me on my head, and send me on my way. Right now, all I really knew was that those men had been homeless and that they'd drowned. Had it been suicide? Again, doubtful. One, yeah, but three? I guess it was possible, but not very likely. Okay, then…foul play? There'd been no buzz either way. Maybe no on knew for sure, or if they did, they weren't saying. As far as I'd heard, the authorities hadn't even been able to notify next of kin because the men hadn't been carrying ID. Apparently, no one knew who these guys were. They'd died without identities, no one to mourn their passing. The thought depressed me.

No! Someone *had* to know who they were. They must've had some friends, some other homeless guys they hung around with…

Yes! That was it! I'd sleuth around town and interview other homeless people. Surely, one of them could shed some light on what had happened to these guys. At the very least, I could find out who they were, put a name on the graves.

It wasn't much, but at least I had a plan.

****

Some plan! I was ready to give up. I'd just spent the most frustrating week imaginable. I'd had no idea how tightlipped and unapproachable homeless people could be. Oh, some of them seemed happy to strike up a conversation, but as soon as I started asking questions, they clammed up tighter than…well…a *clam*. It was like they all belonged to some private club and I didn't know the double-secret password to get in. These people definitely looked out for each other. I guess that was both good and bad at the same time. Good for them; bad for me. I was going to have to rethink; come up with some other way to infiltrate their tight little group. That was the only way I'd ever get my story. But how?

Chapter Three

Lily

That girl's following me. She thinks I don't notice her trying to blend in with the crowd, but she's wrong. Hunh. More like sticking out like a sore thumb. Stay alert...that's the rule. She doesn't know it, 'cause she's not homeless. Stay alert...we have to live by that. If we don't, we wind up dead; like the fella they just pulled out of the river. He's the third one who didn't remember the rule. Doesn't matter if it's New York City or Mayberry; rule stays the same. Me? I'm always alert. Even at night...*especially* at night. Sometimes you see things...*bad* things. He didn't see me, though...I hope.

Why is she following me? What does she want? Doesn't look like one of the mean ones who hurt Big Jim. All that blood...mmm. They beat him up so badly, he landed in the hospital...in a *coma*. Finally got out of there, but he's not the same.

Three men in the river. Media should be all over that. Not, though. Like to sweep that sort of thing under the rug. Been keeping an eye on the papers at the library. If it's mentioned at all, it's only a sentence, maybe two, buried in the back with tire sale and palm reading ads. Not surprised. The men were homeless. Homeless people were unimportant unless it involved a cop shooting; not like the moneyed crowd.

Pfft. I know how *they* think. Three homeless men in the river meant three less nasty derelicts hanging around the squares. A person isn't important unless he has an address.

Hmph. Street person is just as much a person as someone who lives in one of those fine, fancy houses; they're just desperate. Being desperate makes him a sitting duck, ready and willing for bad people to use. Flash a little money under their nose and they'll do 'bout anything. They're willing and expendable. That's the scary truth of it.

Well, not me! I stay alert. Keep my eyes and ears open like I have for years.

I was walking past a large SUV parked beside an expired parking meter. Its mirror-like dark windows reflected an image of a wiry old woman wearing layered shabby clothes and a jester hat. Sunshine sparked off the little bells dangling at the pointy ends. The vision stopped me in my tracks.

Was that me? I looked so *old*. Made sense. I *was* old. Sixty-eight my last birthday. Forty-eight since the day my life changed…the day my sister, Rose, died.

Almost half a century and I can still remember it like it was yesterday. It had been Rose's birthday. I'd planned a party for her at her favorite Mexican restaurant, Sol y Luna. Lots of friends. Lots of laughter. Lots of doting on her, which she loved. While she said her goodbyes, I'd loaded the car with her gifts. We had just left.

"I wish you could've seen yourself in that gigantic sombrero," I said as I backed my car out of the parking space. "I didn't know they made hats that big. A family of four could live under that thing!"

"I would've liked a tiara better," she sniffed. "But it *was* a Mexican restaurant. Sombreros kind of go with the territory." Then she grinned. "I probably made even that ratty thing look good. You got pictures, didn't you? Let's stop by the drug store. They have one-hour developing there. We could kill an hour shopping and swing back by to pick them up. What do you say?"

"You're the birthday girl!"

An hour later we were back on the road with Rose flipping through the stack of photos.

"Oh, you're right! The sombrero *is* huge! I look like a mushroom," she giggled.

"You're right!" I had to agree. "But a very beautiful mushroom," I hurriedly added, not wanting to ruffle her feathers. She was touchy about things like that, even if she knew you were joking.

She shrugged as if her beauty was a given, and kept right on flipping through the stack. "Oh, here's a good one!" she held it out for me to see.

The traffic light had just turned green for us, and I was moving forward into the intersection, but I allowed myself a quick glance.

Something made me look past Rose, through the passenger side window where I had a perfect view of the big, black pick-up truck rocketing past the other stopped cars, sun glinting off the heavy chrome grille, the iconic head of a ram zooming toward us.

I stomped the gas. One thought screeched through my brain: *Move! Get out of its way!*

BLAM! It hit with the ferocity of a freight train. The world tilted. My head crashed against the side glass. A kaleidoscope of flashing lights exploded in my brain. Sensory overload. The squeal and crunch of metal folding in on metal. The scent of gasoline mixed with the smell of blood. Rose's sightless, staring eyes, her head hanging at an angle that it shouldn't be. Screaming...endless screaming which I finally realized was coming from me.

Not one detail had faded in all these years. I could still see the way my car was wrapped around the front of his like half of a metal inner tube. The front passenger seat, where Rose had been sitting was gone. There are some things wearing a seatbelt can't help.

Both the other driver and my sister had died instantly; he, from being thrown through his windshield and slamming against the side of my vehicle; Rose...well, if her neck hadn't broken, the massive body trauma would've killed her. In a way, I was glad it had been quick. At least she hadn't suffered. Why had I made it, though? I could still feel the rage and anguish and guilt that came with the knowledge that I was only one who had made it out of that crash alive.

I fisted the blur from my eyes, not really surprised at the dampness on my hand. Even after all this time, remembering brought tears.

Sniffing, I reached for my bag of glitter, grabbed a handful, and sprinkled it around the base of the expired meter before continuing down the street. Knew it made me look crazy. Part of the reason I did it. Helped with the image. Main reason, though, was because Rose told me the ghosts of Savannah liked the way it sparkled.

She should know. She was one of them.

The day after Rose's funeral, I was still reeling from survivor's guilt. That was its official name, what the doctors called it. My world had already been rocked by my recent breakup with my ex-fiancé, Michael, something I wouldn't let myself think about. Then the accident. It was too much. That was the day I gave up on God. I'd always believed that He was a God of love, and that since I was His child, He would keep bad things from happening in my life. That theory, bent by the Michael-heartbreak, got damaged beyond repair by my sister's violent death; my heart right along with it. How could God say He loved me, and let something like that happen? If that was how He showed His love, then I wanted no part of it.

Then, without any warning, Rose was standing right in front of me.

I gasped so hard, I choked, and spent the next several seconds coughing, while I scrambled crab-like across my mattress in wide-eyed terror from the very real-looking figment of my imagination. My back was soon pressed against my bedroom wall.

"Surprised to see me?" the vision laughed. "You should see your face. No, you're not crazy. You're not having a mental breakdown, either. It's me."

"Rose?" There was no way this was real "How? I saw you. You were dead. Your neck was very obviously broken."

"I'm still dead." She said the impossible words matter-of-factly. She could have been discussing the weather. "I'm a ghost…one of the thousands who wander around Savannah."

"That's just a tourism ploy. Ghosts aren't real."

She whooshed forward and pinched me.

"Ow!" I rubbed my arm and glared at her. "What was that for?"

"Did that feel real enough for you?"

****

Over the next few days, Rose helped me make the change. I no longer wanted to live the life that I'd always lived. I chose a path that would allow me to shut myself off from interaction with people, and at the same time, blend in. In a city full of eccentrics, I chose a way that my peers just couldn't accept.

I glanced at my squeaky metal cart. Rescued it from a pile of garbage sitting at the curb. It had been in multiple pieces, then. Nothing duct tape couldn't fix, though. Stuff could fix anything. Titanic would probably still be floating if they'd had it on board.

My sister had helped me find my "costume."

"No, no!" Rose exclaimed. "It's not just a matter of you pushing a cart around with your belongings in it. You have to *look* the part. Nobody will believe you, otherwise."

I eyed the ragged outfit she'd displayed across the bed like an ad for a clothing magazine, complete with accessories. "Where did you find these?"

"In the dumpster behind Goodwill," she answered happily. *Too* happily, in my opinion. "It's called dumpster diving."

"You went in a dumpster?"

"Well," she shrugged. "It's easier when you're a ghost. You can hover...not actually get *in*. This..." she waved a flash of color in the air like a banner. "...is your *pièce de résistance*; the best part of the ensemble."

"What is it?"

"Your hat." She hurried forward, and pulled it down on my head. "One of those jester hats, complete with bells." She flicked one with her perfectly manicured fingernail before turning me around to face the mirror. "See? Isn't it perfect?"

My reflection's eyes widened. "Did you get this out of the dumpster too?"

"No. This I found in the alley behind Kittens."

"The strip club?"

She nodded with a delighted smile.

I wrinkled my nose as I stared at the hat. "What kind of acts do they do in there?"

"Don't know, but their loss is your gain. Want to try on the rest of the outfit?"

****

Beep-beeeep!

The sound forced me back to the present. I'd walked right out in front of a car. My eyes met those of the angry driver who was mouthing words that were easy to understand. Hmpf. Probably a Yankee. I glanced down at his front bumper, which was only inches away from my metal cart. Yep. New York tag. Plain as day. I shook my head, which sent the little silver bells a jingling, and kept right on walking.

People thought I was crazy. I talked to Rose, and because they couldn't see her, it looked like I was talking to myself. Something a crazy person would do. Randomly blurting out quotes and sayings I'd memorized over the years—another of Rose's ideas—reinforced that opinion. Mental illness wasn't uncommon among the homeless, so I fit the mold of public opinion. I'd done reading on the subject. If a person lived on the streets long enough, he usually ends up with some kind of chemical dependency. And if he uses long enough, he develops some type of mental illness. I'd been lucky. When I talked to Rose, I just *looked* crazy. The hat just reinforced that. No sane person would wear it.

My new persona was complete. The "homeless" version of Lily Telfair-Gordon was born. People who hadn't known me before, had no problem accepting this colorful new addition in town. People who *had*...well, they just pretended they didn't know me. Like I was contagious. It wasn't the first time in the city's history that one of their own had fallen from the top to the bottom, and they didn't want to get close enough to catch it.

I stopped again to sprinkle glitter around a meter. I considered it doing my part to keep the ghosts happy. According to Rose, ghosts had mood swings. Don't ever provoke one, she said. They have good memories and they can be mean. Hold a grudge a long time. Bad thing to get them mad at you. If glitter made them happy, I'd give them glitter. Small price to pay. Had an agreement with a nearby craft store owner. Buy it in bulk at the wholesale price. Sprinkling glitter helped my "crazy" image, too. I patted the sequined bag that hung from my waist, reassured by the bulge that I still had a ready supply.

Savannah had more than its fair share of spirits. No one really knew why, but it was a proven fact. Ghost hunters and scientists—people who specialized in that sort of thing—were always around. Visited spots frequented by "haunts;" did tests and studies funded by various grants, then published their findings. Pictures and video footage, included. Didn't need all that proof, though. Had all the proof I needed. Rose had introduced me to several of her friends. The ones I could see. According to my sister, only the ghosts with strong personalities *before* their deaths could make themselves visible afterwards. Had the ability to *control* whether or not they were seen. Only a few of them could do that, which meant there were many, many more out there that you *couldn't* see. More than people realized. Ghosts everywhere. Moving among them in the streets, crowding into businesses, homes, churches, and schools throughout the historic part of the city. Freaked me out.

Good thing I had Rose to protect me.

Having a sister who was a ghost made me privy to some juicy gossip—some of it centuries old. Made me nervous at first. What might someone do to keep some of this stuff quiet? Didn't take long to realize regular folk think the homeless are invisible. Deaf and dumb, too. Why else would they say and do some of the things I'd heard and seen? Maybe it's because no one would believe a homeless person anyway. No credibility. If we tried to report a crime, the police wouldn't believe us, like there was an unwritten rule. Had to have a roof over your head to be believable. Had I acted like that before my transformation? Probably, and it made me ashamed.

Most people like me sleep beneath underpasses, or in abandoned cars, or in the woods, but I have a little place of my own. Wasn't technically "homeless," even though that's how I saw myself. My tiny, airless, fifth-floor room on Oglethorpe Street was home, at least during the short winter. Rest of the year, it was cooler sleeping outside.

I was in my room that night last week. The moon was full. Bright enough to read by. That's when the shouting started.

"Where's the bag?"

Bag? My heartbeat quickened and I hurried to the

window. The moon's silver highlights and deep shadows made the alley behind my building look like an x-ray. I could see exactly what was happening through my red curtains.

"I'm tellin' you…this is where I put it. Right here in this can!"

"Then that's where it should be, but it's not."

"Someone must've took it."

"Who'd you tell?"

"No one! I'm not an idiot."

The bigger man grabbed the front of the other's shirt, jerked him forward until they were nose to nose. "Who'd. You. Tell?"

They grappled around until I heard a muffled "pop." The smaller man fell.

I froze. Couldn't look away. The big man looked every direction, finally turned his face up to peer at the building's windows. The moon was a spotlight on his face. I gasped in recognition and instinctively stepped back, trembling behind my thin, red shield. Had he seen me? No. My room was too dark, and the moon too bright. That didn't make the fear go away, though. My heart pounded. I pressed a hand to my chest trying to calm it.

I understood part of the argument. That's what had me gnawing my bottom lip. The bag…they'd been shouting about the bag. I'd been out there the night before, digging through the neighborhood trashcans. The best time for treasure hunting is at night. I'd found a garbage bag—the heavy lawn-and-leaf kind—only a third full and knotted at the top. Heavy for its size. Made me curious. I wished I hadn't looked. Now that bag was buried in the bottom of my metal cart. A secret

I couldn't tell anyone. Tried not to think about it, but couldn't help it. I was sure it was the bag they'd argued about. Afraid it was a link to the body of the homeless man they found in the river the next day. And the one they'd found last month, and the one before that. Was someone targeting the homeless? People no one would miss?

No! I shook my head. Stop thinking that way. It wasn't linked. It couldn't be. Rose was right. I worried too much. Wish Rose were here. She'd help me out of this mood, but she was out helping sad, little Alice Riley find her baby. That's right. Think about Alice. That'll help.

Alice was one of the strong personality ghosts. She could control whether people saw her or not. She and her husband had come to America back in the 1700's as indentured servants. They'd been sent to work for a horrible man who mistreated them badly, making their lives a hell-on-earth. After a year of the abuse, life became intolerable, and they searched for a chance to escape. It came in the form of a bucket of water. While grooming their master, the husband held the man's head down in the water bucket until he drowned. Alice and her husband fled for their lives, but were caught and sentenced to death. They hanged her husband first, but when it was her turn, they discovered she was pregnant. They had to wait eight months until "justice could be served." In spite of her continual claims that she hadn't committed the crime, they carried out her sentence in Wright Square right after the baby was born. Some folks claim that she's the reason no Spanish moss grows around the spot of her death. Legend has it that moss won't grow where innocent blood has been shed.

Whether that was the case or not, I had no way of knowing, but there was definitely no moss dangling from a single tree in that square, and it was always eerily quiet...except, of course, when Alice showed up—screaming and crying—looking for her baby.

Today, Rose was busy helping her, so I would have to get myself out of this mood. The bag, the men arguing, and the homeless man in the river didn't have anything to do with each other, and if they did, I couldn't do anything about it. The identity of the man I'd seen in the moonlight made sure of that. If he was involved, then no one could be trusted. No one would believe me anyway.

"Lily Telfair-Gordon," I whispered desperately to myself. "You just keep your head down and your mouth shut."

****

Chippewa Square...where they filmed the bench scene from "Forrest Gump." Right over there Tom Hanks said his famous line about life being "like a box of chocolates." Well, not on *that* bench. Had to move the real one. Just like with the Bird Girl statue from that other movie—"Midnight in the Garden of Good and Evil." Bench and statue were nice and safe in the Savannah History Museum. Jerks couldn't steal them in there.

Raymond was on the bench now. He was homeless too. My only true friend. He sat there everyday, turning palm fronds into roses. Sold them to tourists. That's where I was headed. Good place to rest. Good place to wait and see what that girl would do, too. She was still back there, pretending to read a bronze plaque.

I wheeled my cart behind the bench and plopped

down next to my friend with a sigh. "H'lo, Raymond."

He didn't answer. He had good days and bad days. On his bad days, he just sat and scribbled in a notebook. He was working and not scribbling, so this wasn't a bad day, but maybe he just didn't feel like talking. Or maybe he sensed the girl easing toward the bench and figured he had a potential customer. Saw him reach for a new length of palm leaf and knew he was about to begin his spiel. Soft voice kept time with nimble fingers as they performed their magic.

"Come on closer. You can't see back there. That's right. You know, many folks has tried all sorts of substitutes over the years to make these fine roses, but my granny say you can only use palmetto leaves to make it a work of art. Oh, yeah, folks has tried to use other leaves, but nothing beats palmetto fer makin' a perfect rose. That's what my granny always tole me."

I'd close my eyes and just listen, except I wanted to keep an eye on the girl. I loved the way his voice emphasized certain syllables. Made his sentences ebb and flow like the tide. He rolled the long, folded section, tightly at first, then looser as he reached the outer portion of the rose. Saw him do it a million times. Still mesmerized me.

Selecting another thin strand, he wrapped it around and around the base of the flower, knotting it and pulling it tight after every couple of wraps. "Some folks 'round here—I ain't namin' no names, now—but some folks do shoddy work...*real* shoddy. Not like this here. This here be art. My granny say, Raymond—that be my name—she say, Raymond, "You gots to wrap and tie, son; wrap and tie." If you don't, when it dry, it all come undone on you. If you wrap and tie it enough, it'll stay nice and tight. And then..." he leaned forward and whispered confidentially. "...this be my secret—you tell your customer to dip it in polyurethane to perfect it. It'll stay perfect...just like this!" He presented his completed rose with a flourish, grinning from ear to ear, exposing several places he should've had teeth.

"How much?" the girl asked.

He squinted and pretended to think hard about it. "Mmmm...most folks give ol' Raymond five dollars 'cause they be "art," and they last."

"Five dollars it is, then. I'll trade you." They exchanged money for rose, then she turned slightly toward me, acting as if she'd just noticed me. "Oh, hello there." Her voice sounded nervous.

I just nodded, making the bells on my hat jingle. She was a cute little thing, friendly smile, a sprinkling of freckles across her nose, and the most unusual eyes I'd ever seen. About the same color as a turquoise brooch I used to have. "A girl without freckles is like a night without stars."

She jumped like I'd stuck her with a pin and her eyes went wide. She looked to Raymond for help.

He chuckled. "Don't mind Miz Lily, none. She always talk like that."

"Oh."

The girl struggled for something else to say, opening and closing her mouth several times. Looked like a fish. Finally, she sort of squared her shoulders, and with a determined look on her face, said, "Lily? Oh, I love flower names."

"Birth name is Calla Lily. Go by Lily," I blurted. "Mother liked flowers." Now, why'd I tell her that? I never told anyone before. Not even Raymond.

She held out her hand. "Very nice to meet you, Lily."

Why was she so nervous? Her hand was actually trembling. She was forcing herself to maintain eye contact, too. I could tell. Her nervousness was rubbing off on me. No time for that.

I slowly got to my feet and stepped forward until my nose was almost touching hers. Had to give her credit. She didn't step back. Looked like she wanted to, but she didn't. I grabbed her hand, clamping it tightly, and asked, "What's your name, girl?"

"C-c-cleo," she stammered.

Over her shoulder, I could see I'd surprised Raymond. His eyes were so wide, I could see the whites all the way around his brown irises, and his mouth was gaped open. He'd never seen me interact with anybody, other than spout one of my quotes. That had always been my safety net. He knew my motto: "If they can't get close, they can't hurt you."

I dropped her hand like it was a hot coal and spun around so I could grab my cart, then barked, "C'mon."

When she hurried to catch up with me, it felt like someone poured warm honey over my head. That scared me.

What was I doing?

Chapter Four

Cleo

How old is this woman, anyway? I panted. *She sure moves fast for her age. I can barely keep up with her. And where the heck are we going?*

There was no time to ask her, and I wouldn't have the breath to do it even if there was. Thank goodness it was December and not July when the heat and humidity would be sucking the life right out of me, melting me into a puddle of sweat.

If we'd slow down some, I could savor my favorite thing about Savannah: its squares. They were tucked here and there, all around the historical part of the city. The first four were laid out by James Oglethorpe way back in 1733. That's when he founded both the colony of Georgia and the city of Savannah. As the city grew, more squares were added, each one honoring specific members from Georgia's history books. There'd been twenty-four of them all together, but three were demolished back in the 1900's for the sake of "progress." A few years back, though, they'd reclaimed one of the "lost squares." That was Ellis—one of the four original ones. They'd made a huge deal over it; lots of hoopla at the official unveiling. Now we had a grand total of twenty-two little green oases, plus Forsyth and Emmett. Savannah has a thing for parks.

Jeez! What is she? A robot? Where does she get her stamina? Weathering Savannah summers must've toughened her up. Tougher than me; that's for sure.

"Lily," I wheezed. "Don't—you need—a breather?" Translation: I'm about to drop. Can't we rest?

She didn't answer, but I guess she must've deciphered my silent plea, because as soon as we entered Reynolds Square, she veered off toward the nearest bench, wheeled her cart to its end, and plopped down.

I sighed with relief. "You might be onto something, Lily," I said as I tried to catch my breath, noting with dismay that she wasn't even breathing hard. "I bet no one's ever tried combining an aerobic workout with touring historical downtown. You'd have to get people to sign a waiver, though. So they won't try to sue you if they collapse en route."

She still didn't answer. A light breeze swayed the gray clumps of Spanish moss like rags on a clothesline. It was getting colder. I shivered and pulled the collar of my jacket closer around my neck. I was glad I had it, but what about Lily? How in the world did she stay warm in the winter? Savannah has a temperate climate, generally not getting below freezing, but still... I eyed her outfit. I guess, wearing multiple layers helped make the winters bearable, but how did she cope during the long sweltering summers when it's difficult to stay cool even with air conditioning? Minnie liked to say a person could sit—stark naked in the coolest shade he could find—and sweat like a mule eating briars. It had to be nearly unbearable with no place to escape the heat.

The sun had set, but it was still light enough to see her. Shrewd gray eyes stared at me, seeming out of place in a face made up of at least a thousand wrinkles. Her skin looked like a brown paper bag that had been wadded up, then smoothed out, over and over until it was soft. Maybe she wasn't as old as she looked. The Savannah sun was cruel. Years of over-exposure, without the benefit of sunscreen, could fast-forward the aging process.

"Pay no mind to those who talk behind your back," she stated without preamble. "It simply means that you are two steps ahead."

The random, out-of-context words jolted me out of my revelry. "Uh…good one, Lily," I responded, trying not to get freaked-out. Raymond had said not to worry about it, but normal people didn't do that, did they? Was she schizophrenic? Was I putting myself at risk by being with her? I knew next to nothing about any kind of mental illness. I needed to Google it when I got home, just to be on the safe side. I gave a nervous laugh. "I guess you've been sharing these quotes for years. How many have you memorized?"

"It always seems impossible until it's done."

O-kaaay. Her quirky sayings would take some getting used to. There was a plus to all this, though. I hadn't had a chance to be shy around her. I'd been too busy trying to keep up with her—both literally and figuratively. Good trade off, if you ask me.

It was the sudden silence that caught my attention. I'd already grown used to hearing the constant jingling of her hat's bells. Not hearing them felt strange to my ears. "What's wrong?" I asked her.

"Why must there be something wrong?"

I gave an unladylike snort. "Well, for one thing, you're not jingling. But more importantly...you just answered a question with a *real* answer. One that makes sense. One that I didn't have to stop and mull over and get all deep and philosophical before figuring out the relevance."

Did I really see what I thought I saw? Was that a smile tickling the corners of her mouth? A real smile? Before I could ask her about it, her eyes hardened. "Tell me," she demanded.

"T-tell you what?"

"What you want."

I briefly considered pretending I didn't know what she was talking about, but felt that would insult her intelligence. She might be crazy, but she certainly wasn't dumb or oblivious. She'd known I was following her the whole time. I was suddenly sure of it.

I took a deep breath and blew it out. *Here goes nothing...* "I-I'd like you to model for me." There was no sense beating around the bush. Lily didn't seem like the type of person who'd appreciate that sort of thing.

She didn't say anything, but her demeanor didn't shut down, either. That was a good sign, right? She didn't immediately refuse or get up in a huff and leave. Not yet, at least.

I hurried to explain. "Here's the story. I'm a senior fine art major at SCAD and I have an important assignment to do over the holidays. The problem is...everyone has left campus, headed home for Christmas. I don't really have anyone I could ask—"

"The only people you need in your life are the ones who need you in theirs," she interrupted, her eyes never breaking contact with mine.

What was that supposed to mean? That she needed me? Doubtful. That I needed her? Well, yeah...I needed her for this project, of course. Did I need her for more? No! No way! How could she know that I was a loner? That it was difficult for me to make friends because I wouldn't open up, wouldn't allow myself to need anyone? She couldn't know that asking for her help with this project was one of the hardest things I've ever done, could she?

Whoa! Get a grip, Cleo.

I was definitely reading too much into her comment. She couldn't know that. For heaven's sake, I'd never even seen her before today, though how I could've missed that hat around town was a mystery to me. I pressed my lips together into a straight line and studied her through narrowed eyes. Her expression gave nothing away. Could she really be that astute? I shook my head. No. Impossible. It was just a coincidence that her quote was so insightful.

I cleared my throat and curved my stiff lips into a smile. "Like I was saying, I'd love it if you could help me out. I could pay you if you'd like. You'd make the perfect model—fun to paint and all—and I'm sure we could come up with a story that you could tell. What do you say?"

"If Plan A fails, remember that you have twenty-five letters left."

I cocked an eyebrow at her. "Does that mean, yes?"

That netted me a *real* smile.

"Yes."

"You'll do it? Really? Yippee!" I squealed. "Okay. We need to brainstorm. What story can we tell? Hey, I know. Why don't you come to my house for dinner?

Minnie won't mind. At least, I don't think so. I've never done anything like this before. Aunt Patricia used to spring last minute dinner guests on her all the time and you've never heard such ranting and banging of pots, but one guest shouldn't set her off." *Careful, Cleo...you're making her nervous. And you're rambling. You* never *ramble!*

"Who's Minnie?"

"She and her husband live with me. Well, not exactly *with* me. Minnie cooks and takes care of the place and Tobias used to be my aunt's driver. The gardener, too, I think, though mostly what he does is piddle. They have an apartment on the ground floor of my house."

"They *work* for you."

It wasn't a question, but I felt an irresistible need to answer it anyway, to explain. I couldn't have stopped myself if I'd tried. "Technically, yeah, but they're really like family. I wouldn't have made it without them. Minnie is kind of why I got interested in art in the first place. For my eleventh birthday, she gave me my very first paint-by-number set...a wolf standing in snowy woods. Never had a young girl worked so hard on something as I did with that painting. I wanted it to look perfect, alive and ready to jump off the canvas. I still have it; the painting. It's a sort of talisman to me. A turning point...the moment I decided I wanted to be a painter."

"Where?"

Huh? "Where, what?"

"Your house. Where's your house?"

"Oh. On Gaston. Right across from the park." *Uh-oh. Her expression just shut down. Why? My house?*

She'd been fine until I'd told her where I lived.

"No." Her voice and mannerisms were nervous, agitated. "Chippewa Square. Eleven o'clock. Tomorrow."

Before I could do more than gape at her, she turned and scurried into the twilight.

I watched her leave, awash in a haze of numbness and confusion. What just happened? I replayed the conversation in my mind. What went wrong? Well, besides the fact that I talked *waaay* too much. I couldn't believe that the chatterbox from minutes before was me. I *never* did that, especially with a complete stranger. If I talked at all, I usually tried to keep it monosyllabic. But I don't think that was it. She'd been fine until I mentioned my house. What was it? Did she not want to eat with me?

I pushed my hurt feelings away. My questions would have to wait. I wouldn't be getting any answers tonight. Lily shuffled away from the square even faster than her usual hurried pace, and never looked back. Though stung by her refusal, I couldn't help worrying about her. Where did she sleep? What and where did she eat? Her clothes looked like they came from a dumpster. Did she get her food there too?

Ick! I sure hoped not.

Maybe there was a homeless shelter or soup kitchen nearby where she could grab a bite, but why would she rather eat there than with me? Maybe the thought of coming to my house was too intimidating. After all, she didn't really know me.

It wasn't just the fact that she'd said no; it was the way she'd said it that gave me a sinking feeling, like a balloon with a slow leak, all of the air escaping, leaving me feeling flat and deflated. I thought we'd been developing a sort of camaraderie, maybe even the beginnings of a friendship, not that I had much expertise in that area. It was a little embarrassing to admit it—even to myself—but, I was actually starting to feel pretty close to her, closer than I'd felt toward anybody in years, besides Minnie and Tobias. It was a sad commentary on the state of my life when after only a couple of hours spent with a complete stranger—a *homeless* woman, who may or may not be crazy—I was ready for us to be BFFs.

Jeez. I'm pathetic.

It was when Lily turned left at the corner, that a little tremor of panic started vibrating in the pit of my stomach. I hurried to catch up with her. I needed to make sure everything was still okay. What if she'd changed her mind? What if she didn't show up tomorrow, and I had to start back at square one in my search for a model? What if I'd lost my friend? That last option was the worst one of them all. Definitely more painful that it should be.

When I reached the corner and faced left, I fully expected to see her strange silhouette outlined against the street lamps, but there was no one there. I shot a glance the other directions, even though I knew she'd gone left, but that sidewalk was empty, too.

I turned back to the left, facing the empty sidewalk. The feeling of deflation felt even stronger. My pace slowed, almost to a stop, before I sped up until I was nearly running, peering into every shadow, every doorway, any place I thought it might be possible for her to slip into and hide, but she was gone. Disappeared without a trace. How was that even possible? I'd been only a few steps behind her. She was an old woman, for heaven's sake. Yes, I knew she was fast, but not *that* fast. An all-star sprinter couldn't have accomplished such a feat.

An unwelcome idea was trying to push its way into my brain, and I was trying just as hard to keep it out.

"It's not possible," I spoke the words aloud, hoping that hearing them would help me believe them.

It didn't.

Savannah had the reputation of being the most haunted city in America. I'd never encountered a ghost before. I didn't believe in them, but Minnie swears she's seen several and there were always stories in the local news, with verifying photos, in some cases. Had I spent the last several hours with a ghost? The sane part of me refused to believe it, but what other explanation did I have? How else could she have disappeared like that?

A gust of wind hit me in the face as I made my turn onto Drayton Street, and I wasn't sure if it was the cold or fear that made me shiver as I hurried toward home.

****

I was gasping by the time I turned right at the corner of Gaston Street and Aunt Patricia's house loomed into view. That was probably due to the fact that I'd been flat-out running the last several blocks. I stumbled to a stop, breathing hard and bending at the waist, trying to ease the cramp in my side. I wasn't a runner by any stretch of the imagination, normally only doing so as a last resort, but with each step of tonight's trip home, I felt more and more like every ghost in town—real or imagined—was watching me, lurking in every shadow, ready to pounce, if that's what ghosts did. This "feeling" gave me incentive to move quite a bit faster than I normally would have.

I cast a wary glance back over my shoulder before turning toward the house. It felt safer here, sort of like the ghosts wouldn't *dare* tread on Aunt Patricia's turf. They were probably scared of her. They *should* be.

Light glowed from nearly every window; Minnie's attempt at making it look "homey," though I doubted I'd ever consider this house my home. In my mind, it belonged to my aunt and always would. But after tonight, I was never so glad to see its hulking mass. I drew a long breath, feeling more at ease than I had since Lily had disappeared.

It wasn't that I didn't like the house; it was beautiful. I'm talking, *Architectural Digest* sort of beautiful, even at night when I couldn't see all the magnificent details, it could still knock my socks off. It's never lost its "wow factor."

"So why did mentioning it scare off Lily?" I muttered, then shook the question away. It wouldn't do any good to think about that now.

Aunt Patricia had always had a professional decorator keep the front door—and stairs leading up to it—decorated according to the season. As a teenager, I remember asking my aunt if I might try my hand at it, but she'd flatly refused. You'd have thought I'd asked to set up a stone altar and sacrifice puppies the way she'd reacted. I never made *that* mistake again, just resigned myself to the decorator's elegant, but stuffy, style. After Aunt Patricia's funeral, I thought I'd finally get my chance, but I should've known better. I was informed that my dear aunt had a non-negotiable, non-breakable written contract with that decorator, valid for the next fifteen years! Another example of my dear aunt's ability to control things from the grave. I guess I should be used to by now, but I wasn't.

But back to the house itself...like most of historical Savannah, it's been around a while. William Brantley built the four-floor showplace back in 1857 with coveted Savannah pink-tinged, gray bricks. Of course, it was located across the street from Forsyth Park just north of Gaston Street because every true Savannahian stayed "NOG" (north of Gaston). The first time I heard that statement, it sounded silly to me too, but it didn't take me long to realize that these people were serious about it, almost fanatical, really. All shopping, dining, any business dealing or socializing was done in the old part of town. To a true Savannahian, anything south of Gaston Street was just north Jacksonville. They looked down their noses at anyone or anything not located NOG. The closest comparison I can think of is an Amish shunning. They're that serious.

My stomach growled, interrupting my musings as I unlatched one side of the double gate and sped up the stairs, two at a time.

As I swung the door open my cat, King Tut was there to greet me. Yeah...King Tut. Hilarious. I decided to continue the Egyptian theme my mother so kindly began when she named me. I scooped him up from the faded red Oriental rug, touching my nose to his and giving him an energetic scratch behind his ears. His loud purr showed his appreciation. "Did ya miss me, Tut? 'Course you did, you big lug."

Oh, how I loved this cat. Aunt Patricia hadn't allowed me to have a pet; never allowed animals in the house, period. But shortly after her death, I made a trip to the local animal shelter with a goal of getting a dog. I'm still not quite sure how I ended up with Tut, but it doesn't matter. We were meant for each other.

I took a deep breath, nearly fainting with hunger. The tantalizing aroma of garlic mixed with the citrusy bite of lime made my mouth water. Mmm-mm...I recognized that smell and it was just what I needed to recover from my nerve-racking trip home. Nothing can get you over a possible close encounter of the spectral kind like Minnie's yummy garlic-lime chicken. It was one of my favorites. I whispered to Tut, "You think she knew I needed it tonight, boy? Yeah, you're probably right."

"That you, Miss Cleo?"

I rolled my eyes. *Who else?* "Yes, Minnie," I replied as I sat Tut on the floor, then turned to hang up my jacket. "Mmmm. Something smells dee-LISH-us! I'm starved. You can probably hear my stomach grumbling all the way in there. How'd you know I needed this particular meal?" I followed my nose to the kitchen, Tut right on my heels.

She chuckled, "Honey, if I've told you once, I've told you a thousand times; I got the gift. Got it from my momma, and she got it from hers. When someone's got the gift, they just *know* things."

As soon as I entered the room, I planted a kiss on the top of her head. I had to lean down in order to do it and I wasn't that tall myself. At four feet, nine inches and nearly the same measurement around, Minnie was—as she liked to say—"longitudinally-challenged." She always left out the latitude part. "Can't argue with that, but I've got to say, I don't think I've ever needed it quite as much as I do tonight."

She glanced over her shoulder at me as she was dumping drained pasta into a bowl, then froze, nearly dropping the pot. She managed to set it back down on the stovetop before turning to face me head-on. Her eyes were so wide that they sort of bulged out with the whites showing. Uh-oh! What did I look like? Maybe I should've detoured by the bathroom mirror to make sure I was presentable first.

She stared at me like that for a long minute before narrowing her eyes. That was my cue to move. I headed to the sink to wash my hands, ignoring her and trying to act like nothing was out of the ordinary.

"What on earth happened to you, child? You feelin' all right?" she demanded.

Jeez, I really should've checked a mirror first. "Hmm? What do you mean?" I replied, reaching for a towel. I was striving for nonchalance, but it was pointless. I'd never been able to fool Minnie.

Her hands went to her hips. "Now, don't you be tryin' that with me, little girl. I been on this here earth for long enough to know when someone is tryin' to pull a fast one on me. You forgettin' I practically raised you the last eleven years? You ain't any good at actin'. You should know that by now and you might as well quite your tryin'. You ain't no Julia Roberts."

I could tell she was upset. Minnie usually practiced pretty good grammar. Aunt Patricia had insisted on it. I knew it required her to pay attention and concentrate since it wasn't the way she'd talked growing up, but when she got riled, like she was now, her subject/verb agreement went south in a hurry. I just kept quiet, hoping she'd get it out of her system.

"I mean…have you *seen* your face? It's *white!* And

63

I ain't talkin' white-person white. I'm talkin' white like a...like a ghost!"

At the word, ghost, my mouth instantly dried out and I had the dickens of a time working up enough spit to swallow. I opened my lips to reply, but she waved away anything I'd planned on saying. She wasn't finished yet.

"...and that ain't even the worst part. Your eyes are too bright. Shiny...like marbles. You got a fever? 'Cause that's what it looks like...like you're burning up with a fever. Now, you jest set your fanny down at the table right this minute and tell Minnie what happened. Make it snappy. No lollygagging!"

"Oh, Minnie," I whined. "Please? Can we eat first? I promise I'll tell you, but if I don't get something in my stomach soon, it's going to start eating itself. I didn't have time for lunch today, and that granola bar I had for breakfast was gone a long time ago."

I could see the battle raging within her, but she finally relented and served my plate, thunking it down in front of me and glancing pointedly at her watch. There would be no leisurely enjoyment of *this* meal. I sighed and picked up my fork.

****

I'd no sooner put the last bite in my mouth, than my plate was whisked right out from under my nose. It should be against the law to make a person rush while they're eating something as delicious as garlic-lime chicken. Holding out my fork, I glared at her. I couldn't help it. "You want this too?" I snipped.

She ignored my attitude, crossing her arms expectantly under her prodigious breasts. "You've had your supper, now. Start talking, missy."

"Shouldn't we clean the kitchen, first? Wash up the dishes?"

She tilted her head and gave me her "look." "The dishes can wait."

Hoping to stall a little longer, I opened my mouth to ask her where Tobias was, but she arched an eyebrow at me, her short, silver-dusted hair almost bristled with agitation, her fingers drummed impatiently along the side of her meaty arm. I decided that I'd probably pressed my luck far enough and that I shouldn't try her patience.

"Okay, okay." I blew out a breath to calm myself. "I think I met a ghost."

Her posture relaxed immediately and she collapsed into a chair opposite me, her weight causing it to emit loud creaks and groans of protest. "Is that all? You got me all worked up over you seein' a *ghost?* And here I thought it was something serious. Honey, you *do* live in Savannah, you know. It's about *time* you seen a ghost. I can't believe you've lived here all these years and *haven't* seen one yet."

Her attitude, combined with the fear I'd experienced earlier, made my hackles rise. "For your information, I think meeting a ghost *is* kind of serious. It's not something that happens every day; not to me, anyway. And besides, now that I'm home and not out there walking dark streets, I'm not completely sure it even *was* a ghost. There might be a perfectly logical explanation—there probably *is*—I just don't know what it could be, yet."

Minnie's expression changed and she smiled sympathetically. She could afford to be benevolent, now that she knew it wasn't "serious." Reaching across the table, she squeezed my hand. "Maybe it'll help if you tell me about it."

I shook my head a little defiantly, trying not to pout. Her lackadaisical response to my announcement was like rubbing a cat's fur the wrong way—me being the cat—and I hadn't decided whether or not I'd forgive her yet. My gaze dropped to where our joined fingers rested on the tabletop, and my resentment melted away. The color of her skin was like warm, thick caramel, her hands capable, but worn and wrinkled against my own pale, thin fingered ones.

"Thanks, Minnie, but not right now. I think I'll wait to see what happens tomorrow, first." I looked up, meeting her concerned gaze and forced a smile. I just couldn't explain all the emotions I was feeling at the moment. I didn't want her to know how much this whole thing was bothering me.

She nodded, giving my hand another squeeze. "If you change your mind, honey…"

"Yeah, I know," I muttered as I got up from the table and turned to leave. "Thanks, Minnie."

Chapter Five

Lily

I stood at my window, too busy arguing with myself to notice the weak morning sun struggling to warm the alley. Supposed to be at the square at eleven. That's what I told the girl. Need to head out if I want to make it on time. That's the question, though, isn't it? Do I *want* to make it? Should I go or stay? Why am I being so indecisive? Never used to be like this. Until I found that bag, I made a decision and stuck with it. Never a question. Now *everything* is a question…voices arguing in my head, mixing me up. Should I tell someone what I saw, show them? Who'd believe me?

Maybe I could tell the girl.

No. Stay away from her.

But why? Because that's how its been for almost fifty years? That's not a reason. It's an excuse. Because Rose won't like it? That's not a reason, either. She doesn't like me talking to *anybody*, not even Raymond. The plain fact is that I need help. Has to be a credible source, though. Means it can't be a homeless person…or a ghost. Eliminates two of my three possibilities. Cleo is my only other choice. She needs me for her project, too. Which makes it even better. I help her, and she helps me…even trade. The solution sounded fair, but it scared me.

Her invitation to supper caught me off guard. That was bad enough, but then she told me where she lived. It's why I ran off and hid last night. Even now, thinking about it had me gnawing my lip. Still…no reason to sneak off into the shadows and watch the girl look everywhere for me. Why was this scaring me so badly? Why did it feel like a storm was brewing?

Because cutting myself off from people after Rose died was the safe way. No interaction meant I couldn't be hurt. If I met her this morning, told her about the bag and what I'd seen in the alley, I'd be opening myself up to change, and change was unpredictable. Cleo was the only person—other than my sister and Raymond—who I'd talked to in almost half a century. It stirred up emotions I thought had died along with Rose. I'd actually *enjoyed* the time I'd spent with the girl. I even laughed. Couldn't remember the last time *that* had happened. It felt good.

But if I allowed one emotion to slip through, wouldn't others follow? Could I do it? Did I want to resurrect old feelings and all that went with them?

Scary to think about. Change always was. Like in my dream last night.

I stood in front of a door. The word, CHANGE, was written in big, bold letters on a sign over it. My hand was on the doorknob. Should I turn it? Step through? No turning back, if I did. No way to undo the decision. Once I took the step, the door would lock behind me, and I didn't have the key to open it again. What was on the other side? Good or bad? Happiness or doom?

Doom? I snorted. For heaven's sakes, get a grip, old woman. Cut the melodrama. Just go meet the girl, already.

I grabbed the doorknob.

"Where are you going?" Rose demanded, popping out of nowhere and scaring the living daylights out of me.

"Oh, Rose!" I gasped and pressed my hand to my chest. "You almost gave me a heart attack. You need a hat like mine. The bells would give advanced warning so I could hear you coming. You wouldn't be able to sneak up on me."

"There *aren't* any other hats like yours, and don't try to change the subject," she snapped. "Where are you going?"

"Out." I picked at invisible lint on my overcoat, avoiding my sister's eyes. Rose had the uncanny ability to transform me back into the gangly eight year-old version of myself, malleable, able to be bossed around by my big sister. "Why?"

The air between us fairly crackled with tension, I could almost see the sparks. She was incredulous at my response. I'd never stood up to her before. I always capitulated to her wishes. She studied me through narrowed eyes, then suddenly changed tactics. "We-ell..." She made her voice soft and pitiful. "...I was thinking we could spend some time together. I was gone all day yesterday—"

"*And* all night."

She arched a perfectly tweezed brow at me. "*And* all night, and I thought we could have a girl's day. You know...like old times," she wheedled.

I opened my mouth to relent, then snapped it shut. No. Not again. I knew what she was doing, and I wouldn't let her get away with it this time. One of her ghost friends must've seen me with Cleo yesterday and told her about it. That's the only reason she'd pull this trick. She didn't do, "girls days." "Sorry, but I already have plans."

"You're going to meet her."

It was a statement, not a question. I was right. She already knew. Wasn't sure how, but she knew. I raised my chin a notch. "I told her I would, so I am. Why is it okay for you to talk to people and not me?"

"Why is—" she broke off, then shook her head. "I can see your mind's made up," she sniffed. "If you're not going to listen to reason, then…" her voice trailed off.

I knew what she was waiting for. It was the same thing she always waited for, but this time it wasn't going to happen. I *wasn't* giving in.

Silence was a rubber band stretched between us. I clamped my lips in a stubborn line and gave her a defiant glare.

Finally, Rose huffed, "Fine! Whatever happens is on your head. Just don't come running back to me, expecting to be babied when it all hits the fan!" Then she disappeared in an angry flash of red.

I let out the breath I'd been holding, unaware that I'd been holding it. Wow! I did it. I actually stood up to my sister for maybe the first time in my life, and it felt good. Really good. It had been years since I'd made a decision on my own. I'd forgotten how it felt.

"Okay, Lily," I whispered while squaring my shoulders as I faced the door, hand on the knob. "Time's a wasting. You have a meeting to get to."

Chapter Six

Cleo

I didn't think I'd ever get to sleep, but I guess I did. I remember the numbers on my alarm clock telling it was 2:47, and the next thing I knew there was weak, winter sunlight streaming through my window. I fumbled for my phone and squinted at the time.

"Ten o'clock!" I shrieked, flinging the covers back and leaping out of bed. Tut gazed quizzically at me from his spot on the other pillow. "How could it be ten o'clock? Why'd you let me sleep so late? I'm supposed to meet Lily in an hour and the walk itself will take over half of that time."

My cat just blinked at me. Some help he was.

I raced into the bathroom, tossing my pajamas on the floor before hurrying into the ridiculously large, walk-in shower. Every action needed to be done in triple-time if I didn't want to be late. I was off-schedule and I didn't like it. My morning routine rarely varied. I liked to rise early, take a leisurely shower, enjoying the intense drenching that the dinner-plate sized shower head always gave me. Not this morning, though. Time was of the essence.

I probably would've stayed in my own suite of rooms on the third floor after Aunt Patricia died, but for this bathroom. Besides the luxuriant shower, there was a massive claw-foot tub, practically big enough to swim in, double dressing tables (don't ask me why…maybe wishful thinking on my aunt's part), and a large crystal chandelier hanging from the ten foot ceiling! Yes, a chandelier in the bathroom. This room was what prompted my move downstairs to the master suite. I just couldn't resist it.

I was in and out of the shower in a jiffy. Grabbing a thick towel, I gave myself a brisk rub-down before wrapping it around me and zipping a comb through my hair, then blasting it with my hairdryer. I eyed myself critically in the mirror and then shrugged. There was no time for make-up.

Racing back into the bedroom, I snatched a pair of jeans and my red SCAD sweatshirt out of the closet, rather than my usual frilly layers. That could wait for another day. If Lily showed up, I'd probably be outside all day, so I needed to plan for warmth rather than style.

Tut lost interest in my zooming around the room like a crazy woman, and began his morning ablutions. I ignored him, concentrating on dressing instead. Thick socks and my trademark boots finished my attire. I glanced at the clock and couldn't help a smirk. Less than ten minutes. Not bad.

Luckily, I always kept a backpack loaded with art equipment, so at least that was one thing that I didn't have to spend time doing. Slinging it over my shoulder, I turned toward the bed where my cat was washing behind his ears. "Bye, Tut. Be good!" He paused a moment when I flung him a kiss, then went on with his bath like I wasn't there. I guess he was mad at me. I hadn't paid enough attention to him this morning, but there wasn't time now. I'd make it up to him later. I'd give him a slice of cheese, his favorite thing.

I clattered downstairs, almost knocking Minnie down when I burst through the kitchen doorway.

"Well, well, well…look who decided to put in an appearance this morning. Wait. *Is* it still morning?" She exaggeratedly pushed up her sleeve so she could peer at her watch.

I groaned. "Oh, give me a break, will you? I didn't shut my eyes until almost three this morning and it caused me to oversleep. Can you help me? I've got an appointment and I'm going to be late."

"Sure, honey. What you want me to do?"

"Can you get me a couple of your home-made granola bars?" I asked as I wrenched the refrigerator open and grabbed a bottle of water and two apples. Unzipping one of the outer pockets of the backpack, I shoved my items in, holding it open for her to do the same, then I gave her a smile and leaned forward to kiss her cheek. "Thanks, Minnie."

She cocked her eyebrow. "Where you rushing off to in such an all-fire hurry?"

I shook my head, grabbing my jacket as I headed for the door. "No time. I'll have to tell you later. Wish me luck."

"Luck!" I heard her shout just before the door banged shut.

As I barreled down the front stairs, I tried to push her worried expression out of my mind.

****

By the time I reached Chippewa Square—our appointed meeting place—I was regretting my clothing choice in spite of the nippy temperature outside. The sweatshirt was definitely living up to its name. For all the good it was doing me right now, I could've skipped my shower this morning. If that wasn't bad enough, I'd worked myself into a frenzy over this appointment: worried that Lily wouldn't show, and in an oxymoronic way, worried that she *would*.

My heart sank when I entered the square and swept my eyes from corner to corner. No flash of pink and green. You couldn't hide a hat like that. Wait! It *was* this square, wasn't it? Not Ellis? Or Wright? No, I distinctly remember her saying Chippewa. She just wasn't here. The disappointment made me feel like I was wearing my heart on the bottom of my boots and walking over broken glass. What now?

I felt a tiny surge of hope when I caught sight of Raymond sitting on the same bench he'd sat yesterday. Maybe he could help me. She might've left a message with him.

I opened my mouth to greet him, but paused. Something was different. He had none of his rose-making supplies spread out on the bench. Instead he sat hunched over a spiral-bound notebook, clutching a pen and writing as if his life depended on it. What in the world was he writing? Could he be an author in disguise? Maybe he was in the process of penning the next New York Times best seller.

At first I thought my eyes were playing tricks on me, that he was writing in some foreign language, that that's why I couldn't read it. I wish that were the case, but it wasn't.

Scribbles! Nothing but scribbles. Both pages were filled with line after line of squiggly curlicues!

My jaw dropped. I watched in a sort of horror as he flipped the page and started on the next sheet. I'd be willing to bet all the previous pages were filled with more of the same.

He was completely oblivious to me—to anyone— although I was the only one who stopped and stared. It hurt my feelings a little. Why? Well, he'd been so connected, so *aware* of everything when he'd fashioned my rose yesterday, so unlike *this*. It felt like a betrayal of some sort. Crazy, I know, but that's how it felt.

I turned away, dejected, eyes on the sidewalk, just ahead of my toes.

Before I could take a step, a pair of very worn, cracked-leather work boots came into view and my wilted spirit felt instantly revived. My eyes snapped up to meet Lily's shrewd gray ones. Relief. Happiness. A smile spread across my face, and a sudden sting of tears that had me blinking rapidly.

Wow! Over-react much? Was it the lack of sleep? Maybe. I become a tall two-year old when I don't get enough rest, but this seemed a little over-the-top. Yes, I'd found the perfect model for my project, but this wasn't my usual shy, stand-offish behavior. It made me nervous. I cleared my throat before attempting to speak. "G-good morning, Lily. I was beginning to think you'd stood me up."

"The grass isn't greener on the other side. It's greener where you water it."

Another one of her quotes. I nodded and grinned. "Well, in that case, I'm glad you decided to water *this* grass."

****

We sat side-by-side on another of the square's benches munching the apples I'd brought. I could see Raymond from where we were. He was still hunched over his notebook, scribbling away. I lifted my chin in his direction. "Why does he do that?"

"Why does who do what?" her answer sounded juicy, spoken around a bite of apple.

"Raymond. Filling that notebook with scribbles. People are going to think he's crazy."

She swallowed before answering. "They already do, and it's not scribbles."

"Ha! What do you mean, it's not scribbles? I *saw* it! It's page after page of squiggles and curlicues!"

At her somber gaze, my smile grew uncertain. "They are scribbles, Lily." But my statement sounded hesitant, almost questioning...like I was doubting myself.

"In order to be irreplaceable, one must always be different."

"Well, yeah. That's different, all right. Wouldn't be my adjective of choice, but if that's what you want to go with, be my guest. But I...uh...I have to ask. When you say they're not *scribbles*, are you saying that they're *words*? That you can actually *read* whatever it is that he's writing?"

She didn't answer, but started her bobble-head routine that sent the little bells to jingling. She took another big bite of her apple, her cheek bulging with it as she chewed. She looked like a chipmunk.

"Okay, then, what does it say?"

"You won't believe," she finally muttered.

"Try me."

Her eyes flitted back across the square to Raymond. "He writes down what the ghosts tell him."

My heart did a flip-flop in my chest. "What the ghosts—" I broke off and pressed my lips together, trying to get a grip. My mouth went dry. After last night, I wasn't sure I wanted to hear this, but I had to ask. "How do you know?"

Her eyes met mine again. "Because they talk to me too."

"They talk to—" I shook my head. I didn't want to believe it. The whole thing was getting too weird. "Uh, I think we need to change the subject, talk about something a little less crazy."

Lily cocked her head and smiled like she was privy to a secret I didn't know about. "If it's important to you, you'll find a way. If not, you'll find an excuse."

I jumped to my feet. "Okay. Let's go find a way."

****

Lily's capacity for trivia rivaled her list of memorized quotes.

"Did you know that pearls melt in vinegar?

"Nope."

"Did you know that a snail can sleep for three years?"

I shook my head.

"How about that a tiger's *skin* is what's striped, not just his fur?"

Where did she *get* this stuff? "Nope. Didn't know that either." I'd stopped and was leaning against an iron railing in order to make a quick sketch of her while she sprinkled glitter beside a parking meter. My goal was to capture the movement more than the actual details. I wanted to compile as many "fluid" drawings as possible before starting on the actual assignment. It was something I always did before beginning a painting. It was my own technique, allowing me to get to know my subject better: their movement…their essence, if you will. It helped me make them come alive on the canvas.

"You mind if I ask you something, Lily?" I purposefully kept my eyes on the bold, sweeping strokes my pencil was making on my drawing pad, keeping my voice light and airy. Maybe if she didn't thing I was intensely curious about it, I'd have a better chance of getting a real answer instead of one of her quotes.

I took her silence as an invitation to continue. "Why do you sprinkle glitter like that?" I held my breath, waiting for her answer.

"Rose told me ghosts like the way it sparkles. They really like anything sparkly—diamonds, gemstones, gold and silver in the sunshine—but glitter is easiest to find."

Ghosts again! But at least she gave a real answer. I kept my face composed with an effort, concentrating on my sketch. "Who's Rose?" my voice shook a little.

"My sister."

I looked up, startled. "Sister? Does she live here too?"

"Guess you could say that, although "live" isn't the right word. She's been dead for forty-eight years. She's here, though. Well, not *here* right now. Here in Savannah."

"Dead?" I swallowed noisily and dropped my gaze back to my drawing. I hoped I looked like I was absorbed in my work. In reality, it could have been a blank sheet of paper. I gave up that façade pretty quickly. I knew I wasn't a great actress. I tend to wear my emotions on my face for all to see. That being the case, I knew that Lily could see that I was totally freaked out, so why bother acting? I finally whispered,

"You say she's not here now. Um, if she ever shows up when we're together, will you tell me? In case I can't see her myself, that is."

"Is that what you want?"

"Yeah…I think."

A tiny smile curved one side of her mouth. It gave me a shot of courage that I needed for my next question. "Okay. I've got to ask this, especially after last night. Are…"

My voice cracked and the word came out high-pitched, like an adolescent boy whose voice is changing. I stopped, cleared my throat, and tried again. "Are you a ghost?"

The other side of her mouth tipped up. "No, child."

The breath that I'd been unconsciously holding *whooshed* out. "What a relief! I cannot tell you how much of a relief it is. You have no idea how spooked I was last night when you took off on me like you did. I tried to catch up with you and when I looked down the street, you were *gone!* Poof! Without a trace. You just disappeared. And you know, people, especially *older* people—not saying that you're old or anything—but people your age can't generally move that quickly. It was so fast. You turned out of the square and you were gone. It was almost supernatural…something a ghost would be able to do. That's why I asked. I'm not trying to pry or anything. I was just curious as to how you did it. Disappear, I mean. Where'd you go?" I was blathering and I knew it, but couldn't seem to stop myself. A bad case of nerves can do that. It's as if my brain short-circuits and my mouth goes out of control. *Somebody stop me, please!*

She took my arm and pulled me over to a sunny

spot on the stairs, sitting me down. "Tell me about your home," she changed the subject as she settled down beside me.

I snorted. Well, that was a sure-fire way to halt a runaway mouth. "Okay, you don't want to tell me. I get it. At least you didn't throw another quote at me." I drew a deep breath and blew it out. "You want to know about my home...well, like I told you before, it's right across from the park on West Gaston. Built back in 1857 by one of my aunt's ancestors, though I'm not sure how the Davenports got added into the Brantley mix; by marriage, I guess. I'm not up on all the genealogy. I only know that the house has always been in the family. You probably don't know this, but certain people in Savannah take tremendous pride in having that kind of history."

Lily got the strangest look on her face. "Pride. Enough to choke a horse. Know about that crowd. Same thing with money. They love it, but hate to spend it."

"Yeah," I answered, surprised. "The only thing they love more is gossiping. It's as vital as breathing, but how did you know about the money part?"

"Nevermind. You were telling me about your home."

I studied her through narrowed eyes before continuing, "My parents died when I was nine, and I was sent there to live with my aunt—no, my *great* aunt—my *mother's* aunt. And well...she hated me."

"Hate is a strong word."

I nodded. "Yup. And she was pretty obvious about it."

"Was? Is she—"

"Dead? Yes."

"Don't be so broken up about it."

I laughed without humor. "It's hard to be broken up about the death of someone when you feel nothing but relief."

She let that slide. "So you're by yourself?"

"No, not by myself. Remember I mentioned Minnie? She and her husband, Tobias, live there too. They're family. Oh…and Tut, of course."

"Tut?"

"King Tut…my cat."

Her eyes twinkled.

"I guess that's all."

After a thoughtful gaze, she asked, "Why did she hate you?"

"Aunt Patricia?" I shrugged. "I wish I knew. I'm pretty sure it had something to do with my mother, but no one ever told me and I didn't dare ask."

"Holding a grudge is like letting someone live, rent-free, in your head."

I had to chuckle. "I was wondering how long you'd be able to go before giving me another of your quotes."

She just smiled, looking very wise in her comical hat. "What else?"

"What do you mean, "what else"?"

"You're a senior at SCAD. How'd you get there?"

"Well, I wanted to be a painter, but I needed some training. SCAD is right here; spread out all over the town. Did you know that they've reclaimed over sixty historic buildings that would've been torn down otherwise? Very eco-friendly, if you ask me."

"Mm-hmm. But there are better art schools. Why not choose one of them?"

"Not you, too," I cried. "I know SCAD sort of has a bad reputation with some people. Strict Southern decorum doesn't mix well with free spirits. Sort of like oil and water. I'm sure Aunt Patricia wanted me to choose a "good" college, an ivy-leagued one, preferably one that was on the other side of the Atlantic Ocean, or at least several states away so she'd be rid of me. Not only did I pick a school close by—parts of it almost within rock throwing distance of the house—I picked SCAD. I guess she considered it a slap in her face. Anytime she or her snobby friends even said the name, it was spoken in a nasty tone and with the same expression worn whenever passing the paper mill."

Lily chuckled. "Think you're exaggerating."

"I'm not!" I insisted. "It's true." At her look, I laughed. "Okay. Maybe I slightly exaggerated. The good part is it's all paid for. My school, that is. Remember the pride we were talking about? Well, Aunt Patricia wouldn't hear of me "begging for money," which is what she called any type of student loans. The phrase, "what would people think?" played a big role in her decision-making process."

"I see."

"Yeah. It was a surprise, all right. But not as big as the one I got after she died. I figured she'd have donated the house to the Daughters of the American Revolution, or one of the long list of committees she chaired, and that I'd have to find another place to live, but the fine folks at Groben, White, and Jones, Attorneys-at-law told me the house was mine. As long as I continued living there. All Aunt Patricia's assets had been put into a trust from which I'd get a meager living allowance until I married, at which point my *husband* would take charge of the purse strings."

"Husband?" she looked startled. "Anybody in mind?"

"Hah!" I scoffed. Her question proved how little she knew me. "That's not the point. It bothers me that Aunt Patricia—a dyed-in-the-wool spinster who'd never had to answer to anyone her entire adult life about how she chose to spend her money—put that kind of stipulation in her will."

"You're not one of those feminists, are you?"

"No, but—"

"But nothing. Your college is paid for, right?"

"Yeah," I grudgingly saw her point. "And any costs associated with the house are taken care of by a fund she set up with her attorneys. *And* I don't need a car because I can walk anywhere I need to go."

"Pretty sweet deal."

I burst out laughing. The phrase sounded hilarious coming from her lips.

"What? That's what they call it, right?"

"That's what they call it," I nodded, still chuckling.

"Be thankful for such things as you have." The words hung in the air. She clapped a hand over her lips, the oddest expression on her face.

Hmmm. What was *that* about? "Another quote? Okay, okay. I get the message."

I could tell she didn't want me to pursue it—whatever *it* was, so I didn't. I picked up my sketchpad instead, flipping the page over to a clean, white surface. As my pencil captured the pensive expression on her face, I replayed our conversation in my mind, skipping over that last quote. I'd heard it before, but couldn't remember where. I knew it would come back to me later.

I knew the only reason I had a roof over my head was because Aunt Patricia feared the wagging tongues of Savannah. Her pride wouldn't allow her to be the focus of gossip even after her death. And while I'm thankful I didn't have to scramble for a place to live, I think being talked about is probably the last thing she needed to worry about now.

I drew in silence for a while. When I finished the sketch, I picked up the conversation where she'd so cleverly changed the subject. "So…how'd you do your smoke act last night?" I gestured with my hands. "Poof! You just vanished."

"Not so fast. I've got one more thing to say."

Her expression looked so serious, she instantly had my undivided attention. "Okay."

"You said you wished you knew why your aunt hated you. Did you mean that?"

The question caught me off guard. I swallowed hard before stuttering, "I g-guess so."

Lily cocked one eyebrow and waited.

"Okay, yes! It would be nice to know. Maybe, if I knew, it would help me understand why she treated me the way she did. It wouldn't change anything, but at least I'd know."

She nodded once. "I'll find out."

Okaaay…A heavy silence hung between us. What do you say after something like that? I had nothing.

"The best things in life are unseen. That's why we close our eyes to kiss, laugh, and dream."

Leave it to Lily to fill in an uncomfortable blank with one of her quotes. I laughed in relief, thankful for the break in the tension. "I'll probably never know about the kiss part of that statement, but I finally understand your game. Whenever you feel uncomfortable or don't want to answer my question, you respond with one of your little proverbs. That's pretty sneaky, you know, but I'm onto you now, so you can stop hiding behind them and start answering when I ask you something. Where. Did. You. Go?"

Boy, that sounded bold! What's gotten into me lately? Where's the quiet, introverted, push-over? *That's* me, not this demanding, bossy person that seemed to emerge in Lily's presence. The dual-personality thing was disconcerting, to say the least. Maybe it was just the intensity of the previous moment that caused me to react this way.

She studied me carefully before rising to her feet. "Come. I'll show you."

Chapter Seven

Cleo

"Almost there," Lily called over her shoulder. "One more flight to go."

I didn't answer. I was too out of breath, sucking wind to beat the band and Lily wasn't even breathing hard. How embarrassing. "Where are you...taking me?" I finally panted. "Are these stairs...even safe? It's a fire...escape. Has the fire marshal...checked them lately? Seem kind of...rickety to me. Seems like they're...just clinging to the back of the building...sort of like ivy."

Lily was muttering something. I think I heard the word, "wimp," but didn't have the energy to ask.

"We're here." She held a door open and I dragged myself inside.

Once my eyes adjusted to the darkness, I could see that we were standing in a slanted-ceilinged room that was smaller than my closet. The only spot where you could stand fully upright was directly in the center, where the ceiling reached its apex. A pallet of blankets lay on the floor. A mostly-melted candle sat in a cracked Tybee Island mug, a book of matches beside it. A single burner hot-plate was plugged into the only outlet I could see, a beat-up aluminum pot sat atop it. A few dented cans of Campbell's soup were stacked on the floor to one side, a plastic milk jug, half full of water on the other.

"What *is* this place?" I asked, once I'd caught my breath.

"I live here."

"What? I thought you were homeless," I blurted. "I mean, I'm glad you have a roof over your head, but...I don't understand."

"You don't have to," she answered brusquely. "No questions. Only reason I brought you here was to show you something."

"No questions?" I whined, ready to argue, but one look at her expression made me change my mind. She meant it. "Okay," I sighed. "No questions."

She gave me a single nod and turned toward the window, her back facing me.

I tried to satisfy my curiosity by studying the room. To say that the furnishings were merely Spartan would be the greatest of understatements. The only thing "decorative" in the room were the curtains at the single window. Though faded, the dark red fabric still had a lustrous sheen that seemed out of place, too fancy for the rest of the décor...if you wanted to call the contents of the room, décor, that is.

Now I understood how she'd disappeared the night before. The doorway that led between this building and the one beside it was basically invisible, hidden completely behind a huge camellia bush. It took less than a minute after leaving the square for us to vanish from the street. A narrow walkway led to the rear of this large five-story house. Her room was in the attic.

Cardboard boxes were stacked along one wall, nearly bursting with no-telling what. The one closest to me had a collection of colorful Savannah area brochures fanned-out beside a book that was turned face-down. I couldn't read the title.

What sort of book would she have and why didn't she keep it with the rest of her things in her metal cart? I couldn't help myself; I reached for it, turning it over.

Holy Bible?

My gaze dropped to the bottom right corner where her name was stamped in gold: *Lily Telfair-Gordon.* I spun around and stared at her back as she stood at the window, silently gazing through the faded curtains. I was confused. With Lily, every step forward came with twice that many backward steps. She *had* to be the most multi-layered person I'd ever encountered. Worse than an onion.

She had a Bible—with her *name* stamped on it, no less—very much like the one I had packed away in a box somewhere in my closet.

My mind suddenly slipped back to a time when my parents were still alive and I was about five or six years old. Every Sunday morning we had waffles for breakfast, then put on our best clothes, tucked our Bibles under our arms, and headed off to church. I loved the separate service they had for kids—His Kids is what they called it. There was always lots of singing, and wonderful stories told with the help of puppets. Sometimes these stories were illustrated with chalk drawings, which were my favorites. They'd turn all the lights off except for the single spotlight on the artist. Vibrant colors seemed to flow right out of his fingertips as he painted a beautiful pastel illustration. Unknown to us children, he used some fluorescent chalk for unseen details. At just the right moment, a black-light replaced the spotlight and the hidden parts appeared like magic accompanied by gasps of surprise and lots of *oohs* and *ahhs*. It was after one such presentation that I'd asked Jesus into my heart.

I shook my head to dispel the memory. When my parents died and I came to live with my aunt, we attended her church every Sunday morning, because that's what people did; it was *expected*. But it wasn't the same. Though beautiful, Aunt Patricia's church was as cold and dead as a package of frozen peas. I felt myself becoming just as wintry as the rest of the congregation, and I made a promise to myself that as soon I could manage it, I'd never step foot into that church again. When I walked out after Aunt Patricia's funeral, it was for the last time. I'd kept that promise to myself and never looked back...until now.

Finding out that Lily had a Bible unearthed some guilty memories as well as more confusion about my new friend. Just when I thought I was starting to figure out her "pitching style," she'd throw me a curve ball. How could she make me feel confident and off-balance at the same time? It didn't make sense. I wondered if it ever would.

She seemed deep in thought. I waited for her to break the silence.

"You can't start the next chapter of your life if you keep re-reading the last one."

Her voice was barely louder than a whisper, as if she was talking to herself, as if I wasn't meant to hear. I was about to throw my hands up in exasperation and stomp out of the room, when I stopped and allowed her words to penetrate my mind: *You can't start the next chapter of your life if you keep re-reading the last one.*

The words were a mental forehead smack.

The message pealed out in bell-tones, loud and clear, making me completely forget my attempted psychoanalysis of *her*, and focus on *me*. It shot like an arrow, straight to the center of my heart...*bull's eye!* She was talking about my life before meeting her. Did she know that? I'd done nothing, but re-read the same boring chapters over and over. *Poor me...my parents died and I had to go live with my mean, old aunt who hated me. <insert pout> She treated me sooo bad. It's no wonder I'm shy and have no friends. It's not my fault. Poor, poor pitiful me!* Then suddenly—was it only yesterday?—Lily shot into my life like a rocket, blasting away all the smudged, dog-eared pages of that old chapter, revealing the crisp, clean pages of a new one and making me excited to begin reading it. Maybe it was all her little oddities that finally opened my eyes; I didn't know and I didn't care. I was just suddenly very grateful that Lily had jingled into my life, sprinkling glitter along the way.

What an epiphany!

"Can I show you something?"

Lily's voice sounded...what? Choked up? A little scared? I wasn't sure. Maybe she'd had an epiphany too and was just as emotional as I was.

"Yeah," I croaked, and then cleared my throat. "Sure you can."

She held out the black plastic garbage bag she'd retrieved from her cart before we'd started up the stairs. It was one of those thick lawn and leaf kind, but only a fraction of it was full. She held it out to me without a word, pulling back slightly when I reached for it. I shot her a glance, and let my hand drop. What on earth was wrong? It was clear that she was fighting some inner battle; it was painted all over her face. It took several seconds for her to decide the outcome of the struggle, but then she squared her shoulders and almost forced the bag into my hands. But by that time, I didn't want it.

"What *is* this?" I asked. "Something you found in someone's trash?"

She didn't answer, just turned back to the window, leaving me with my questions.

I tentatively hefted it from hand to hand. "It's heavy for its size. And lumpy, though I can't tell what it might be through this thick plastic. Can you give me a hint? Animal, vegetable, mineral?" I joked, trying to lighten the atmosphere that now seemed too heavy to breathe. "Nothing? C'mon, Lily. You're scaring me. Why are you acting so skittish?"

She never moved, just kept staring out her window. It looked like I'd have to open the darn thing if I wanted to know what it was. It was bad. I knew it. She didn't have to say the words to tell me. Her actions screamed it. Did I really want to know? No, but it was something that I had to do.

My fingers fumbled with the knot that held it closed before finally managing to untie it and peer inside.

It was like staring into a bucket of black paint. I couldn't see a thing. The thick plastic bag seemed to absorb any available light like a sponge. A glance overhead told me there was no light fixture, and the candle by her pallet of blankets wouldn't be much help. The only other source of illumination was the window, so I moved to stand beside Lily.

At first, I didn't understand what I was seeing. Booklets? Flyers that someone had printed out? It was thick stacks of paper, with rectangular designs printed on top, several per page. "Huh. Looks sort of like sheets of play-money from a board game...a bunch of hundred dollar bills."

I pulled the bag closer, studying it more carefully in the dim light.

"Wait a minute... Lily, this is some pretty realistic play-money. It looks *a lot* like hundred dollar bills."

My hands went a little numb and I clumsily turned the bag upside down, dumping the contents to the floor, then gawking with a mixture of fascination and horror at the uncut sheets covered with little portraits of Benjamin Franklin.

"Oh, my God! This isn't play-money!"

My legs turned rubbery, and I sank quickly to the floor, sitting there in a shocked heap, amidst a small, counterfeit fortune.

It took a while, but the reality of it finally penetrated my foggy brain. "Counterfeit! Someone's printing counterfeit money. Where'd you find this? In the trash? Oh, God! Did anybody see you? Please tell me no one saw you take it. If the people who printed this know you have it, you're dead meat, Lily. They won't take a chance of you telling someone."

I expected a response, a retort, justification...*something*, but I might as well have not been in the room for all the reaction I got. She stood like a mannequin in front of her window, seemingly deaf and dumb. Her silence made me angry. Didn't she realize the danger she'd put herself in? She'd stumbled onto evidence pointing to a significant counterfeiting operation. What was *wrong* with her? *She* might not be scared, but *I* was. Actually jittery with it.

"Lily," I tried to speak more calmly than I felt, but my voice still shook. "I'm no expert, but I *am* an artist. I know high quality stuff when I see it. These people even used paper that feels right. And the color's perfect. The only wrong thing that I can see is there's a *very* slight misalignment—a printing plate malfunction, most likely. Other than that, you'd be hard pressed to find anybody who wouldn't believe these were anything other than real hundred dollar bills. They're obviously test-sheets; rejects that were never meant for circulation. Someone used a Sharpie to make sure of that." I touched the big, black, diagonal lines drawn across each rectangle. "More than likely, whoever printed these will have tweaked their process by now, and will be able to produce sheet after sheet of perfect bills."

Lily finally turned from the window. Maybe it was the light—or *lack* of it—but I swear she looked older, the wrinkles deeper, her face more drawn. She *was* scared. It was obvious. And here I was reading her the riot act.

"Okay," I said gently, patting the floor beside me. "Let's talk."

"Oh, no, Lily…are you sure?"

She nodded once, her jaw set stubbornly. "I know you think I'm crazy, but I'm not stupid. There's no mistaking that face, not when you see it on signs everywhere you look."

"But, but…*Mark Spencer?* Why would he do something like this? He's the police commissioner—has been for years—and he's even running for re-

93

election!"

"How should I know? Ran out of campaign money? Someone's blackmailing him? Greed? Who knows?"

"But why didn't you report it?"

She gave me a "how-dumb-can-you-be?" look. "I didn't report it because he *is* the commissioner. I mean, what can you do when the good guys are really the *bad* guys? That's *one* of the reasons. The other is that no one will take a homeless person seriously. They think we're all crazy." She sighed and sat quietly, deep in thought. "Don't you see? With him involved, I didn't know who I could trust. Didn't want to end up in the river with the other homeless people."

I gasped. "What?! You don't think there's a connection with *that*, do you?"

She shrugged. "Very next day they pulled the last guy out. Just saying."

The possibility scared me to death, and I found myself gnawing my thumbnail, a habit I thought I'd finally kicked. Apparently not. I sat on my hands to keep from doing further damage and stared at her. "What are we going to do?"

"I don't know," she shook her head, sadly. "I just don't know."

****

I exited Panera with a large sack and two drinks. Lily wouldn't enter the restaurant to eat with me, so I was bringing it out to her. "I got us some soup to go with our sandwiches. Warm us up inside."

She nodded eagerly. I could tell she was hungry and wondered if she ever ate anything besides cans of Campbell's. Maybe I'd ask her someday, but not now.

We found a bench and I doled out napkins, spoons, and a bowl of soup along with a sandwich for each of us, we ate like cavemen for a while; with only an occasional crunch or slurp punctuating the steady hum of traffic. It was only when the last bit of soup was scraped from the cardboard bowls and the final swallow of sweet tea sucked through our straws that we leaned back and breathed a big sigh, at exactly the same time, almost as if we'd rehearsed it. We laughed when our eyes met.

I started gathering up the trash, stuffing it into the bag, then held it out for Lily to add hers. "I don't know about you, but that hit the spot. I'll be able to think better now."

"Thank you for lunch. It's been a long time since I ate that well."

I hopped up and deposited the bag of trash in a nearby can and smiled at her. "No problem. Glad you enjoyed it." I didn't add that it was just a tiny fraction of what I felt I owed her after my recent epiphany. There was enough of my shyness still in there, that I couldn't bare my soul to her yet. I'd just have to show her instead. "Now…we need to figure out what to do…how to handle this thing you've stumbled into." I glanced meaningfully at her cart; the black plastic bag once again buried somewhere in its depths. "It doesn't give me the warm fuzzies to think about your cargo, if you know what I mean."

She nodded and rose to join me, grasping the cart's handles firmly. "Me, either. High blood pressure? Yes. A stomach ulcer? Probably, but definitely not warm fuzzies."

We'd taken about three steps when someone

tapped me on the shoulder. "Excuse me, Miss?"

Turning in surprise, I faced a broad expanse of black and red plaid flannel. I tilted my chin upward, but that movement had me squinting directly into the sun, unable to see anything, but blinding light.

"Oh, gosh! Sorry!" I heard a deep voice say, before a hand turned me away from the brightness. "Better?"

Once I was out of the glare, and I'd blinked a few times to get rid of the dark spots in my vision, I could see that the flannel shirt belonged to an absolutely drop-dead gorgeous hunk of a guy.

His eyes widened and he gasped, "You!"

Oh, no! It was the guy I'd crashed into at school yesterday—the Adonis—and he was even better looking up close. I mean…imagine the combination of the five best looking men you know and multiply it by a hundred! His thick, dark brown hair was cut almost military short, which might've been an attempt to control the curliness. Even as short as it was, I could see it was trying to show its natural tendency. His eyes were a warm, delicious brown—like chocolate—and his smile revealed a set of beautifully even teeth. All in all, he knocked my socks off, and all I could do was nod in answer to his question because my tongue was too tied up in knots to do anything else.

Not so, Lily. "What?" she demanded belligerently. Her gruff voice sounded even rougher than usual. I wanted to scream the same question back at her. *What?!*

His movie-star smile faded a little at her nasty tone. He glanced between the two of us, his expression, uncertain. "Uh…sorry. My name is Jonas Holmes." He reached into his shirt pocket and handed us both a card. "I'm a reporter for the Savannah Tribune, and in light of the three men they've recently pulled out of the river, I'm doing an investigative article on the plight of the homeless in Savannah. Do you think I—"

"We have nothing to say to you," Lily cut him off.

I turned to face her, my eyes wide and pleading, my hand gripping her arm. "What are you doing?" I kept a forced smile on my face, murmuring in my best ventriloquist imitation, barely moving my lips.

She shook her head, her mouth in a tight line, back ramrod stiff, arms folded under her breasts. She was trying to look severe and disapproving. She'd evidently forgotten about her hat. It was pretty much impossible to look stern wearing a hat like that. Her attempt was foiled before she even started, but that didn't stop her from *trying*. At least the hat provided some comic relief from the rest of her demeanor.

I turned back to the reporter, and gave him an apologetic smile. I couldn't speak to him yet. I was still too tongue-tied, but I help up a finger that silently asked him to give us a moment.

At his nod, I clasped her arm tighter. "Let's talk in private, shall we?" I murmured as calmly as possible. The serene demeanor was a lot harder to pull off than you'd think. What I *wanted* to do was shake her until her eyes popped out like champagne corks. It was only by using supreme effort that I was able to keep my fake smile in place until I'd dragged her a few feet away. Turning to face her with my back toward him, I shouted a whisper, "You mind telling me what you're doing??"

"I don't want to be in his article," she spoke through stiff lips. "I don't want to draw any attention to myself."

"Seriously?" I wanted to laugh and cry at the same

time. My recent epiphany was the only thing helping me keep myself together. "You don't want to draw attention to yourself?" I repeated her words so maybe she'd *hear* them. "Have you *looked* in the mirror lately?" I gave a derisive snort. "Great! Now you've got me sounding like Chandler Bing!"

"Who?"

"You know…Chandler…from *Friends* reruns? Oh, never mind. Lily, your hat screams, "Look at me! Look at me!" and you're worried about calling *attention* to yourself? If that's your aim, you need to lose the hat. It's defeating the purpose; definitely drawing more looks than any newspaper article *ever* could."

She beetled her eyebrows and glared at me, arms crossed even tighter.

I tried another tactic. "Okay, listen. Maybe he can *help* us."

Her glare grew darker. "You just think he's cute, is all."

That gave me pause. Was she right? Did I just want to help him because he was the hottest thing I'd seen in a long time and he actually talked to me? Probably, but I didn't think it would help my cause to tell her that, so I forged ahead, ignoring the accusation.

"Look, you know we can't go to the police with what you found, right?" I glanced pointedly at her cart. "Now, listen. He's an *in-ves-ti-ga-tive* reporter." I drew the syllables out slowly, then paused, giving her a minute, hoping she'd put it together on her own.

She didn't.

I sighed and rolled my eyes. "Don't you see? We can give him something to *investigate*. It won't be about the homeless—well, not *totally*, anyway—but it'll definitely be worth reporting. If this story gets out in the paper where every person in Savannah—including the tourists—can read it in black and white, the police will *have* to pay attention, arrest the guilty parties, and thus, stop the counterfeiting. Granted, it's kind of a round-about way, but at least we'll achieve our purpose, which is shutting it down. *And...*" I added quickly when I saw her mouth open, thinking she was about to voice some protest. "...if Spencer's operation *is* connected with these homeless guys ending up in the river, well, it's sure to come out in any subsequent investigation, and that'll stop too."

She was no longer glaring at me, which I took for a good sign. "Well, what do you say? Can we work together with him?"

"We'll catch Mark Spencer?"

"I haven't exactly got that part worked out yet. In case you haven't realized it, I'm making this up as I go, but I'm pretty sure it'll bring him down. At the very least, he won't be re-elected commissioner. I doubt Savannahians will take kindly to learning that not only was a major counterfeiting operation going on right under the commissioner's nose, but that he was *in charge* of it. Stuff like that doesn't get you re-elected; it gets you in jail."

I glanced over my shoulder to where Jonas waited, wearing an uncertain look on his face. "Can we tell him yes?"

She gave me a long look before answering, "Yes."

Chapter Eight

Jonas

I was getting nowhere fast, and I was ready to give up. What was the problem anyway? Was I wearing an invisible, "Don't talk to me" sign? Jeez! Talk about a dead end! It was time to cut my losses, and come up with another plan. This one obviously wasn't working. For all the good I'd done so far, I might as well be back at my desk tapping out another brilliant article about the latest bank robbery or home invasion or gang fight or…or…just fill in the blank with the headline of choice. My shoulders slumped with discouragement and I sighed, feeling beaten, practically incapacitated.

Heading through Chippewa Square, on the way to where I'd parked my car, I spotted a possible contact and decided to give it one last shot. Couldn't hurt, right? The man was obviously homeless…dirty, clothes tattered and shabby, the typical metal cart stuffed with plastic bags pulled up next to the end of the bench where he sat hunched over a notebook, writing as if his life depended on it. Maybe I'd luck up, and this guy would actually *talk* to me.

The flicker of hope fizzled as soon as I got near enough to see what the man was doing. A double-page spread of indecipherable scribbles told me what I needed to know. I'd get no help from this one, either. I stared at the man, fuming...mad at everyone and everything. I was even angry at the dappled sunlight dancing around me on the sidewalk. How *dare* it look so happy? I raked a hand through my hair, frustrated beyond belief, then turned on my heel, muttering to myself as I continued on the way to my car. A flash of color in my peripheral caught my attention; a casual glance became a double-take that had me veering around the statue, pausing in front of a bronze plaque, pretending to read it, trying not to gawk.

A young, dark haired girl, wearing a blazing red sweatshirt, sat on a bench, nearly shoulder to shoulder with an elderly woman who was wearing an obscenely bright pink and green hat, practically capable of retinal burning. But it wasn't the colors that grabbed my attention—okay...maybe initially that's what did it, but what *kept* me staring was something entirely different. The older woman was homeless. If ragtag clothing and weird hat didn't give her away, that two-wheeled metal cart sitting beside her sure did, but that wasn't why I stared, either. No, it was because that homeless lady was *talking*—having an actual conversation—with the slim girl in the sweatshirt...who obviously *wasn't* homeless.

It was hard to stay calm and unobtrusive when what I wanted to do was jump up and down, whooping and waving my arms in a victory dance. Though outwardly cool, my heart was pumping like a steam locomotive, making me feel like I'd just run the Rock and Roll Marathon. *See...?* I mentally sashayed, punching my cynical, glass-half-empty self in the shoulder...it *is* possible to get them to talk. Here's proof in living color, and boy, did I ever mean *color!*

They were eating something—apples, from the looks of it—a companionable snack between friends. *Were* they friends? They both seemed pretty relaxed. Their body language had an open, friendly feeling, but how had it happened? How had that girl broken through the wall when I couldn't? I wished I could hear what they were saying, but I didn't want to draw attention to myself by moving any closer.

I eyed the girl, fighting a touch of jealousy. She looked familiar. I'd seen her somewhere before...and recently. Where? It wouldn't come to me. Maybe later.

What was her secret, anyway? What did she have that I didn't? Maybe I'd learn something useful if I just watched her a while. Yes, that's what I'd do...watch and learn.

****

The girl was an artist—the drawing pad in her hand gave that part away. I'd be willing to bet she was a SCAD student, though she looked too young to be in college. Slender, graceful...like a wood nymph or a fairy. *Not big as a minute,* as my dad would say. Maybe she looked older up close. Was that the SCAD insignia on her sweatshirt? It was. Okay, so...yes, she was probably a student there, but that still didn't answer the burning question: how had she broken through the invisible barrier I'd been encountering everywhere I'd turned? Guess I needed to keep on watching.

Uh-oh...they stopped. I ducked into a doorway so they wouldn't notice me. Peeking around the corner, I could see the young girl leaning against a stair railing, holding her sketch pad across her left arm. Her right hand held a pencil that swept broad, sure strokes across the page, supposedly capturing her subject in black and white, but I couldn't tell for sure from where I stood.

Wait a minute! What was the old woman doing? She'd pulled out a sparkly bag and was reaching into it, pulling out a handful of whatever was inside. Now she was...sprinkling it around a parking meter?

Huh?

I fidgeted, waiting impatiently for them to move on, curious to see what that stuff was. It was several minutes before they moved down the street, allowing me the chance to vacate my hiding place. I approached the parking meter and stared.

Um...yeah.

Guess it was safe to say that more than just the old lady's hat was weird.

****

I was sitting inside Panera, spooning thick chowder into my mouth as quickly as possible. Sunlight poured through the window, painting a warm, yellow band across my table. My speedy eating had a two-fold cause. One...I was famished. The only thing I'd had for breakfast was an oatmeal bar and a cup of coffee as I headed out the door, and two...I wanted to make sure I finished my meal before my targets finished theirs. On the other side of the glass, two heads were bent over their own lunch; one glossy brown, the other capped in lurid colors that would look right at home in an LSD hallucination.

I broke off a hunk of bread, soaking up the remnants of my soup, then popped it into my mouth, chewing slowly, staring at the two outside. I couldn't help it. The longer I watched, the more it piqued my interest. What a mismatched pair! What on earth had brought these two together? All my stalking still hadn't answered that question. I'd been around enough affluent folks in my life to be pretty good at judging who came from money and who just wanted people to *think* they came from money. The girl was in the first category, and as a general rule, there wasn't a lot of intermingling between her group and the homeless. So...there must be a very good reason for them to be together, but what could it be? My writer's curiosity trekked down several unlikely paths, rejecting each one and returning to contemplate some more.

The girl had been drawing the older woman. Could that be it? Maybe a class assignment? Possible. I studied her profile, her animated expression. She didn't *look* like she was being forced to do something she didn't want to do. On the contrary, she was enjoying herself, and...wow! Now that I could see her better— her profile rather than a back view—she really *was* a pretty little thing. She—

Cut it out, Holmes! Don't get sidetracked. You don't have time for that. Remember the article you're writing. Syndication...think syndication...stay on track.

Right.

It looked like they were almost finished, which meant it was nearly game time. My plan was a back door approach, get to the older woman through the younger one. All I had to do was somehow convince her to help me. Piece of cake, right? So how come I wasn't oozing confidence? Probably due to the fact that all of my other interview attempts had crashed and burned.

I slurped the last of my drink before gathering my trash, and heading toward the exit. After sliding the tray's contents into the can and adding my tray to the stack already there, I drew a deep breath, muttered, "Here goes nothing," and pushed out into the bright sunshine.

I reached out to tap the girl on the shoulder, startled at the jolt that rocketed through my hand. *What was— No! Figure it out later.* "Excuse me, Miss?"

She whirled to face me, squinting through unbelievably long, thick lashes. The sun was blinding her.

"Oh, sorry!" I turned her to face away from the glare. "Better?"

"You!" I gasped. It was the girl who'd crashed into me while I was doing that interview about the bike thefts at SCAD. The most amazing set of eyes I'd ever seen stared up at me. Dark-lashed, turquoise…dazzling. She had perfect features, a faint sprinkling of freckles across her nose and cheeks now suffused pink with embarrassment; soft lips that were curved into an enchanting smile.

I stared—I *think* my face still wore a smile, but my inner self was absolutely slack-jawed…dumbfounded. For a long second, I forgot how to speak. Heck…I almost forgot how to *breathe*. I hadn't felt like this since—who was I kidding? I'd *never* felt so bowled over before! When my sluggish brain finally kicked back into gear, a single thought flashed red, over and over like a railroad warning: Danger, danger, danger!

"What?" The old woman growled, breaking the spell.

"Uh…sorry. My name is Jonas Holmes." Numb fingers fumbled in my shirt pocket, trying to locate the business cards that I knew were there, but couldn't feel. "I'm a reporter for the Savannah Tribune…"

****

Later, I tried to remember the rest of the conversation I'd had with Cleo and Lily, but it was mostly a blur. The gist of it was that I'd be meeting them later. I grinned at the thought, but then I gave myself a mental head smack. *Get a grip, man!*

The meeting place was an alley where Lily had seen a homeless man being beat up. It wasn't much, but it was a better lead than anything else I'd come up with in over a week, and it meant I'd get to see Cleo again. That was the good part. The downside was that the old woman didn't like me. I know, I know…what's not to like? But she didn't. At all. The negative feelings had been instantaneous, and as far as I could tell, it wasn't from anything I'd done. Maybe she had something against men.

Whatever the reason, it made things tricky. It meant a tight-rope walk for me if I wanted to work with them. And since I saw no other means of getting any help with my story, I guess I needed to find an umbrella or some sort of pole to help me keep my balance. I was definitely going to need it.

My thoughts were interrupted by my cell phone. My brother, Andrew…the pediatrician. What did *he* want?

I answered. "What's up, bro?"

"Just checking on you, man."

"I'm fine. Did mom put you up to this?"

"Do I have to have a reason to call my brother?"

I rolled my eyes. "No back-peddling. You said "check on," not "call." And since when do you ever check on me unless coerced by mom?"

"Technicalities. I'm crushed, but yeah…mom

might've mentioned you were a bit down...you know...three years since the Jill thing."

"I'm fine," I repeated. "And I'd be a lot finer if you guys would give it a rest. I mean, I'm glad you're concerned and all, but honestly...I really *am* fine."

"Okay, okay. I get the message. I'll try to convince mom to back off."

"Good luck with that, but give it a shot."

"Job going all right?"

"As a matter of fact, it is. I'm working on a pretty big story right now. Have a meeting with a source later on tonight."

"A source, huh?"

"Yeah, tracking down leads on homeless men who keep ending up in the river."

"Oh, yeah. I heard something about that on the news. You mean there's more to it?"

"That's what my gut's telling me. Plus, I've got a source I'm checking out. I'll let you know."

"Again with the source? What kind of source are we talking about?"

"A homeless woman, and before you ask...she's old. I'm supposed to meet her and her friend when it gets dark."

"Is the friend old too?"

"Um...why do you ask?"

Andrew laughed. "Curiosity more than anything. You sound different, and I'm trying to figure out the cause."

"I'm just feeling good about this assignment, that's all."

"Whatever you say." He sounded unconvinced. "Well, be careful. Anything you want me to pass on to mom?"

"Just get her to stop worrying."

Andrew laughed again. "Like *that's* going to happen."

"I know, right? Well, give her my love, then."

"Will do. See ya, man."

"Bye."

I shook my head with a rueful smile, as I hung up. Moms…can't live with them, can't live without them.

Chapter Nine

Cleo

"Why is it so dark?" I whispered, glaring upward in an accusatory manner. The high, thin clouds we'd had for most of the day had thickened as night fell and were now thwarting the attempt of moon or stars in shedding their light. "Isn't there supposed to be a streetlight back here? Oops...sorry," I apologized after bumping into Jonas for the fourth time. *Not really.* He was wearing some delicious-smelling cologne, and every time I jostled against him, I got a fresh wave of it. It made me want to press my face against his neck and take deep breaths until I got light-headed. I wondered how many more times I could get away with my bumping routine before he caught on.

After our discussion earlier that afternoon—*YES, I talked to a guy! My mouth had actually formed coherent words that made sense! I know, I know! I can't believe it either! Especially once I knew he'd recognized me as the idiot who'd slammed into him yesterday at school.* Anyway, we decided to meet and hide in the alley behind Lily's building. That's where she'd found the bag; that's where she'd witnessed Mark Spencer beating and then shooting the mystery man. It only stood to reason that's where we needed to start. We were looking for a clue and not having much luck with it yet.

I'll admit, we didn't tell Jonas *everything*. Only that this was the place where Lily had seen a homeless man being beat up. Okay, so we didn't *know* it was a homeless man, we just *suspected* it, stretching the truth a little. We also didn't tell the part about the man being shot, thinking that Jonas might not be so gung-ho if he knew there was real danger involved. We just didn't want to show all our cards yet...at least Lily didn't. I went along with her because that was the only way she'd work with Jonas. We'd tell him the truth soon, I promised myself.

"There used to be a light," Lily pointed over our heads. "Someone shot it out."

"Ahh..." I responded. "To keep it as dark as the ace of spades. I see. They need it pitch black in order to cover up their clandestine shenanigans."

Jonas chuckled, "Did you really just say "clandestine shenanigans"?"

I was saved from having to respond when a car stopped at the end of the street, waiting to make a turn. Without a word, we all leaped behind a bank of city regulation sized trashcans lined up and awaiting a visit from the sanitation crew the next morning. Our backs were pressed into the grape ivy that covered the wall like thick shag carpet. I was never so thankful that we didn't have to contend with Lily's cart. I was still amazed that she'd actually cut the umbilical cord and left it in its hiding place in the alley.

My heart was lodged in the vicinity of my throat, and it was having a difficult time beating properly. The car eased past us, pulling to a stop right beside the stairway Lily and I had climbed earlier in the day. Four car doors slammed in quick succession, then there was a confused shuffle of footsteps; loud at first, then fading away.

I was straining my ears so hard, listening for something else, that I jumped when Jonas broke the silence with a whisper. "Sounded like they went down a set of stairs. Is there a basement in this building?"

"Yes," Lily answered. "Small window in the alley on the left side. Hasn't closed properly in years. Always open a little bit. We need to get near it. It's privacy glass, so we won't be able to *see* anything, but that means they can't see us either. If we can get close enough, maybe we can hear what they're saying."

"Great!" he replied. "Let's move!"

We were able to scurry from the trashcans across the street in a surprisingly quiet manner, considering the way we moved, like we were all joined at the hip. Once we rounded the back corner, we spotted the slightly open window, just like Lily had said. A light clicked on behind it just as we were crouching down, startling me, and making me jump. I quickly clapped my hand over my mouth to keep from gasping out loud. I stared into two sets of very wide eyes; I'm sure mine looked similar.

Someone was talking, but it was mostly a hum at first. *C'mon...* I mentally urged them closer to the window. *Over here...that's it...a little more. Good!*

"No, I was lucky to get this place. Renting it. I'd buy it if I could, but no one seems to know where the owner is. Been empty for years, and apparently the owner's flown the coop. Since it's owned outright, and the taxes and insurance keeps getting paid on time, it's got the city's hands tied. Until they figure out how to handle it, I thought it'd be the perfect base for my little enterprise."

That was Mark Spencer talking! With all the campaign commercials on both TV and radio, I'd heard large doses of his coastal drawl. I'd recognize it anywhere.

"Now," he went on. "...the reason you're here is because my man, Al, recommended you for the job and you've already signed the agreement. Consider this your introduction into the business. Ready?"

I couldn't hear any answer, but apparently Spencer had gotten one. "Right. This is the printer I was telling you about on the way over here...eleven by fourteen offset. Got a plate in place already. Two negatives for the portrait side and one for the back side. I paid two grand for that set," he bragged. "Another fifteen hundred for each plate. But look at this quality, will you? You only get something like this if you're willing to pay for it."

There was a muttered response, with only a word here and there that I could make out, nothing that made sense, then Spencer's smooth voice took over again. He must've been standing just on the other side of the window, and the others were across the room. "Yeah, you're right. The paper's one of the most important things. Even if everything else is perfect, if the paper's off, it's no good. It has to be twenty-five percent rag content. Disaperf's the best."

A different murmurer spoke. This one was slightly higher pitched than the other one. Again, I could only make out an occasional word. How many were in there? At least four, since we'd heard four car doors slam. This guy made three. Where was the fourth?

Spencer laughed, interrupting my wonderings. "Nothing you need to worry about, right Danny?"

A chuckle. "Yeah, boss."

Ah…the fourth voice.

I swallowed hard and glanced at Jonas. I wondered if he'd figured out what they were talking about yet; that this was much bigger than a homeless man being beat up. His grave, brown eyes met mine, and I had my answer.

Yep, he knew.

Spencer went on, "You wrap it around the cylinder like this…and then load the black ink. Make sure you run more than you need because you'll have a lot of rejects." He gave an evil sounding laugh. "And just remember…it's not good for your health to get any bright ideas about the rejects. You understand what I'm saying? You can ask Al and Danny about that."

A quiet response. Did I hear the word, *swim?*

"Yeah. Okay…while the black is printing, you mix the ink for the serial numbers. A little white, maybe some yellow. Experiment 'til you get it right. Next, clean the press and print the other side. You'll end up with a bill with no seal or serial numbers. Print a few with one number, change it, print a few more and then repeat that until you have as many numbers as you need."

Murmur. I couldn't tell whether it was the high or low pitched one.

"Not to worry. I have a list of all the numbers to use. Next, is the cutting process. It has to be exact and I mean *exact*. No mistakes. You'll use that paper cutter over there for that."

Another answer too quiet to make out.

113

"Of course they're white, stupid. They're not done yet. You have to mix up hot water and teabags and probably…uh…sixteen to twenty drops of green food coloring. Al knows the exact amount. He'll show you, and you can experiment with some of the reject bills to get it right. After you've made any necessary adjustments, you'll dye all the bills. Once they're completely dry, you'll have to crumple them up several times and rub them in coffee grounds, you know…to make them look used. If you follow these steps, it's a pretty simple process. But you *gotta follow the steps*. Any questions?"

Again, the reply too indistinct to understand, but I could tell it was the low one.

"No, not tonight. I just wanted to give you an overview before you start tomorrow. Al will show you everything nice and slow. Do exactly what he says and you'll do fine. Right now, there's someplace I need to be, so we have to go. Just remember what I said about keeping your mouth shut. I think we understand each other on that point, don't we?"

I was listening so hard for the response, that I was surprised when the light clicked off. The sudden darkness disoriented me, but I managed to scramble to my feet. Jonas had turned to dash back the way we'd come, but Lily grabbed his arm in one hand and mine in her other one, then pushed me and pulled him toward the front of the building along the same narrow space I'd trod earlier today. We were strolling along Oglethorpe Street within seconds. I just hoped we didn't look as suspicious as I felt.

"Okay," Jonas shoved an ice cream cone into my hand after giving one to Lily. "Which one of you wants to start?"

I was going to try to play innocent, to claim ignorance about all that had transpired the last hour, but I gave up before I started. It would be pointless to try. I gave Lily a look, but she just shrugged, too busy eating her cone.

"Well, I guess you could say that we weren't entirely honest with you."

"Oh! You think?" His eyes shot chocolate sparks at me.

"You're angry," I said, stating the obvious.

He opened his mouth, then snapped it shut, pressing his lips together, and breathing deeply through his nose, apparently trying not to explode. He stared at me through narrowed eyes, waiting.

I nodded once. "Yeah...so...where should I start?"

"Try the beginning," he ground out through clenched teeth.

Uh-oh...time to quit stalling. "Okay. Just so we're clear, a man really *was* beaten in that alley, but we don't know *who*." He opened his mouth to reply, but I held up my hand to stop him, hurrying on. "However, Lily *did* see who was doing the beating...and the shooting."

His eyes bugged out. "Shooting?! There was shooting too? Oh, jeez..." He squeezed his eyes shut and rubbed his forehead like he had a headache.

"Do you want to hear this or not?"

Those brown eyes met mine again. The muscle in his jaw tightened, and he gave me a curt nod.

"That's better." Was that *me* talking? How'd I get to be so sassy? This new Cleo handled impertinence like a pro; thinking nothing of spouting off smart aleck responses to this Greek god in flannel. Well, she better not quit on me, now. I couldn't do this without her. "Now, the person Lily saw was Mark Spencer...you know, Police Commissioner Spencer? That was the smooth voice we just heard."

His mouth gaped, and I blurted, "But that's not all. The day before that, she found a black trash bag containing rejects from the little operation we heard about tonight. Lily picked up enough of the argument that preceded the attack to realize it was connected to the bag of money she'd found. Then the next day, a homeless man's body was dragged out of the river. The news didn't mention whether or not that man had been shot, but we're afraid it's all connected." I took a deep breath and huffed it out. "That's all. Now you can talk."

Jonas turned to Lily and demanded, "Why didn't you tell the police?"

She just rolled her eyes, gave him a "you've got to be kidding" look, and kept eating her cone.

I watched, waiting for him to make the connection. It didn't take long.

"Right. Mark Spencer...police... I guess telling the cops is kind of out, isn't it?"

I touched his arm and felt tingles travel from my fingertips to my shoulder then radiate out. It made me lose my train of thought for a second. "Uh...that's why we told *you*. You're an investigative reporter. You can help us by doing what you do best, and once you get all your facts, you can report them, bring it all out in the open, and the police will *have* to arrest him, no matter *who* he is. They'll have no choice."

He rubbed his eyes a little tiredly. "This is big, you know...*huge!*" He stared off into space, and never even noticed it when the big scoop of ice cream slipped right off his cone and plopped onto the sidewalk.

I decided not to point it out.

"Do you realize what this means?" he finally said. "How dangerous it could end up being? Somebody's already been shot! Maybe more than one person!"

I nodded. "Yeah...we needed help in the worst kind of way. And then, at exactly the right time, you arrived on the scene...a veritable knight in shining armor, ready to slay the dragon."

The smile he gave me made my stomach do a flip-flop and my toes curl up inside my boots. I shivered. Time stood still.

Then he blinked, giving his head a slight shake before responding, "Knight in shining armor, huh? Well, let's hope my sword is sharp enough."

Out of the corner of my eye, I saw Lily stop licking her ice cream, look up at me, and smile. I knew what she was going to say by the way her eyes were sparkling. I felt a laugh bubbling up inside me, but it fizzled a little when I realized my mind was traveling along the same path as hers. Yikes! I was thinking like Lily! That was a little scary.

"The pen," she intoned, "...is mightier than the sword."

I couldn't help it. I burst out laughing, and after a startled moment, Jonas joined in.

Lily just grinned and went back to eating her ice cream.

Chapter Ten

Cleo

After Lily finished her ice cream, she gave an exaggerated yawn and announced that it was past her bedtime. I *assumed* she'd say goodnight, disappear like she was so good at doing, and I'd get to spend some quality time with Jonas, all to myself. Though nervous, I was already dreaming about it.

Well…you know what they say about a person who assumes.

Lily rose to her feet and stood there, staring at me like she was waiting for something.

Oh! She wants to know what time to meet me in the morning, I thought, naïvely. "Same time; same place tomorrow?" I asked, giving her my best smile.

"Well?" she demanded, ignoring my question and asking one of her own. "You aren't going to make an old woman walk home by herself now, are you?"

I blinked at her, not really understanding. After all, this was a woman who had been walking the streets of Savannah on her own for nearly half a century. "What?" I finally asked, keeping my smile in place, but it wasn't without effort.

I wouldn't have believed what happened next if I hadn't actually seen it with my own eyes, but she actually *pouted*. "Aren't you going to walk me home?"

Her low voice was almost a whimper.

My mind scrambled in a million different directions for a response. I felt my mouth drop open, and then snap shut when I realized what she was doing. I narrowed my eyes and glared at her, furious. She was trying to keep me away from Jonas! Why? Who could know that, but maybe in some warped way, she thought she was protecting me. But protecting me from *what*? It wasn't like he was some perverted psycho out to do me harm. I know I'd just met him, but the circumstances that we'd already gone through together had sort of cemented the friendship...*quickly*. How could I make her see that I didn't *want* to be protected from him?

I turned to Jonas. "Um...I guess I've got to go. Let me give you my cell number." I picked up a napkin and printed my number carefully, in big, bold characters. I didn't want him to not be able to read it. I could see Lily fidgeting out of the corner of my eye. She didn't like this at all. Our eyes met and I gave her a tight little smile as I handed Jonas the napkin. I wasn't about to let her have her way with this.

I turned back to him. "I know you thought you were going to be *getting* help with this article rather than *giving* it, but I've got to say, I'm very glad it was you who galloped into the arena to help us slay this dragon, *and* that you didn't get scared off by the idea. Will we see you tomorrow?"

His gaze went from me to Lily, then back to me. He gave me a crooked smile and nodded his head a little helplessly, his eyes like warm chocolate. "Yeah...see you tomorrow."

****

"In the words of Ricky Ricardo, "You got some

'splainin' to do!'"" I fumed the minute we were out of his earshot.

"I don't know what you're talking about."

I gritted my teeth. "The heck you don't! You're sabotaging my attempts at getting to know Jonas better. You're like a submarine, sneaking around, undetected, and then *whoosh*...here comes a torpedo! I can't believe that you pulled the "poor little old lady" routine! Who do you think you're kidding?"

"Don't do something permanently stupid just because you're temporarily upset."

"Argggh!" I threw my hands in the air, stomped a few steps ahead, and then stopped. *I'm gonna kill her... No one will blame me. That's what I'll do. Epiphany or not, I'm gonna kill her!* I whirled and got right in her face, my nose almost touching hers. "You like your stupid little sayings so much, well, here's one you might not have in your repertoire: *Some people are so full of crap, they need their own sewer system!*" I glared at her for a long minute, then turned and stalked away.

I could hear her shuffling behind me, her bells barely jingling.

We walked in stony silence for about a block. Well, maybe a stiff-legged *march* would be a better description, at least as far as I was concerned. As my anger cooled, though, I felt my joints loosening up, becoming a little less stiff. I was still walking slightly ahead of her, but I was eventually walking *normally*.

Finally, Lily sighed. "Apologizing doesn't always mean you're wrong and the other person's right. It just means you value your relationship more than your ego."

"Does that mean you're sorry?"

"Yes."

I snorted, stopping to wait until she caught up with me. "That's about the most pathetic excuse for an apology that I've ever heard, but I guess I accept."

She smiled and waggled her head, making her bells jingle. "Good."

As we strolled along a few minutes, the silence became less strained, and was practically back to normal by the time her building came into view. I broke it with reluctance, crossing my fingers that what I was about to say wouldn't re-freeze the atmosphere. "I think he's really nice, and I like him, you know."

She didn't speak for a minute, but finally gave a sigh and said, "I know, but I want to share one last saying with you before you leave. It'll give you something to think about on your way home."

"You mean, like today hasn't already given me enough to think about?"

"Well, I guess you have a point there, but this is a good one."

"Okay," I heaved an exaggerated sigh. "Go ahead."

A streetlight shone through the tree limbs above us, the ghostly drapery of Spanish moss casting long, eerie shadows across her face. A moped's high-pitched engine whined past us, sounding like an angry bee trapped in a bottle. Lily's expression was serious, somber; her eyes caught mine and held them. "Follow your heart," she intoned. "But take your brain with you."

I managed to keep my fa   straight for about ten seconds, before dissolving into g   les. "Sorry, Lily," I said, trying unsuccessfully to get myself under control. "I know you mean well and I really do appreciate it. I'll keep that in mind. I promise. See you tomorrow?"

I could see her eyes sparkling a little, so at least I knew I hadn't offended her. She was probably laughing too…on the inside.

"Yes, I'll see you tomorrow. Goodnight."

"G'night."

****

Minnie's inquisition began the minute I stepped through the door.

"Where in the world have you been? I'll have you know, I like to have worried myself to death over you all day. First, you come home last night all white-faced and scared, then you go bustin' out of the house this morning like your hair was on fire, your shirttails hangin' straight out behind you, and now you come draggin' in here, *waaay* after supper time, without botherin' to call and tell me, mind you, and you think you're gonna go straight up to your room? Hmpf! Think again, missy. We need to talk."

She turned on her heel and headed straight for the kitchen, obviously expecting me to follow. My shoulders slumped, and I stared down at my cat. "Do I have to, Tut?" I whined.

Without an answer, he performed an about-face, his nose and tail stuck straight in the air, then followed right in Minnie's footsteps.

"Great!" I muttered to myself. "My cat is ticked off at me too." I gave a huge sigh. "Well, I might as well get this over with."

I entered the kitchen to see Minnie facing the sink, industriously scouring away on a pot that probably wasn't even dirty. If she wasn't careful, she'd end up scrubbing the bottom right out of it. I'd seen her do the same thing on numerous occasions after Aunt Patricia had read her the riot act for one infraction or another. I never thought I'd be the cause of one of her pot-scrubbing fits. Tut sat on the counter beside her, his back to me too.

I sighed again. This was going to be fun.

I thought, briefly about asking her where Tobias was, but nixed the idea. He was probably out driving the limousine, pretending it was a taxi; a practice that began after Aunt Patricia died. Although he didn't need it—my aunt had uncharacteristically provided for him and Minnie in her will too—he was surprisingly successful at giving tours around the city. The fact that Minnie didn't approve of his activities caused me to hold my tongue. I didn't need to give her more reason for aggravation. Instead, I settled onto a barstool and sat facing her stiff back across the marble-topped island. The silence seemed to grow heavier with every tick of the clock. If I didn't say something soon, the air would be too thick for us to breathe.

"I'm sorry I didn't call and let you know I wouldn't be home for supper. To tell you the truth, I never even thought about it. I've been kind of busy today."

Minnie's shoulders relaxed a little as she turned on the tap and proceeded to rinse the pot. Tut watched this action for a minute, then turned his face back toward the wall.

I tilted my chin up and stared at the ceiling with wide eyes. *Why me?* I mentally moaned. Then I remembered what Lily had said after our argument tonight: *apologizing doesn't always mean you're wrong, it just means you value the relationship more than your ego.* "Okay, okay! Tut, I'm sorry I ran out this morning without giving you the attention you think—no, the attention you *deserve.* Will you please forgive me?"

That darn cat immediately turned and jumped from his spot on the counter by the sink over to the bar where I was seated and then sashayed right up to me, touching his nose to mine. I couldn't help it; I scratched his head, whispering, "You little turkey!"

By this time, Minnie had turned to face me. "Did you eat supper?" she asked solicitously.

I winced. "About five licks of an ice cream cone. Does that count?"

Without a word, she turned to the refrigerator and pulled out a plastic container. Grabbing a plate, she spooned out some of the contents, draped a paper towel over it, popped it into the microwave, and punched in some numbers. While it warmed, she retrieved a glass from the cabinet, filled it with ice, and then poured in some sweet tea. When the microwave beeped, she removed the warmed food and slid it and the glass in front of me, following them with a fork and a napkin. "Eat," she ordered.

I stared down at my plate, taking a deep breath of the unmistakable aroma of Italian seasonings mixed with tomatoes and cheeses. Mmmmm…lasagna. I *loved* Minnie's lasagna. Without another word, I dug in, making sure to share an occasional bit of cheese with Tut. He loved Minnie's lasagna too, but he especially loved cheese.

When I finished, I gave her a sheepish smile. "I really am sorry I didn't call you. I'll try my best not to let it happen again."

She nodded and smiled in return, although hers seemed a bit grudging. "I know, child. Now…I'm all ears." She pulled both said appendages straight out from her head.

"You look like Minnie Mouse," I giggled, then sobered, wondering how much to tell her. There wasn't time to plan any sort of strategy for my story; I'd have to figure it out as I went. "You remember that painting assignment I told you about? The one I have to do over Christmas break?"

"Yes."

"Well, I finally found a model. Kind of unexpected, really."

"Who is it? Anybody I know?"

"Uh…I don't think so, although, you may have seen her around town."

The clock ticked a few times before Minnie asked, "Well? Are you going to tell me, or do you expect me to start guessing?"

"Her name is Lily…Lily Telfair-Gordon. I know, weird name, right? She's probably around your age, maybe a little older. She lives down on Oglethorpe Street. As soon as I saw her, I knew she was perfect for this assignment."

"Well, good. I'm glad you found what you're looking for. So that's what you been doing all day? Working on that assignment?"

"Yeah, sort of."

She narrowed her eyes and stared at me with pursed lips before asking. "What do you mean, sort of?"

"Well, part of the day was that, and part was just getting to know Lily better. And then we met Jonas."

Her eyebrows shot up. "Jonas?"

"Um, yeah. Jonas is a reporter for the Savannah Tribune and he asked us to help him with an article he's working on."

"What kind of article?"

"Well, he's doing a sort of investigative story on the plight of the homeless in Savannah."

I could tell by the look on her face that she was confused. "Cleo, honey...how in the world can *you* possibly help him with an article like that; you livin' in this fancy house and all? You don't have any way of knowin' anything about the homeless."

"Yeah, I know. *I* don't, but *Lily* does."

"How's that?"

Uh-oh. This is where it could get sticky. I looked at Tut for help, but he seemed to be waiting for my answer too, his stare seeming even more suspicious than Minnie's. "Um...well, I guess you could say that Lily is an expert, and can provide him with *first-hand* information."

Minnie cocked her eyebrow and gave me that look that only she can give. "And why, pray tell, would her information be first-hand?"

"Well, I guess that would be because she's, um..." I dropped my gaze to the counter top, tracing a finger along the design in the marble. "Because she's...*homeless.*"

I kept my eyes on my finger, twirling around and around in the stone's pattern. The silence grew a little oppressive. I heard the distinct, soft thud of Tut jumping to the floor in retreat.

Traitor! I hissed mentally, before continuing to follow the convoluted lines of the countertop.

The silence stretched tighter and tighter. *Say something!* I screamed inwardly. *Go on...say something!*

I felt like I'd nearly rubbed the pattern off the marble slab when Minnie did something totally unexpected.

She laughed.

I'm not talking about some mild little lady-like chuckle. I'm talking about a Santa Claus kind of laugh; a "shook like a bowlful of jelly" kind of laugh; a "rip-roaring, leg-slapping, eyes crying, leaning over, holding your stomach because it hurts" kind of laugh. And it was so *not* what I expected.

I lifted wondering eyes to her, amazed that tears were actually running down her wide cheeks. Her head dropped to the counter, atop her crossed arms and her shoulders shook in uncontrollable hilarity.

I have to tell you; I was amazed. Thoroughly and utterly amazed.

I waited the storm out. It was a pretty long wait. She finally lifted her head and took a deep shuddering breath that actually had a chuckle or two attached to its end. She used her sleeve to wipe the tears from her cheeks and gave me a wide smile. "Thanks, honey. I needed that. It's been a long, long time since I laughed that hard. Maybe never."

I pressed my lips into a straight line and gave her a rather exaggerated nod. "Uh...you kind of took me off guard, there, Minnie. You mind telling me what in the world was so darn funny? And for heaven's sakes, don't start again," I ordered when she snorted and seemed to be fighting off a fresh bout of giggles.

"I'm sorry...I can't help it. I keep picturing the

look on Miz Patricia's face if she knew you were hanging around with a homeless lady. I almost wish she was still alive just so I could see it. *Almost,*" she tittered. "I bet it's killing all her rich lady friends too."

"Why? I'm the one "tarnishing my good name." Why should they care?"

"Because you won't play their games. You made *that* clear right after your aunt's funeral. They can't snub you by *not* including you in their soirees and teas and such if you won't play. I bet they're fit to be tied. Your ears should be burning plum off your head."

I shrugged, grinning. "So you're okay with it, then?"

"Honey, I couldn't be *more* okay with it. I'm real glad you found you a model and I'm even gladder that she's homeless." She thought a minute, then frowned. "That didn't sound quite right, but I think you know what I mean."

"Yeah, I do. Thanks, Minnie."

"You're welcome, child. Now, you probably need to go smooth out things with Tut. I don't think he has my sense of humor, and he's feeling a little bent out of shape with you right now. You got yourself one spoilt cat, honey."

"Yeah, tell me something I *don't* know." I hopped up and planted a kiss on her cheek. "Goodnight, Minnie. Thanks for understanding. I love you."

"I love you too, child."

****

I closed my bedroom door and leaned against it.

Wow! I hadn't seen *that* coming. I'd pictured many different scenarios, but uncontrollable laughter certainly wasn't one of them. Was it a good reaction? Yes, but very unexpected. Of course, I hadn't mentioned the counterfeiting operation or its possible link to the homeless ending up in the river. I mean, Minnie didn't need to know everything, right? Somehow, I doubted that laughter would be the dominant reaction if she did.

I closed my eyes and drew a deep breath, letting it out slowly. A small, cat-type noise drew my attention and I peered across the room at Tut sitting at the end of my bed. The way he stared at me made me feel as if he knew everything. Not just what I'd told Minnie, but *all* of it.

Ridiculous! How could a cat know?

Even so, his golden gaze made me feel uncomfortable...guilty. I crossed the room and plopped down beside him, running my hand down his back several times, hoping that a rub-down would help me get back into his good graces. But even though he began purring, the accusation never left his eyes.

"Listen, Tut, Lily is great; you'll like her. Believe it or not, I think she's helping me be the person I'm supposed to be...maybe the person I would've been if my parents had lived. I don't know. I'm going to try to get her to come here to visit sometime, okay. You'll need to be on your best behavior when that happens. I know, of course you will."

I pulled him into my lap and scratched under his neck, just the way he liked. "I guess you want to hear about Jonas." Tut's purring suddenly stopped and my fingers did likewise. I touched my nose to his and smiled. "Don't be jealous. You'll always be my first love. I promise." He looked relieved at that and started purring again.

This cat was unbelievable!

My fingers moved from under his neck to the sides of his head and around behind his ears. He closed his eyes in ecstasy, purring like an Evinrude boat motor.

"Jonas…well, Jonas is pretty amazing. Not only is he the best looking guy I've ever seen. Well, besides *you*, of course," I added hurriedly, when he slit his eyes at me, almost glaring. "I'm able to *talk* to him, Tut. I know, I know. Me? Talk to a guy? Amazing, right? But he's different. Or maybe it's that *I'm* different. After my epiphany up in Lily's tiny, little room…You know what an epiphany is, right? Well, I guess I *am* different. I refuse to read the same old boring chapters anymore. It's time to move forward. And I'm hoping that Jonas will be part of that."

I paused a minute, scratching away at Tut's head, barely aware of it, then I shrugged. "But even if he's not—and I hope that's not the case, mind you—but even so, I've got to move forward. I can't keep putting all the blame on Aunt Patricia. I don't know if I can ever forgive her for how she treated me, but I can stop re-reading those chapters and flip forward to a new part of the story."

I lay back on the bed, settling Tut on my chest, and continued scratching. He was in hog-heaven now, eyes closed in utter contentment, his emotional tank registering "full" from all the attention he was getting. I was back at the top of his favorite persons list, and I smiled. "Lily's weird habit of quoting proverbs is enough to drive a person crazy, but she's exactly what I needed to wake me up. And I'm excited to see what will happen next.

"Everything's going to be okay. I promise. I'll tell you all about it later. I need to get ready for bed. I've got another big day tomorrow and I'd like to get enough sleep tonight. But you'll see. It's a win-win-win. I have the perfect model for my assignment so I'll get a good grade; we're going to stop the counterfeiters as well as keep the homeless guys safe; and at the same time, we're going to help Jonas get his story. See what I mean about win-win-win? Oh, and you don't have to worry about the ghosts."

Tut's contented, golden eyes suddenly went perfectly round, his pupils dilating to the point where all I could see was black. It was uncanny the way he seemed to be able to understand me; unnerving too, in this case. I gave a nervous laugh, hoping to reassure him, as well as myself.

It didn't really work, so I leaned my head forward a little and touched my nose to his again, staring straight into his eyes. "Lily said most of them are nice and they like the glitter she sprinkles around."

I sat up and pressed my cheek to the top of his head, whispering, "I hope she's right."

Chapter Eleven

Jonas

After detouring by the fridge for a Pepsi, I somehow made it to the couch where I collapsed, sprawling in a sort of semi-reclined position, too tired to even drag my feet up high enough to prop them on my second-hand coffee table. Just as well. As rickety as it was, the darn thing would probably collapse if I tried it.

I fumbled around with the bottle cap until I finally managed to unscrew it, then took several big gulps. Groaning, I flopped my head backwards and as my eyes closed, I considered whether or not to just remain where I was for the night and save myself the trouble getting up and folding the futon out into a bed later. Hmph…that wouldn't work for several reasons. Besides the fact that the darn thing wasn't all that comfortable even when it was in bed-form, it wasn't long enough like this, it sagged in the wrong places, bulged in others, and its narrow depth made it a gamble as to whether I could make it through the night without face-planting on the floor. No, I'd just rest here for a few minutes.

The wind was picking up. I could hear the hollow knocking of the scraggly palm tree fronds just outside. The air fluted around my apartment's ill-fitting windows like someone blowing over a bottleneck. I held my own bottle up to my lips and blew across the top, echoing the sound whistling around the panes of glass. If I had the strength to open my eyes, I knew I'd see my curtains slightly swaying. This place definitely didn't get high marks in energy efficiency. My usual response to the cold was to add more layers of clothing, but at the moment, my tired-meter placed any concern about the room's temperature down in the "I don't care" range. It just wasn't a priority at the moment.

Well...I'd wanted a lead for my story, but I'd gotten more than I'd bargained for...*much* more. The police commissioner involved in a counterfeiting ring? Possibly even murder? Before tonight, I would've called anyone crazy if they'd suggested such a thing, but now...? I didn't know what to think. The conversation we'd overheard outside that small window in the alley was pretty damning, as far as evidence went, but I didn't have the energy to figure it all out right now.

My machine was blinking, so I punched the button, listened to the mechanical voice tell me I had one message and waited.

"Hi. It's Mom. I just wanted to warn you. Your brother ran into Jill today, and he...uh...he *might've* let it slip that you live in Savannah now. Don't hate him. Bye."

Terrific.

"Yeah, and don't think I didn't notice that you didn't say *which* brother, Mother, dear," I glared at the machine. "...but then, you didn't have to. I already know. Thanks for being such an idiot, Phillip."

Of all my brothers, why'd it have to be him? Any

of the others would've known better than to give out any details about me. How in the world did the man make it through medical school? Oh, I knew he was an excellent orthopedist, and a genius, to boot...IQ just under 160, but when it came to everyday living, I'd swear he needed someone to remind him to breathe in and out so he wouldn't suffocate. The term, "common sense," was definitely an oxymoron where Holmes son number two was concerned.

But as for Jill knowing I was living in Savannah...I didn't care.

I glugged another swallow of Pepsi, and leaned my head back again, expecting the familiar flicker of pain that always came when I thought of Jill. I waited, and waited, and...

It didn't come.

Really? I waited some more.

Mmmmm. Nothing.

Wow! What a freeing moment! It really didn't bother me. Why was that?

An image of a small, dark haired, turquoise-eyed girl came to mind. I tried to convince myself that it wasn't about her, that she wasn't the reason, that it was just because I'd finally found a real story to sink my teeth into, but I soon gave up and let my mind go where it'd wanted to go ever since I got home.

Cleo...Dear God! Every time she pressed against me while we were hiding behind those trashcans, tonight, it had been nearly impossible to think. The tickle of her breath each time she whispered in my ear, that gentle, floral scent that radiated from her skin, her hair...it nearly drove me mad. The urge to grab her, press her close, breathe her in, taste her...

I groaned. Maybe it was a good thing it *was* so cold in here.

I'd had to fight it the entire evening. Maybe that was part of the reason I was so darn tired now. It wasn't just physical exhaustion…it was mental and emotional, too. I wasn't sure how long I'd be able to keep my defenses up. I wasn't sure I *wanted* to keep them up. That was the problem.

But *why* was it a problem? Was there some reason it *had* to be? Ethics? A good reporter wasn't supposed to get involved with a source, right?

Well…heck with the ethics—

The phone rang. If that was Mom again, I'd—

Tilting my head, I slit my eyes just enough to read the screen.

Jill?!

I jerked to attention, eyes wide and staring now…gaping at those four little letters, while my phone rang a second time.

What did *she* want?

Third ring…

I reached over and turned the ringer off, then tipped the bottle up, swilling down the last gulp, my heart feeling lighter than it had in years. Heaving myself off the couch, I patted my pocket where I'd tucked the napkin with Cleo's phone number on it, and smiled. It was time for bed. I was too tired to think anymore. I'd face it better tomorrow.

****

After an amazingly restful night of sleep with some pretty intense dreams in which Cleo played a starring role, I was in my cubicle, before the building was officially opened. I'd already written my assigned article about the problem of poachers illegally digging up pitcher plants and Venus flytraps from the Savannah River basin wetlands.

Yes, there was an actual "black market" for that sort of thing.

Anyway, these swampy areas were on public lands managed by the Georgia Department of Natural Resources, Georgia Forestry Commission, U.S. Fish and Wildlife Services, and other conservation organizations. The Marshland's Protection Committee was having a benefit barbecue to raise money to support efforts to nab these "criminals." Their slogan for this dinner was...wait for it..."Eat some hog and save our bog."

Yes, *really*.

It's not that I'm against conservation and saving plants, and all that. I like flowers and trees as much or more than the next guy, but I say take it in moderation...don't go overboard. Concentrate on catching some *real* criminals. And as for them having a barbecue as a fundraiser? Well, it seemed a little like the group was talking out of both sides of its mouth. I mean, nature was nature, right? Why should pigs die in order to save some plants?

Whatever...

See why I want my own feature column?

My phone rang. Again? I glared at the name on the screen. I had nothing to say to Jill Parker. Everything had been said three years ago on the night before our wedding was to have taken place.

It'd been raining. A real, round-up-the-animals-Noah-it's-starting-to-flood, sort of rain. Jagged arcs of lightning volted between the black clouds. The car's tires had slashed along the rainy highway, shooting twin rooster tails of water into the air behind us. We'd been on the way to our rehearsal dinner, chatting about this and that, when Jill had mentioned a house she'd gone by to see that afternoon...

"As soon as I saw it, I knew it was perfect for us. Yes, it's only five thousand square feet, but as a starter home—"

He nearly choked. "Jill, I already told you, we're not staying in Charleston. I've got to get away from this place. Start somewhere else."

"But I thought—"

"And besides," he interrupted. "We won't be able to afford something that big. Not on my salary. I've told you that."

"What? What do you mean? You have plenty of money!"

"Uh...no...I don't. My parents *have plenty of money."*

"I thought you were joking about that," she whispered.

For a long moment, the only sounds were the persistent, annoying drum of rain on the roof, the metronomic smear of wipers on the windshield, the whoosh of cars flashing by in the other direction. Jill just sat there, wearing the strangest look, then all of her features sort of hardened. "So, you're telling me that we won't be getting money from your parents. We'll be living on what you earn as a journalist?" She almost sneered the word.

He went cold and still. "Yes," he answered quietly. "That's exactly what I'm telling you."

She drew a deep breath, then blew it out. "Take me

home, Jonas. There's not going to be a wedding."

My phone beeped, rousing me from my reverie. Without hesitation, I deleted the voice mail without listening to it. There was nothing she had to say that I wanted to hear.

****

I spent the next hour surfing the Internet, searching for more information about the homeless, educating myself.

The societal problem seemed to be snowballing. No matter what the city leaders did, no matter what programs were put in place, the supply of help couldn't keep up with the demand. The homeless demographic used to be made up mostly of men, but there were growing numbers of women and children living in their cars—if they had one—sleeping in front of twenty-four hour a day shopping centers and restaurants so they could have access to a bathroom, napping in air conditioned libraries in the summer to escape the heat.

I thought about the unbearable summers in Savannah and winced. The heat was bad enough, but the humidity and the gnats…ugh!

I looked back at my notes. It was a vicious cycle; one that was being repeated at a sickening rate. The husband would take off—if there ever was a husband— leaving the woman with a passel of kids that she can't afford childcare for. She juggled bills, deciding which ones she could pay and which ones she couldn't, trying to make ends meet with a minimum wage job—that's if she *had* a job—and the "past due" notices kept piling up. Sooner, rather than later, she got the dreaded eviction notice, which she had seven days to respond to, but she couldn't get an appointment to seek help for thirty days, so another little family ended up on the street. No wonder the numbers were growing. They hardly stood a chance. The decks were stacked against them, defeated before the game had even started.

Something had to change, but what?

Chapter Twelve

Lily

I fumbled for the book of matches that was supposed to be right beside the candle. "Where *are* the darn things? Should be right here."

"Looking for something?" Rose's voice came from the darkest corner of my room.

"Gah!" I jumped. "Stop *doing* that! I think you're *trying* to give me a heart attack! Give me the matches."

"Oh, don't be ridiculous. Here…"

Though it was too dark to see them, I felt the matchbook bounce against my chest. I clapped my hand over them before they fell to the floor.

"Thanks for nothing," I muttered, as I held the flame to the wick. I stared at the warm, dim glow that bathed my sister's face. "Why are you here?"

Surprise widened her eyes, dropped her mouth open. "Do I have to have a reason?"

At my silence, she huffed, "If you must know, I was worried about you."

"Why?"

"Why? You know…that girl, and well…" she spluttered. "…you're not usually out so late. I know you've been with her all day, and—"

"How do you know that? Have you been following me?"

"No, but I have friends. They keep me informed."

"So, *they* follow me."

One brow arched. Her expression clearly said, *what's your point?*

"Why is it okay for *you* to have friends, but not me?"

I'd surprised her again. Her mouth opened and closed several times before she finally snapped, "I don't think I appreciate your attitude." Her eyes shot angry sparks at me, and I glared right back.

After a long fuming moment, she gave me a pretend smile that didn't reach her eyes. "Lily." Her voice took on a wheedling tone. "You're my little sister. I only want what's best for you. You know that. All I've ever done was help you. Remember? We agreed: people can't hurt you if you don't let them close. That was our agreement, but you're letting her close. Talking with this girl, spending time with her will only hurt you. Remember what happened the last time."

"Cleo won't hurt me. I told you. She needs me for this assignment. I'm helping her."

"Yes, and when the assignment's over, she'll drop you like a hot potato," Rose insisted. "She's *using* you, Lily. Don't you see that?"

"And I say, she's not," I argued, just as insistent.

"Well," she sniffed. "I can see that we're getting nowhere." She studied me through narrowed eyes. "You've changed, and I don't mean just arguing with me, which—FYI—I *don't* like. You're different...you even *talk* differently. I don't like it," she repeated. "It bothers me that that girl can have such an impact on you after you've spent less than twenty-four hours with her."

I turned away from her and tugged off my hat, pulling a thick wool sweater from one of my boxes, replacing my overcoat with it. It was ratty, and oft-repaired, but warm.

The argument with my sister had me feeling fidgety. Proud that I stood up for myself, for once, but on edge. I didn't like Rose being mad at me. I should try to smooth her ruffled feathers.

Turning toward her, I reached for her hand, glad that it felt solid. Sometimes it didn't, and I hated that. It was like holding soft Jell-o. Sometimes even, smoke. "Rose, I really want you to meet Cleo. I know you'd like her if you just got to know her."

"Lily, I—"

"But if you don't want to," I interrupted, talking over her. "I guess that's okay, but I have a favor to ask."

"Fine. What is it?"

"Will you see what you can discover about Cleo's aunt? Find out why she hated the girl? You remember Patricia Davenport, right?"

"The Brantley house across from the park?"

"Yes, that's the one. She died last summer, so it should be easy for you to nose around, see what you can come up with." I gave her hand a squeeze. "Can you do that for me?"

Before she could answer, a sudden *whoosh* swept through the room, causing my candle to sputter and dance, almost go out. A flashy, Clark Gable-ish young man postured before us, acting like we should be asking for his autograph. His dark hair was parted in the middle and slicked back with more than just the prescribed dab of Brylcreem. He wore a thin mustache, a velveteen cutaway over a silk striped vest. A white ruffle frothed under his chin, and leotard-tight pants accentuated the fact that he was a man. I averted my eyes, a little embarrassed.

My sister's expression went from disgruntled to simpering in an instant and she hurried to his side. "Barry! You're late," she pouted. "I was beginning to think you'd stood me up."

He reached for her hand and gave it a lingering kiss, while his dark eyes devoured her. "Nevah, my dahling."

Oh, brother!

"Lily," she turned to me, her voice a little breathless. "I'd like you to meet, Sir Beryl Belvoir, from Charleston. Barry, this is my sister, Lily Telfair-Gordon."

He clicked his heels and bowed his head slightly my direction. "Verrah pleased to make your acquaintance, ma'am." He glanced down at Rose. "Shall we go?"

"Yes. I want to show you the bridge I was telling you about."

"Oh, mademoiselle, as I told you, Chahleston's Ravenel Bridge is both biggah and longah than your little bridge he-ah."

"And like I told you," she tucked her hand in the bend of his arm and turned him toward the door. "Talmadge Memorial came first. That makes it the original. The Charleston folks had to make theirs bigger to hide the fact that they couldn't come up with anything better than a copy. Just a minute, Barry." Rose sent me a considering glance. "In answer to your question...maybe. I'll think about it."

Without opening the door, they were gone, and I was alone with my thoughts.

****

The wind trundled the last of the clouds out toward the Atlantic Ocean. There was Orion. The three stars that make up his belt were barely visible above the roofline of the building next door. It was the only constellation I could always find. More stars were blinking into view as the clouds moved east. The scene was the perfect analogy. I felt like those stars, straining through the clouds, to light the path in front of me, fearful of the next step, afraid of the future. Following my sister's advice, I'd kept myself in a safe little cocoon, sealing others out and myself in. I'd done it for years, and other than giving me a very lonely life, it'd caused me to nearly lose myself, as well as the art of conversation. I'd forgotten how much I enjoyed people, *needed* them. Rose said that I sounded different now, and it was true. Cleo had dragged me out of my cocoon. That child had done and said *exactly* the right things, pulling me back into *living* life instead of watching it from the sidelines. She'd saved me...was *still* saving me.

I wanted to include my sister in my friendship with Cleo. It's the reason I'd asked for her help. Would she be able to find out anything? I hoped so, for Cleo's sake. I knew, first hand, the results of bitterness. I was living proof of it. I'd been blaming God for Rose's death and Michael's betrayal for all these years, and look where it got me. I couldn't help but wonder what my life would've been like if I'd chosen a different path.

But I couldn't go back and undo the past.

My fingers rubbed the red fabric of my curtains, enjoying the silky feel. They used to be a deep, rich color, like burgundy wine, almost the exact shade of Rose's hair. I found them stuffed in someone's garbage can years ago. Grabbed them up, quick as a flash, and brought them back here. They've faded a lot over the years, sort of like me. I touched my face, traced the grooves. Time had sure etched its mark. Not like Rose. She'd forever be young and beautiful. Never old and wrinkled like this.

If she'd lived, she'd be seventy-two now. Seventy-two! I tried to imagine her that age, and couldn't. There'd have been no aging gracefully with her, either. Every wrinkle, every age spot, every gray hair, she would've fought with the diligence of a Roman soldier. She'd have *hated* growing old.

Up until the day of the wreck, she'd led a charmed life, It wasn't that people overlooked her faults; they didn't even *see* them. Her smile did it. She'd turn on that smile and all annoyance would melt away. Yes, she was a bit of a diva, but that came with the territory, right? That's what actresses did. She was spoiled and had an ego as big as the state of Georgia, but everyone ignored that in the face of her beauty.

"I'm a people person, Lily." I heard her say it a million times. "I *need* people. Can't help it. It's in my DNA. The doctor told me. I have an actual, physical need for people, just like breathing." She's always used this "proof" whenever I compared my near-exile with her ever-growing list of ghost-friends.

Whatever the reason, she'd been perfect for the limelight; receiving rave reviews for every performance; her fans and paparazzi clamoring to see her. All she had to do was hint at something she wanted, some tiny desire, and people scrambled to make it happen. Maybe that made it harder for her to die so young.

Part of me envied her. I tried not to; after all, she was dead, and she deserved a few perks, but it almost seemed like Rose was jealous of *me*.

Ha! Even thinking such a thing was ridiculous. Why should she be jealous of me having a relationship with Cleo? It didn't make any sense.

Well, whatever the reason, her advice had been wrong. Shutting down and living life in my own little world was not the answer. It only shut off my senses…my awareness. If I'd been aware of things like I should have been, the counterfeiting activity going on in the basement would've never happened. I'd have noticed. Oh, it might've happened somewhere else in the city…wickedness will always work its way to the surface, like a splinter under the skin; bad guys will always find a way to be bad, but it wouldn't have happened *here*.

But because I'd met Cleo against her advice, Rose was mad at me, which was novel for both of us. She was so used to people obeying her every command, bowing to her every whim, that she didn't know how to handle someone overriding her guidance. Had it always been this bad? Or had she just gotten worse about it after she died? I racked my brain, trying to remember something specific. Well, of course, there was the issue with Michael, but I didn't like to think about that. It made me feel so blind and stupid, even now. How could I have been so naïve? I thought he loved me. I'd been planning to marry him, for heaven's sake. Thank goodness Rose showed me what kind of a man he'd *really* been.

But had she?

No! I squashed the little voice as soon as it whispered the question. Rose loved me. She'd never do anything to hurt me. Michael had been no good. Hadn't Rose proven that when she'd seen him with that other woman? She'd helped keep me from an even bigger heartbreak.

Really? The little voice whispered again.

I whirled from the window. My impatient fingers fumbled with the laces of my boots before kicking them off. Shivering, I crawled onto my pallet, and huddled under several layers of threadbare blankets, staring at nothing.

The niggling doubt that I'd never allowed myself to even consider before, loomed to the front of my brain. If Rose had been wrong about Cleo, could she have been wrong about Michael, too? There'd never been any proof other than Rose's word. No pictures...nothing. Only her word. I didn't even give him a chance to defend himself. As soon as she dropped the bombshell, I immediately broke things off with him. That had been Rose's advice too. She vowed that a clean break was the best way; that listening to his lies would only prolong the pain; that she only wanted what was best for me. She didn't want me to be hurt.

I compared that long ago advice to that she'd given concerning Cleo. What if I'd listened to her? Look at all I'd have missed. All the emotions I never would've felt...

My mind and heart rebelled at the idea that was

trying to form. No! It was impossible! Rose would never do something to deliberately hurt me. She was my big sister and she loved me.

Didn't she?

Wavering shadows, created by candlelight, danced along the walls, and seemed to only intensify the question. I rolled to my side, blowing out the candle with a single impatient *puff*. A ribbon of smoke scented the air with melted wax as I lay on my pallet, eyes wide and staring at the dim light filtering through the red curtains. Doubts mushroomed, crowded my mind. My heart pounded.

What if Michael had never been false? What if Rose had made up the whole story? My heart clenched. No, why would she do that? Rose had everything...beauty, confidence, a star-spangled career, crowds clamoring to see her...everything!

Everything...but a man who truly loved her, the little voice argued. Oh, yes, there were always throngs of men following around after Rose, men like Barry Belvoir, vying for her attention, plying her with flowers, and even jewelry, hoping for her favors in return...a smile, a kiss...more? But there'd never been one special man, someone like Michael, someone who—

Stop it!

Too late. The thoughts kept coming, relentless as the tide.

Was it possible that Rose had been jealous because I had something she didn't? Or maybe she'd not wanted to share me with Michael. Maybe she'd wanted *all* of my love, not just part of it. Rose never liked to share. Whenever there was any sharing to be done, it had always been me who'd done it; never the other way around.

And Michael...I pressed my fist to my lips, trapping the cry of anguish. Sweet, sweet Michael... If Rose had lied, and he'd never been untrue, that would mean I had been wrong about love all these years. It *wasn't* doomed from the start. It *didn't* have to end in heartbreak.

I squeezed my eyes shut and groaned, "What have I done? What have I done?"

Tears coursed down my cheeks, dampening the blankets as I faced my greatest fear...the fear that I'd wasted my life on a lie; that Michael had never done anything wrong.

Pain ripped and squeezed my heart; regret lashed at me. I choked back the sob that wrenched up from deep inside me, but wasn't strong enough to fight for long. The pull of despair was too great, and I finally gave in to the storm of emotion washing over me. It pulled me down, down into its depths.

I think I slept a while, but when I awoke I drew a deep, shuddering breath, sleeving the tears from my face. My mind was made up. I'd face Rose later, confront her with my suspicions...demand the truth, but even if Rose had been right and Michael *had* played me false, I had no reason to undermine Cleo's interest in Jonas...an interest he obviously returned. I didn't want Cleo to be hurt, but I'd been basing all romantic relationships on my supposed failed one with Michael. Jonas was a different man, and Cleo deserved a chance to make her own mistakes, her own discoveries...whatever they might be.

"I won't torpedo...that relationship...again," I

whispered brokenly in the dark through trembling lips. "I promise."

****

"G'morning, Raymond," I called out as I approached his bench. He wore a Santa hat and was busily folding palm fronds. He raised a hand in greeting, but kept right on working. *No time,* he told me without speaking. *Customers are waiting.* Yes, and he was delivering. His musical voice was casting its spell, and he glowed with pride and satisfaction.

Raymond's "good days"—the days he was in his right mind and aware of his surroundings, the days he made roses as opposed to the days he spent scribbling in his notebook—were infrequent at best, so I changed directions, aiming toward another bench to wait for Cleo. I wasn't about to mess up his chance at making a little cash. As far as I knew, it was his only income and five dollars a pop wasn't much.

Rose never showed up this morning, which was probably for the best. I wasn't ready to face her just yet. I still had a lot of things to process before I could get my thoughts in order. Right now, everything was still too chaotic. It would take some time.

I found a bench with a clear view of Raymond and took a seat. I couldn't help my grin as I watched his performance. I'd never really appreciated his showmanship before. When I'd shut down my emotions all those years ago, it seemed to have blinded me as well, so now I watched with new eyes…eyes that could really see.

"When you change the way you look at things, you change the way things look," I whispered the words aloud, meaning them like I never had before.

150

Raymond smiled his snaggle-toothed smile, presenting his finished masterpiece to his delighted audience, and receiving his payment with a humble nod. He tucked the bill discreetly into his pocket, and bid them a Merry Christmas, as they strolled away, chattering their admiration for his work. He was definitely good at what he did. I couldn't remember ever seeing him not getting paid.

The whole scenario reminded me of the quote by Henry Van Dyke: *Use what talents you possess. The woods would be very silent if no birds sang except those who sang the best.* Raymond might have problems on his bad days, but on his good days, he lived out Mr. Van Dyke's message to the fullest.

"It's fun to watch him in action, isn't it?"

I jumped in surprise, putting a hand to my heart. "Gracious, child! Are you trying to scare a poor, old woman to death? You need a hat with bells on it, too, so I can hear you coming."

Cleo laughed. "I hate to be the bearer of bad news, but don't think they make hats like that anymore."

"That's exactly what Rose said."

Cleo's smile faded a little and her eyes darted around.

I laughed. "Don't worry. She's not here."

"Okay…sorry I startled you," her voice sounded relieved. "Ready to go?"

"I kind of wanted to pay a visit to Raymond first, if you don't mind. I was waiting for him to finish with those customers." I nodded toward the departing tourists. "His good days seem to be getting fewer and farther between, so I feel like I need to take advantage of this one. You don't mind, do you?"

"Not a bit."

Raymond looked up with a grin as we approached. "Top o' the mornin' to you ladies and Merry Christmas! How in the world are you?"

"Doing fine, my friend…doing fine," I replied as I settled on the bench beside him. "I like your hat. You look very Christmas-y."

His grin widened and his booming, "Ho, ho, ho!" caused Cleo to dissolve into giggles.

I just smiled and shook my head. "So what have you been up to lately?"

His face instantly sobered and he glanced around as if making sure no one could hear before leaning toward me and whispering. "I may not be havin' to do much more of this rose-makin' gig. I got something in the works that's gonna have me sittin' in high cotton soon." He nodded his head, giving me an exaggerated wink.

"What do you mean?"

He sat back, hooking his thumbs under imaginary galluses, fingers waving proudly. "Ol' Raymond…he's gettin' ready to make his way down easy street. Can't tell you no more than that. Just that I won't have to be makin' palmetto roses for five bucks a pop no more. Maybe on the side, but not for a livin'."

"You have a rich uncle die and leave you millions, Raymond?" Cleo kidded.

He shook his head. "Nah! Don't need me one of them."

"C'mon, Raymond," I cajoled. "Give us another hint. You can't leave us hanging like that."

"Nope, my lips are sealed. I been sworn to secrecy, you know." He pulled an imaginary zipper across his mouth.

Before I could question him further, a man approached the bench. It seemed a little odd that he was by himself. Most of Raymond's audiences were couples or groups or families, but this fellow was alone. A wary expression crossed Raymond's face for a split second before he turned on his showmanship appeal.

I studied my friend carefully. Did his smile seem forced? His performance a little too enthusiastic? The thought made me glance back at his intended audience. The man had that muscle-bound look that serious body builders have. He was wearing a black leather jacket, stretched taut over his muscular shoulders. I prided myself on being able to read people well, and I was willing to bet this guy was a bouncer for some exclusive club or else a bodyguard. Whoever he was, his expressions never lightened, even when Raymond switched on the charm. "Good morning to you, sir. Would you care to have me demonstrate the art of creating a rose from this ordinary palmetto palm leaf?"

I motioned to Cleo. "Let's leave him to his work." Then I tapped him on the shoulder. "Bye, Raymond. See you around."

He reached up and tipped his Santa hat. "You have yourself a good day, Miz Lily...Miz Cleo. Merry Christmas!"

"Yeah, Merry Christmas, Raymond," Cleo replied and bounced to her feet.

"Yes, I hope you do, too." I was a bit slower getting to my feet. My glance flicked up to meet the dark, unsmiling eyes of the man in the leather jacket, and I frowned before adding, "...and be careful."

****

Cleo immediately began chattering away about what she hoped to get done for the day; that she had some ideas brewing for the actual story-line for her painting project and wanted to get some sketches to illustrate those ideas. Then there was something about her cat, and something about Minnie, but my mind wasn't really following it too closely. I was thinking about what Raymond said about being on easy street. What had he meant by that? Whatever it was made me nervous, slightly on edge. And that man in the black jacket hadn't helped any.

I shook my head, causing my silver bells to jingle and hoped it would send the negative thoughts flying away. I had another day to spend with Cleo, and I didn't want anything to cast a shadow over it. I could mull over Raymond's words later.

Nudging Cleo with my elbow, I tilted my head at the window of the shop we were passing. Whoever had designed the display had gone completely overboard with way too many Christmas lights, tinsel, Santa, reindeer, Frosty the snowman, and various other holiday related trimmings. "Here's a bit of advice they need to adhere to when doing any future Christmas decorating, and you can use it too: there's a fine line between white-trash and festive!"

Cleo burst out laughing and linked arms with me. "Thanks for the advice. I'll keep it in mind."

Chapter Thirteen

Cleo

"We need to go back to Chippewa Square." Lily suddenly ordered out of nowhere. Her words were clipped and terse. "Now."

I stopped sketching in mid-stroke and stared up at her. "Why? What's wrong?"

She shook her head, agitated. "I don't know. It's a feeling I haven't been able to shake. Something about the way Raymond said, "easy street," and then that man in the black jacket... I just feel like I need to go back and check on him."

"Okay," I shrugged my backpack off and tucked the sketchpad and pencils inside, zipping it closed. "I'm ready when you are."

"Cleo!" a voice shouted from behind us. "Wait up!"

I turned and I swear my heart did the same thing the Seuss' Grinch's did when it grew three times its size within seconds. And let me just tell you, when your heart's that size and it's beating the way *mine* was at the moment, it makes you shake all over.

I somehow managed to raise my hand and wave at him. "Jonas!" I was amazed that my voice wasn't shaking too. Granted, I'd only said one word, but since my voice was the only thing *not* shaking, it deserved some recognition.

I couldn't take my eyes off of him as he jogged toward us. He looked even better than I remembered: perfect-fitting jeans and denim shirt under an Eddie Bauer-looking canvas jacket...definitely easy on the eyes. I'd been trying not to worry because he hadn't called yet, but wasn't having much success with that. I kept trying to tell myself that it hadn't been that many hours since we'd said goodnight, but still... I glanced at Lily, but she looked too worried about Raymond to be thinking of ways to keep us apart.

"Hey," he was a little out of breath, but he grinned as he joined us. "I was just going to call you when I looked up and there you were. Guess it was fate."

"Yeah, I—"

"We were on our way to check on Raymond, remember?" Lily reminded sharply, giving me a pointed look.

"Right! No time for chit-chat. C'mon," I grabbed his hand, trying to ignore the tingling that shot from my fingertips all the way up my arm at the contact. "You can go with us."

My eyes met Lily's, and I raised my brows in a silent question. She gave me a shrug, turned, and hurried away.

"Where are we going?" he asked as we tried to catch up with her.

"Chippewa Square."

"Wait! Why don't we just take my car? It'll be faster."

"Good idea!" I turned to tell Lily, but she was already halfway down the block; her pink and green hat a brilliant splotch of color that was rapidly growing smaller, the farther she got away. Jeez, she wasn't letting any grass grow under her feet. "Lily!" I yelled. She either didn't hear me or chose to ignore me.

"C'mon," Jonas ordered. "We'll catch her at the next square."

****

Once we were strapped in, he chirped away from the curb, moving as quickly as was automotively possible. Since all of Savannah's squares are one-way, and relatively small, cars are obliged to move at a leisurely pace. The corners are just too tight for speeding. At this particular moment, though, I was wishing we could straighten out some of those corners.

"Okay, fill me in before we catch her," he demanded, slamming on his brakes when a truck attempted to pull out in front of him, then surging forward again.

I closed my eyes. Maybe it would be better if I didn't watch him drive. "Lily is worried about Raymond."

"Who's Raymond?"

"Her friend. He's homeless too. You know, he's one of those guys who sit in the squares, folding palmetto leaves into roses. You might be able to use him as another source for your article." Mentioning Raymond's notebook scribbling didn't seem necessary.

"Okay, so why is she worried about him?"

"I'm not really sure. A creepy looking man in a black leather jacket showed up while we were talking to Raymond this morning, and Raymond said "easy street," but that—"

"Easy street?"

"Yeah, Raymond told us that he wasn't going to

have to make roses anymore. That he was going to be sitting in "high cotton," and be on "easy street."" I opened my eyes to peek at where we were, then quickly shut them again. Yeah, it was better if I didn't watch. "I didn't think much about it, but apparently it's been bothering Lily ever since we left him."

Jonas was too quiet. I took a chance and looked at him. A frown was etched between his eyes. "You say there was a man?"

I swallowed hard. His tone had me feeling more and more uneasy. "Yes, he came to Raymond's bench, you know the one from Forrest Gump? That's where he always sits to make his roses. Anyway, this big guy came up and just stood there, which is weird, now that I think about it. I mean, would you, as a single guy, stop to watch something like that?"

He shook his head.

"I didn't think so. There she is. Hurry!"

We were still rolling forward a little, but I wrenched the door open. "Lily!" I screamed. "Over here!"

Her cart practically skidded to a stop, and she whirled it around, speeding over to where we sat with the engine idling. I cut my eyes sideways at Jonas. "What are we going to do about her cart?"

He didn't answer. He'd already popped the trunk latch and was getting out of the car. "Get in!" he ordered. "I'll put your cart in the trunk. Go on," he added when she hesitated. "Don't worry, I'll be careful."

Lily looked undecided for about three seconds, then she relinquished her hold on her precious cargo and scrambled in.

Jonas was back in his seat before she had the door closed. "Ready?" he asked, glancing over his shoulder to make sure she was settled. At her nod, he zoomed away from the curb.

We screeched to a stop beside Chippewa Square. Jonas slammed the car into park and turned on his emergency flashers, probably hoping that it would keep him from getting a ticket for parking illegally. The driver in the car behind us laid down on his horn. I'm sure if I would've taken the time to look back, I'd have been treated to a universally recognized hand-gesture, but there wasn't time. We all jumped out simultaneously and rushed toward the bench where Lily and I had left Raymond earlier that morning. At this angle, the monument blocked the bench from our line of sight, but a few more steps took us to the point where we had an unobstructed view.

The bench was empty.

My heart sank and my feet slowed, but Lily didn't. She made a beeline, nearly knocking down several tourists in her hurry to reach her destination. I glanced worriedly at Jonas before speeding up to join her.

By the time I reached her, she was just standing there, staring at the spot where her friend had been an hour ago. Her breathing was heavy, which struck me as odd, since she never gets out of breath, until I could see what she'd obviously already seen: the bench wasn't as empty as we'd thought.

A plastic shopping bag full of palmetto fronds, as well as an unfinished rose sat there, tossed aside and forgotten. But the thing that really germinated a seed of panic in my stomach was the sight of Raymond's two-wheeled cart partially hidden behind the end of the bench. That seed fast-forwarded through its germination process, unfurling its leaves until it filled every part of me.

I reached over and gently put my hand on Lily's shoulder. My eyes stung as the reality of what I was seeing sank in. If these items hadn't been left, it would've been reasonable to assume that he'd had some other engagement and he'd decided to take a day off. Not likely, but *possible*. Leaving them behind, though…? I shook my head, not wanting to think about it, but not being able to stop myself, either.

"What do we do?" I asked quietly.

"Well, I don't think it'll do any good to report him missing," Jonas answered. "What would you say? *Our homeless friend has been missing for about an hour?* The police would only laugh. Someone's not even technically considered "missing" until they've been gone at least forty-eight hours. And besides, you have no proof of foul-play."

I pointed to his cart. "What do you call that?"

"I know, I know. You and I would call that undisputable proof, but I'm telling you…the police *wouldn't*."

Lily hadn't said a word, and was still staring at the bench. I gave her shoulder another squeeze, and then asked Jonas, "Are you sure? Not even in the face of what's been happening with the homeless?"

He shrugged. "It might make them pay a *little* more attention, but with Mark in charge of the police…" He sighed. "Listen…you know the system as well as I do. Like it or not, a missing homeless guy just isn't a high priority with law-enforcement in this town, probably *any* town. They're not going to waste—"

I opened my mouth to argue his use of that word, but he held up his hand.

"Let me finish. It's a waste to *them*, not to *me*. They're not going to waste taxpayer money looking for someone who the taxpayers would like to forget anyway. Most of Savannah's elite would be tickled to death to round up the whole lot of them and ship them off to Charleston or Jacksonville. But because they can't, they pull their ostrich routine, and try their best to ignore them. That's one reason why I wanted to do these articles. To open their eyes…to make them aware…to spur them on to *do* something."

I stared at him in wonder. His voice was so passionate. He really believed in this. He saw injustice and was doing what he could to change things…kind of like a modern day Robin Hood. He was right about how most people felt, though. Aunt Patricia had looked down her nose at homeless men like Raymond. She'd complained that the city officials should run them out of town, called them "beggars," said all they were after was tourist money. I'd always had to bite my tongue to keep from pointing out that that's what *all* of the businesses in Savannah were after. All it would've done was start an argument. It wouldn't have changed her mind.

I blinked and came back to reality. "We're all thinking the same thing, right? Raymond's gone and gotten himself involved in Mark Spencer's counterfeiting operation. Ugh! Why didn't I see? He said, *easy street*. How else would a homeless man be on easy street? I should've seen it. I should've caught on!"

"Don't beat yourself up, Cleo," Jonas tried to calm me. "All the mental black eyes in the world won't help him right now."

His words didn't help. "Hey!" I gave Lily a little shake. "Is there any other place that Raymond might be? Maybe we could drive around town, see if we find him."

She shook her head. "I don't know. This is the only place I ever saw him. He was always here…good weather or bad; it didn't matter…Raymond was *always* here."

Her comment didn't make me feel better about the situation, but I tried to put it out of my mind. "Okay, let's go. Staring at this bench isn't going to make him reappear. We'll drive around…" I sent Jonas a questioning look and he nodded his agreement. "…and keep our eyes open. Hopefully, we'll see something."

****

Although we spent the rest of the day canvassing old town, questioning any homeless person we saw as we went, we were no closer to finding Raymond than we were when we started. I couldn't speak for anybody else, but I was hungry, tired, discouraged, and growing more worried by the minute. Apparently, Jonas was thinking along the same lines, or at least the hungry part, because he suddenly slid into an empty parking spot and announced, "I think we'd all feel better if we got something to eat. Does Moon River sound all right to you, girls?"

Right on cue, my stomach gave an audible rumble, sounding embarrassingly like a Harley Davidson. "Uh…Moon River sounds great to me." I unzipped my backpack and retrieved my phone. "I just need to give Minnie a call and let her know I won't be home for supper. I don't want to get on her black list again."

I hit my speed dial and watched Lily while the number rang. Knowing how she had refused to go into a restaurant with me, I wasn't sure she'd go along with Jonas' idea. Minnie picked up on the other end. "Hello?"

"Hi, Minnie. It's me. I just wanted to let you know that I won't make it for supper."

"Again? Honey, you got to quit skipping meals. It's not good for you."

"I'm not skipping. I'm going out."

"Out?" Her tone changed. "You mean, by yourself?"

Uh-oh. Here we go. "No, not by myself."

I was painfully aware that both Jonas and Lily could hear my half of this conversation, and I prayed that Minnie wouldn't give me the third degree.

"With who?"

"Friends."

"Friends? Plural? Or "friend," like on a date?"

I could hear her grin over the phone and felt my face heat up. I was glad it was too dark for the others to see how red I knew I was. Lily's wide smile was clearly visible from the back seat. I couldn't bear to look at Jonas. "No! And I've got to go. I just wanted to let you know so you wouldn't worry."

"Mmhmm."

I rolled my eyes and fought the urge to growl at her. "Uh, could you do me a favor?"

"Depends." She laughed.

I shook my head in defeat and smiled. "Could you baby Tut a bit? I'd like to avoid another scene like last night if I can."

"I'll see what I can do. Thanks for letting me

know."

"Bye, Minnie." I snapped my phone shut, replacing it in my backpack. "Y'all ready?"

Lily unfastened her seatbelt and reached for the door. "I wouldn't miss this for the world."

Now she decides to go into a restaurant. Great.

****

It was crowded and loud. The patrons at the bar had probably been there a while, judging by the volume of their conversations. There seemed to be a direct cause and effect relationship between alcohol consumption and noise level in a place like this. On our way to our table, I saw Ellie, draped like a set of Christmas tree lights, all over some unfortunate guy at the bar, and I stifled a groan. She aimed a fake smile in my direction and gave me a finger wave. I tilted my chin at her, barely managing a tight smile in return.

I watched her as I settled into our booth. Her eyes went from me, to Lily, to Jonas. At Lily, they widened in shock and a mocking smile lit her face. When they moved on to Jonas, her expression changed, became more calculating, like a cat contemplating a delicious bowl of cream. I clenched my fists so hard that my nails bit into my palms.

Do it and die, chick. Do it and die!

The waiter introduced himself and we placed our order. I ignored Ellie as best I could, gazing with interest at the rest of the people, as well as the décor. A long row of varied and colorful beer cans stretched out on a narrow display shelf over the bar. I thought it was a pretty ingenious decorating touch, advertising a large selection of micro-brewery brand names to those who may not be familiar with them, as well as adding a bit of color.

Moon River—the restaurant—was a brewing company, as well. It got its name from the song made famous by Savannah's own Johnny Mercer. With it being right on Bay Street, it was a very popular place to be. SCAD students loved it. I'd been there before, but not often. It wasn't a place to come alone.

As soon as we ordered, Lily excused herself to the ladies' room. I offered to go with her, but she refused and scurried away. I knew she was probably uncomfortable, in spite of her declaration of not wanting to miss this. The stares from Ellie, and others like her, didn't help her comfort level any, I'm sure, making her feel like she didn't belong here—a square peg in a round hole—hopelessly out of place. I hoped she didn't sneak out the back door. I found myself anxiously watching for her return.

"I wanted to ask you something." Jonas smiled at me and spoke loudly to be heard over the din. "Who's Tut?"

"Oh…Tut is my cat. He thinks I'm supposed to spend all my time with him." I wrinkled my nose. "I guess you could say he's a little spoiled."

"Tut? As in *King* Tut? And Cleo is short for Cleopatra, right?" His smile grew wider and he nodded sagely. "Very appropriate name choice."

"Glad you approve, but keep in mind…I didn't have any choice in the first one. That's all the parents' fault."

"No, I like it. It suits you."

"Thanks," I laughed, then made a face. "I think." My eyes slid back in the direction of the restrooms.

"You're worried about her." It wasn't a question. I

guess it was obvious.

"Yeah, a little. I really can't believe she agreed to come in here. I haven't been able to accomplish that feat with her yet."

"Well, to tell the truth, I was surprised myself. I think her usual reaction is pretty typical among the homeless. They know they look different. They feel uncomfortable; other guests feel uncomfortable, and it sort of escalates. I've done quite a bit of research on it, preparing for these articles I'm writing, and from what I've read, it's almost as bad as segregation was, back in the fifties and sixties. Not quite, but almost."

"That's so sad."

We were interrupted by the waiter bringing our drinks, but as soon as glasses and straws were doled out and the waiter had moved away, he continued, "At least we're moving in the right direction with the Stand Down program."

"Yeah…I've heard about that. They have it at the Civic Center, right?"

"Yep. Good Will, the Salvation Army, American Legion, and a bunch of others all work together, pooling their resources, and making at least a little bit of difference. They have volunteers who can talk one-to-one with attendees, and give them information about jobs, veteran services, housing, and a bunch of other programs. They can even get a flu shot, a haircut, and their teeth cleaned while they're there."

"Wow! I wonder if Lily knows about it?"

"Probably." He laughed. "But you can ask her when she gets back."

I glanced to the rear of the restaurant again. "She's been in there a while. Should I see if she's okay?"

"Yeah, but before you do..." He stared at the tabletop like he was trying to memorize it. "I don't know how you feel about this, but I was thinking about hiding in that alley again later tonight. I don't know if it'll do any good, but three inter-connected things have happened there so far: one...Lily found that bag of money; two...she saw Mark Spencer beating up that man; and three...we overheard that conversation last night. It wouldn't hurt to try to make it four for four."

"Sounds as good as anything else. It couldn't hurt, right?"

"Let's hope not." He motioned with his head toward the back. "Maybe you need to go check on her."

"Yeah," I said, as I scooted out of the booth. "I think you're right."

****

Lily was gone, of course. I had a waitress ask in the kitchen, and the cooks confirmed her exit out the back door. It didn't really surprise me.

I also wasn't surprised when I returned to our table and found Ellie sitting in my vacated seat across from Jonas. I *was* surprised she wasn't sitting next to him.

"Cleo!" she greeted me joyously, as if we were long lost friends instead of mortal enemies. "It's so good to see you!"

"Ellie." Her eyes narrowed at my mispronunciation, but she didn't correct me. I gave her a cold stare. The only thing that kept me from yanking her out of my seat by her dark rooted, bottle-blonde hair was sheer, iron will.

"I saw you come in earlier," she trilled in her fake-friendly voice. "I wanted to be *sure* to come tell you "hi." Imagine my disappointment when I finally made it to your table and found you were gone. But luckily..." she gave Jonas an impudent smile. "...this nice man was good enough to let me sit here and wait for you."

Finally made it to my table? Yeah, right. I was sure she'd waited—on purpose—for me to leave before she swooped in. I'd seen this act before, and I thought I was ready for it, but I guess I wasn't. When she finished her little performance with a wink, I think I may have growled.

"Well, that worked out well for you, didn't it?" My smile was brittle. One false move and my face might shatter into a thousand little pieces. I waited stiffly for her to vacate my seat. Could a person's blood actually boil?

Jonas was casting an uncertain look between the two of us. I'm sure he was astute enough to feel the undercurrents. He might not understand them, but he had to be aware of them.

Then he sort of jumped, shoulders stiffening, eyes widening in shock as he stared across the table. What was *that* about? I glanced at Ellie, looking for an answer. Uh-oh. I knew that look. I'd seen her use it often enough. It was her "come and get me" expression—gazing up through her mascara thickened lashes, a seductive smile curving her lips, promising things I didn't even want to know about—the look that reduced men to puppy-like creatures, eager to please. A movement under the table caught my eye and my jaw dropped. Ellie's stiletto-clad foot was rubbing suggestively up and down Jonas' leg. Obviously, Ellie had no intention of relinquishing her spot at the table.

Oh, no you don't, girlfriend! Not this *time!*

I made a totally out-of-character and utterly rash

decision, praying that Jonas would just go with it and that it wouldn't backfire. I slipped into the seat beside him, snuggling up close. "I like it better on this side, anyway."

I'll have to hand it to him. It only took him a split second of startled uncertainty before he dropped his arm around my shoulder, pulling me even closer. He put his lips to my ear, whispering, "I guess you'll explain what's going on later?"

His warm breath against my ear caused goose bumps to shiver along my arms and down my legs, but I dimpled up at him and answered, "You know I will." Turning to Ellie, I almost shouted over an explosion of laughter from the bar. "Isn't he a sweetheart? I just love him to death!"

Ellie's expression had become a bit frosty and I almost giggled with delight. It felt wonderful to be vindicated. Not to mention, it was very, *very* cozy to be snuggled up against Jonas like this.

She slid toward the outside edge of the seat. "It was good to see you, Cleo. Happy holidays. Nice to meet you, Jonas. Maybe we could meet for a drink sometime?"

"Sounds good," he said. "I'll let you set it up with Cleo."

Ellie's jaw tightened. "Of course. See you later." She spun around and stalked away, swaying a little on her four-inch heels.

I turned toward him, nearly beaming. "Thank you so much for playing along. You will never know how much I appreciate it. She's deserved something like that ever since high school!" I attempted to slide away from him so I could move back to my former seat, but his

169

arm tightened. I glanced at him, both eyebrows raised in question.

"Who said I was playing?" he replied, his voice a little gruff around the edges. His chocolate eyes were serious…warm and dark, and my heart started hammering erratically. "Besides," he grinned. "She might come back; you don't want to take any chances, do you?"

As soon as I opened my mouth to answer, I felt a vibration against my hip. It took a couple of seconds for me to realize that it was his phone. He leaned away just far enough to be able to reach it, and gave the screen a brief glance. His eyes narrowed a bit and he clenched his jaw, then he turned it off without answering.

I wasn't trying to look. I really wasn't, but I noticed the name on the screen said, "Jill," and the green-eyed monster reared its ugly head. Who the heck was Jill? Jeez! First Ellie and now Jill? A line was forming!

I silenced my desire to swear by taking a sip of tea.

I didn't trust my voice. I was afraid I'd growl again if I tried to say anything, and since I didn't want him to know I'd seen the name, to think I was nosy.

"So…do you?" he repeated.

"Do I, what?" I asked.

"Want to take a chance on Ellie coming back."

I just shook my head.

"Good answer," he smiled.

Chapter Fourteen

Cleo

Lily was waiting by the car when we came out.

I rushed over to her and grabbed her shoulder, impulsively pulling her close in a quick one-armed hug. "Why'd you do that?" I demanded. "Didn't you think I'd be worried about you? Why'd you sneak out on us like that?"

"Look at me, Cleo. I don't belong in there. You know it…I know it…and so did everyone else in the restaurant. If it wasn't illegal for her to do so, that seating hostess would've barred me from coming in there in the first place."

I couldn't argue with her so I dropped the subject, handing her a doggie bag containing the food she'd ordered before her escape. "Here's your food, at least."

She immediately opened the bag, releasing the wonderful aroma of its contents. Garlic-rosemary fries were a Moon River specialty and I had to admit they were pretty darn terrific. By the next morning they made your breath smell like a troll had slept under your tongue overnight, but it was worth it. She retrieved a fry and popped it into her mouth. "Thank you," she breathed, closing her eyes in apparent ecstasy.

Jonas beeped the car doors open and smiled. "My pleasure."

"So, where are we going now?" Lily asked around another mouthful of fries. "What's the plan?"

I turned around as much as the seatbelt would allow. "Jonas and I think we should hide out in the alley again. That seems to be where most of the action is—or *has* been so far. Maybe we'll get lucky and find a clue that can help us find Raymond."

Lily nodded, sending the bells jingling again. "When nothing goes right, go left."

Jonas looked confused. I cut my eyes at him and shook my head slightly. "Lily has an arsenal of famous—and infamous—quotes she likes to fit into her conversations. Sometimes they're a perfect illustration, but sometimes it takes time to figure out how it fits." I looked back at her. "I don't understand this one."

"You will."

Hmmm.

We were quiet then, each lost in his or her thoughts. My own kept wondering who this Jill person was. Maybe it was a sister. He'd mentioned a sister earlier, right? No, her name hadn't been Jill. It was Samantha, and they call her, Sam. Shoot! I wished now that I hadn't seen the stupid name on his stupid phone. Ugh! I forced myself to focus on the sound of Lily, chomping in the back seat. I hoped Jonas didn't mind people eating in his car.

We reached the spot to turn into the alley and I sprang to attention. "Oh, I get it!" I exclaimed, making them both jump. "*When nothing goes right, go left.* This is a one-way alley with a one-way road approaching it. You can only go left. That's it, isn't it?"

She cocked her eyebrow at me. "Told you."

I laughed. "Yes, you did."

We pulled into a slot reserved for a realty business on the corner, inching forward into the deep shadows as far as we could go. The headlights went off, followed by the engine. The sudden silence seemed very loud to me. I stared straight ahead where Lily's building hulked in the darkness. No lights shone from any of the five floors. A shiver travelled down my spine.

"You have any other wise sayings before we start this stake-out?" I whispered.

"Experience is what you get when you don't stop trying."

I blew out a breath. "Okay, then...Let's go get some experience."

****

For the second night in a row, I found myself crowded behind a line of garbage cans in the dark. My nose wrinkled at the smell emanating from our hiding place. Evidently, the city sanitation crew hadn't made it by this morning, after all. I leaned away from the cans as far as I could—which wasn't far enough—and breathed through my mouth to keep from inhaling the stench. Great! Now I could taste it! I ordered my gag reflex to take a hike, and tried to think about something else, while grape ivy leaves tickled my ears, and sharp stems dug into my back and neck. Thank goodness it wasn't *poison* ivy. I hoped this reconnaissance mission was worth all this.

The alley was as black as my mood ever since seeing that name on his phone. Maybe I should just ask him who this Jill was...get it over with. No! It wasn't my business. If he wanted me to know, he'd say something. It didn't matter anyway. He was just a reporter, doing a story. Once he completed it, I'd probably never see him again.

That thought hurt me more than it should. I needed to snap out of it.

Why was it so dark in this alley? The rest of town wasn't like this. Okay, so there wasn't a streetlight here. You'd think there would be *some* sort of illumination...perhaps a faint glow from a nearby window, or maybe some reflected luminance from the many other streetlights posted at regular intervals around the city.

But there wasn't. All the walls facing this narrow street were just as black as the rest of the alley. For some reason, being tucked between these rows of multi-storied nineteenth century buildings made it as inky as the inside of a coal mine; so shadowy that it was impossible to distinguish one shape from another, everything seemed to merge together. I peered up at the strip of sky above our heads. There were a few weak stars up there, intermittent pinpoints of light, but their dim glow was simply unable to penetrate the gloom down here.

Dark was good, though, I reminded myself. In our present predicament, lighting the alleyway kind of defeated the purpose, and would be detrimental to our health if any visitors showed up since they'd be able to see us. Complete darkness made it much easier to remain incognito, which was the status we were after.

But what were we hiding *from?* There was nothing here, and it looked like that wasn't going to change. Although last night we'd heard Mark Spencer say the work would begin tonight, apparently, the nabbing of Raymond had caused a change of plans. We'd been here nearly an hour with nary a hint of movement anywhere, other than some rustlings in one of the trashcans.

I tried to convince myself it was just a cat.

My legs were asleep, as was my butt. The rest of my body wanted to follow suit, but I didn't think that now was the time or place to mention it. And if that wasn't enough, I was cold. I was trying my best *not* to think of how warm it had been snuggled up next to Jonas in the restaurant. The stark contrast between then and now was just too painful.

Wah, wah, wah! Stop being such a cry-baby! My mental order helped, but if something didn't happen soon, the effect would be short-lived.

I leaned toward Jonas and whispered, "How much longer do you think we should stay?"

"I don't know," he whispered back. "I thought they'd be here by now. Maybe they're waiting a day or two before starting things back up. I knew it was a long shot, coming back here tonight, but I was kind of hoping—"

I was about to ask him why he stopped, when I heard the smooth purr of an engine. From this angle, the only thing I could see was that the car was large and wide, taking up nearly the width of the alley. A Lincoln or Cadillac, maybe? They were both big cars. The color looked dark—black or navy blue—blending in with the shadows except for the faint, twin beams of orange cast by its parking lights. But then again, *everything* looked the same in this alley. That car could probably be *white* and still look dark in here.

It pulled forward until it was directly in front of our shield of trashcans, and then stopped. The engine turned off and there was silence. After a minute or two, I caught a whiff of cigarette smoke.

Perfect. Here we sit, in the dark, in the cold, wedged like paperbacks crammed in a cardboard box, while this joker sneaks a smoke.

That's when I heard a second car.

It moved just as stealthily, but when its engine cut off, there was the sound of two car doors opening, then closing. Footsteps, and the sound of a trunk popping open were followed by a bit of a scuffle, a grunt, and then more footsteps that were accompanied by the sound of something dragging. After they faded away, a door on the first car opened, then closed. Heel clicked against pavement, then nothing.

Silence stretched to the breaking point in this narrow slice of space and my nerves felt just as stretched. I leaned toward Jonas again and whispered, "What now? Sounds like there are at least three of them. Do we make a run for that window again?"

"I don't know," he replied. "What if there are four? What if someone stayed behind in the car as a lookout? We can't see anything from here so we don't know for sure."

"Yeah, but we can't just keep sitting here either. We need to hear what's being said in that basement. They were dragging something. What if it was Raymond? Maybe there's a chance we can save him. We have to try."

I felt a slight movement to my left where Lily was hiding. I reached toward her and my hand hit nothing but air. "Lily," I hissed. My hand waved about frantically, trying to find her in the inky blackness. "No!"

But she was gone.

For a very long minute, we sat in frozen silence, tensed, listening for a shout, a scuffle, something to indicate that she'd been discovered, but heard nothing.

As I waited, it finally sank into my fear-frozen brain, that her exit had been silent, in other words: no bells. She must've taken off her hat. The absence of the familiar jingling that was so much a part of Lily, felt so odd to me that it was hard to concentrate on anything else.

I jumped and barely kept from shrieking out loud, when she touched my arm. "C'mon! The coast is clear. There's no one in the cars."

With the lower half of my body numb and lifeless, scrambling from our hiding place was easier said than done. I took a couple of stumbling steps before collapsing in a heap.

Jonas was right beside me. "What's wrong?" he murmured.

"My legs are asleep. I can't feel a thing."

Without a word, he slung my arm over his shoulder and, with his arm around my waist, he carried me across the open space and over to the small window. By the time we settled ourselves as soundlessly as possible, light was already glowing behind the textured glass. A low voice was speaking, but I couldn't hear it. I was too busy concentrating on staying completely motionless. Blood was finally coursing through my lower extremities and the sensations it was causing made me bite my lip to keep from screaming. I prayed that no one would accidently bump me until it was over.

It seemed like an eternity of complete focus, but it was probably no more than a minute, before I was able to take a deep breath and move a little closer to the window so I could listen.

I heard a voice—not Mark Spencer's, but another man—speaking. "No, he didn't actually mention the money, boss, but he was sure hinting at it. I doubt he could've kept from spilling the beans much longer. He was actually *bragging* that he wouldn't have to work anymore."

"Tsk, tsk…is this true? Even after I warned you about talking?"

I couldn't make out the response, but it sounded like the person was crying. I pressed my fist to my mouth, horrified.

"I know, I know…but even if you didn't actually say the word, *money*, you hinted at it. In my book, that's just as bad."

I strained my ears, trying my best to understand the mewling response, but couldn't.

"I have to tell you, I'm very disappointed. I thought we had an agreement…a mutually beneficial arrangement. I thought we understood each other."

A long pause stretched my nerves to the breaking point, then I heard a sigh. "It's regrettable. You finally understand just how serious I am about my "no talking" rule, but now we have a problem. I don't give second chances. You can't stay in Savannah."

Another whimper.

"No, you can't come back…ever. I'm going to have to insist that you accompany these gentlemen on a little excursion. They're going to take you out of town, and drop you off in a previously determined spot."

I felt a tap on my shoulder, and jumped. In the light from the window, I could see Jonas motioning for me to follow him. I silently crept back a few feet before standing upright, then practically flew, like my feet had wings, along the tiny walkway. Our movement toward the front of the building was a carbon copy of the night before, only faster. When we reached Oglethorpe Street, we turned left and dashed to the corner. I was sure I was breaking all kinds of land-speed records, but Jonas was right beside me and unbelievably, Lily was breathing down my neck. I had no idea that old people could move that fast. She must've run track in her younger days.

We turned left again and sped the remaining few feet to the parking area behind the real estate office on the corner. I pressed myself as flat as possible against the wall, trying not to sound like an emphysema patient gasping for breath, heart hammering in my chest. When I finally got my breathing sort of back to normal, I crept into the inky shadows, hands groping ahead of me, to where I knew Jonas had parked his car. I couldn't see a thing.

Ouch! I bit my lip to keep from exclaiming aloud.

I rubbed my knee with one hand and felt the contour of the bumper with the other. Well, at least I found the car. Keeping my hand out to guide me, I limped around to the passenger side. My hand was on the door, ready to open it, when I heard a car door slam up ahead and instantly dropped to my stomach. I knew they couldn't see us in this black chasm, but I didn't want to take any chances.

We couldn't open our car doors and get inside because the interior light would give us away, so we had to wait an eternity and a half for the two sets of taillights to turn right at the end of the alley before we could move.

I don't remember actually getting into the car, but I must have, because the very next instant we were turning right too, easing out onto the tree lined road—headlights off. I knew Jonas was trying to merge with the shadows so we wouldn't attract their attention on this quiet, residential street. I crossed my fingers, hoping that all the city cops were busy elsewhere.

At a stop sign up ahead, the first car went on around Wright Square, but the second turned right, and stayed straight, heading for Drayton. "He'll be in the second car. Mark Spencer won't take a chance getting his hands dirty," Jonas muttered, flicking on his headlights before turning right to follow the second car. There was a little more traffic now. We'd be able to blend in better. Up ahead, our quarries turned left.

"Hurry! Don't lose them!"

"I won't."

My hands were clamped so tightly on the edge of the seat beside my legs, I was afraid that I might break off chunks of it, but I couldn't seem to loosen my grip. I was too busy trying to figure out what we were going to do; how we were going to pull this off. These men were going to drop Raymond "at a previously determined spot." Sounded innocent enough, right? He might not even realize what that meant. Spencer hadn't really spelled it out. If I didn't know better, I could even believe that he was giving Raymond a second chance. There were, however, three problems with that line of thinking…the three bloated bodies discovered floating in the river. When I looked at the situation in light of the statistics…well, Raymond's chances of surviving this nighttime joy ride, didn't look so hot.

But what could *we* do? We had no weapons;

nothing to fight with, and I was sure that wasn't the case for those goons two cars ahead of us. We couldn't hope to save him...maybe not even ourselves! If it came down to it, I'm sure they wouldn't hesitate to give us a dose of the same medicine they were planning on giving Raymond.

But we couldn't just ignore the situation and let them get away with it, not without at least *trying* to stop them. I didn't know about Jonas or Lily, but I wouldn't be able to live with myself. Granted, I may not be able to live, *period*, but at least I'd know I'd tried. I think there was some famous quote that somebody said about tyranny and good men doing nothing. I was sure Lily probably knew what it was. I'd have to ask her later...if there *was* a "later." Now wasn't the right time.

I glanced at Jonas. His handsome face looked grim in the light reflected from the dashboard; both of his hands held the steering wheel in a death-grip. "Uh...you have any idea what our next step is?" I asked.

"Not a clue. I'm sort of making this up as I go."

I winced. That was *my* line. Up ahead, the dark car turned right on busy Bay Street. "Where are they going?" I wondered aloud, not really expecting an answer—Jonas was busy trying to avoid getting caught by red lights; Lily was busy being silent—but I couldn't seem to keep from asking it anyway.

We'd just crossed the Wilmington River drawbridge and were headed out Highway 80. I started getting a queasy feeling in my stomach. Right now, there were still several roads our target might choose to turn-off on, but for the most part, this road had one destination: the islands...Oakland, Whitemarsh,

Tybee…no farther. Each of them, small slices of coastal real estate, surrounded by nothing but marshes and creeks, a haven for mosquitoes most of the year, but beautiful in a desolate sort of way. One way in; one way out. Raymond's future wasn't looking too good.

But wait! Hadn't all the other bodies shown up in the Savannah River? This was the wrong direction. Anything dumped out here would only head to the Atlantic, so maybe I was wrong, and there *was* another reason that dark car was going this way. Without thinking, I blurted, "Ha! I just realized that none of the creeks out here lead in the right direction, so they can't be planning a body-du—" I broke off when I glanced over my shoulder and saw Lily's tense face.

Good move, Cleo! It took all my self-control to keep from banging my forehead against the dashboard.

There was no need to finish the sentence. The unsaid words hung in the air. They might as well be written in glow-in-the-dark paint. Everybody in the car knew exactly what I had been going to say. On top of that, my logic was flawed. That dark sedan could still be heading somewhere to dispose of a body. Spencer had probably decided to vary his dump-sites to avoid raising suspicions; head them straight to sea rather than through town where they'd be more likely to be discovered. I squirmed a little in my seat, staring blindly at the red tail-lights ahead of us, noting the silver cradle of the new moon suspended in the sky above them. I was desperate for something to erase those invisible—yet very visible—words. "Oh!" I gasped in relief. "They're getting off on this exit."

"Yeah," Jonas agreed, coming to my aide. "It's going to be harder to stay inconspicuous from here on out. I better hang back some. The trick will be keeping the right distance between us. Not so far back that I can't tell where they turn, but not so close that they'll realize they're being followed. This "tailing" routine is harder than it looks on T.V."

He slowed down so that his car was barely rolling down the exit ramp. I kept my eyes on the dark car ahead of us. It turned right, but instead of picking up speed, the right turn signal stayed on and it turned into the parking lot of a truck-stop. From the end of the ramp, I watched as two men got out of the car and headed into the restaurant part of the station. "Are you kidding me? They're going to *eat?* How can they think about food at a time like this?" I demanded. "They have a man locked in their trunk, for heaven's sakes! And they're stopping for a late supper?!"

"Maybe we could get Raymond out while they're inside."

It was the first time I'd heard Lily's voice since we'd gotten back in the car. It sounded low, but determined. "They parked on the side, not in the front with the rest of the cars. That's both good and bad for them. Good...to keep from arousing suspicion in case Raymond makes any noise, and bad...because they can't see the car from inside the restaurant. Maybe we could get the trunk open, get him out, and get away without them even realizing it."

Jonas immediately turned right. "Sounds like a plan to me. Let's go."

My heart was in my throat again, hammering wildly, causing my breath to come in short, shallow gasps. I hadn't fully grasped the magnitude of what we were about to do, but I knew enough to realize that we were putting ourselves in a very dangerous situation.

Jonas wheeled into the spot beside the dark car, and popped his trunk before hopping out. I wasn't sure my legs could hold me up, but I tried it anyway and managed to wobble around to the back of his car. He was rummaging in a toolbox and withdrew a long screwdriver. "Maybe this'll work," he muttered, then turned to me, "Run to the corner of the building and keep a look out for them. Try to be as inconspicuous as possible."

"Right! Look-out. Inconspicuous. Got it." My rubbery legs somehow carried me to the corner and I peered around it. The instant I gave him a thumbs-up, he rammed the screwdriver into the lock. I winced; waiting for a car-alarm, but amazingly, there wasn't one. I could see Lily, still in the back seat. Her eyes were closed and her lips were moving. It almost looked like she was praying. I shrugged, remembering the Bible with her name on it. Nothing she did surprised me anymore.

I gave another glance around the corner.

Still clear.

Back to Jonas. He was shoving the screwdriver, first one way, then another, finally down...with all his strength. I could see how much effort he was putting into it by the look on his face in the glow of the lights around the diesel pumps for the eighteen wheelers.

The latch suddenly gave way and the trunk popped open slightly.

Jonas hurriedly stuck the screwdriver into his back pocket before swinging the trunk all the way open. My heart was about to explode. I peered around the corner again.

Still clear.

Jonas reached into the trunk, grabbed and heaved. When he pulled up the limp form, my heart nearly stopped. Was Raymond already dead? Oh, please no!

I left my post and raced back to help Jonas. It was like lifting a huge bag of wet cement! Though Raymond wasn't a big man, his dead-weight was heavier than expected and very unwieldy. We heaved and struggled, awkwardly dragging the body out of the trunk, somehow managing to get it over to Jonas' car's back door, which swung open at our approach. Lily reached out to help us, pulling as we pushed, and we stuffed Raymond inside. I rushed around to my door and wrenched it open, expecting Jonas to be doing the same with his. When I didn't see him, I panicked. Where did he go?!

Before I could work myself into a tizzy, his head popped up on the other side of his car. "Get in!" he barked, as he tossed the screwdriver into the back and slammed the trunk closed. "Let's get out of here!"

He didn't have to tell me twice.

I jumped in and our doors banged shut simultaneously. He turned his key and the engine roared to life. I expected him to head back the way we came in, from the front of the restaurant; instead, he zoomed around the rear of the building, coming up on the far side, beside the diesel pumps. He barely paused before making a quick left out onto the road, back under the bridge toward the highway. I kept my eyes trained out the back window, watching for any headlights that appeared to be following us. Amazingly, there weren't any. But even so, it wasn't until we got out on Highway 80, heading back to town, that I actually took a breath.

"How is he?" Jonas asked Lily.

"He's breathing. I think they drugged him."

Jonas took a deep breath and blew it out. "I can't believe we pulled that off."

"What were you doing back there?" I demanded. "When I turned around and didn't see you, it freaked me out!"

"I was trying to give us a little head start. I rammed my screwdriver into both right tires. I figured they had one spare, but not two."

I stared at him, wide-eyed. Several emotions fought for first place, but admiration and amazement came out on top. "Are you sure you haven't done this type of thing before?" I laughed.

"Nah," he chuckled. "I just watch a lot of bad guy, suspense-type movies."

"Well, I'm impressed."

He grinned, then reached over and squeezed my hand. "Good."

Chapter Fifteen

Jonas

I had plenty of time to think while Lily and Cleo got a nearly comatose Raymond cleaned up, bandaged, and into bed. We'd taken him to Cleo's house since no one could come up with a better idea. Though the injuries he sustained at the hands of Mark Spencer's henchmen didn't appear to be serious enough to warrant a trip to the ER, they *were* serious and he deserved better than a blanket in some alley. My apartment wasn't an option; there was barely even room enough for me. Lily was homeless. The streets were certainly not safe. Actually, when you came right down to it, there really wasn't a place in all of Savannah where we could be assured of his safety, but as far as we knew, there was no tangible connection between Raymond and Cleo, so we could be relatively certain they wouldn't think to look here. According to Cleo, no one used the top floor of the house, anyway. Since we didn't have too many alternatives from which to choose, this seemed like the most sensible one. Perfect.

Well...*almost* perfect. In retrospect, maybe Cleo should've run it by her housekeeper before showing up at the front door with a mostly unconscious man who left a trail of blood behind him like a macabre version of Hansel and Gretel's breadcrumbs. I guess you could say that our plan hadn't gone over too well with Minnie.

When we'd hauled Raymond out of that trunk, I'd been too busy to pay much attention to how he looked. I'd had other stuff on my mind...like getting the heck out of there before Spencer's hit men came back. Now that I could see him, well...let's say it was going to take a while for him to heal. Small wonder he didn't have any broken bones. Shoot...it's a wonder he hadn't been killed.

For that matter...it's a wonder we hadn't *all* been killed!

What had I been thinking?! That just because I was one of the 'good guys' I'd be okay? That the "black hats" would wind up in jail and everyone would cheer the "white hats" for saving the day? This was real life, not an old John Wayne movie or some police drama on television that they could wrap up in an hour in between commercials. I needed to stop watching so many old NCIS episodes. I was no Jethro Gibbs.

The threat was out there, on hold, perhaps, but still very, *very* real. It hadn't magically gone away just because we'd wrested Raymond from its grasp. Thinking otherwise was wishful thinking. The danger was just skulking...biding its time...waiting for the perfect moment to make its move. There had to be a way to beat this thing, but I was coming up with nothing.

Wait! Of course! The answer hit me so hard and fast, I felt it vibrating throughout my whole body, like a giant gong had just been struck with an equally giant hammer. I knew what I had to do. It was the only way.

I also knew Cleo wasn't going to like it, not one

little bit, but that was okay…I wasn't particularly crazy about the idea, myself. Maybe I just wouldn't tell her.

Yeah, right. Even if, by some remote chance, I was able to get away with it, eventually she'd find out and…

No, I needed to tell her, be up front with her, get it over with. Like yanking off a stuck bandage or pulling a tooth, the quicker the better. Besides, it might not even matter to her. She might not care as much as I hoped.

That thought depressed me more than it should, but then I thought about her expression when she'd seen Jill's name on my phone at the restaurant and my spirits buoyed.

Yeah, she cared. How much? I wasn't sure yet, but it was enough for now.

****

"I've decided to go undercover," I announced quietly once Raymond was tucked in and down for the night, then waited for her response.

Nothing. Maybe she hadn't heard me.

I glanced at Lily. She was sitting by Raymond's bedside, holding his hand. If she'd heard, she was ignoring me, or else she was too focused on the invalid to pay much attention to anything else.

Cleo's face stayed calm, never changing. She kept right on doing what she was doing as if I hadn't spoken. Hmmm. Guess I better say it again. I opened my mouth to repeat myself just as she grabbed my arm and practically dragged me out into the hallway. Clearly, I'd been wrong about the "calm" part. It was all a mask, and as soon as the door closed, the mask came off.

"What, *exactly*, does that mean?" Her question

sounded decidedly ominous.

"Only that I'm going to disguise myself as a homeless man, get out on the streets and see if Spencer will choose me next." I was trying to diffuse the situation a little by forcing my voice to sound offhanded, sort of light and airy, like I was talking about the weather or telling her what my favorite color was or that I like mushrooms on my pizza.

It didn't work. Several emotions flitted across her face, incredulity being the most predominant; fury, a close second.

"You're kidding, right? This is a joke. It *has* to be. Nobody would seriously consider such a suicidal mission, not if he or she had a smidgen of intelligence. I thought you were a smart man, but must have been wrong, because I can see by your determined expression, you are, in fact, *serious!*"

I nodded.

"Are you out of your freaking mind?" she whisper-shrieked. "After what happened to those three men they found in the river? After what almost happened to Raymond? Or what *would've* happened if we hadn't been at the right place at the right time and were able to stop it! Did you hit your head or something? Because you obviously have brain damage. You're not thinking in a rational manner…or *at all!*"

I slipped a hand under her elbow and led her down the hallway to a cushioned bench, tucked into an alcove under a window. When she just stood there—body as stiff and unbending as a flagpole—I turned her around, resisting the nearly overpowering urge to kiss her, and gently pushed on her shoulders until her knees unlocked and she plopped onto the padded seat. I sank down next to her, picking up her hand, lacing my fingers through her icy ones.

"Do you have a better idea?" I asked gently. "Because if you do, by all means share it with me. I'm not one of those crazies who get their kicks by living life on the edge, flirting with danger, doing everything to the extreme. I'm more an "always wear your seatbelt" kind of guy."

All she could do was splutter out partial syllables, words lacking either a beginning or an ending consonant.

I nodded. "That's kinda what I thought you'd say." I traced my finger along the back of her hand, feeling invisible sparks zing at the contact. My heartbeat was chaotic, skipping with some anonymous emotion. "Well…maybe I was expecting a few more actual *words*." I gave her a half-grin, drowning in her beautiful eyes.

"The way I see it," I continued, hoping she couldn't hear how gruff my voice sounded. "Going undercover is the only way to get this guy."

"Jonas, I—"

"No, let me finish. You have to admit that we need to get on the inside of this operation. Am I right?"

"Yes, but—"

"And since—besides those two guys who had Raymond in their trunk tonight—we're the only other people who have figured out that Spencer uses homeless guys. Right?"

"Yeah, but—"

"And he'll be looking for another homeless guy to replace Raymond now that he's out of the picture, right?"

Her sigh was loud and exasperated. She snatched her hand away, crossing her arms, and glared at me.

There was my answer.

"I'm going to *be* that guy, Cleo. Don't worry. I have no intention of getting dumped in the river. I can stay one step ahead of them because I have an advantage those other men didn't. I *know* what's going on. I'll get Lily to help me find the right clothes so I'll *look* the part, but that's where the similarities will stop. I'm not like them. Homeless folks tend to be a little desperate; willing to do almost anything—legal or otherwise—to make money. I'm not trying to be a hero. All I'm after is shutting Mark Spencer down."

She narrowed her eyes. "What about your story?"

I dropped my gaze, feeling a little sheepish. "Well…yeah, there's that, too."

She let that slide, not commenting any further.

She might not like it, but I was right, and she knew it. She'd probably die before admitting it, though. In the eyes of the citizens of Savannah, the name "Mark Spencer" was synonymous with "police." He was trusted to uphold the law—to do what was right—and he was abusing that trust. He'd keep abusing it, too, unless someone did something. *Someone like me.*

Unless we attacked from the inside, there was really no way to stop this mess. The counterfeiting would continue and so would the killing.

"I'm not going to be able to talk you out of this, am I?" she asked.

I shook my head.

"I'd be wasting my breath if I tried, right?"

"Yep."

"There's *nothing* I can do to change your mind?"

Her question sent my heart pounding again, my blood heating in my veins. "Hmmm…I like the sound of that. I'd be willing for you to try."

Her cheeks stained pink, but she ignored my offer. "Would you promise me something?" she finally asked.

I nodded, and she whispered, "Please, be careful."

I reached over and recaptured her hand, releasing another wave of invisible sparks, before giving it a squeeze. "That, I can do. You got it."

Chapter Sixteen

Cleo

"What do you think?" Jonas asked, hamming it up, doing a sort of Vanna White-meets-runway model sort of pantomime, comically showing off his new look. He wore a pair of ragged, loose-fitting workpants that had a strip of worn duct tape acting as a patch over a hole in one of the knees. On his feet, were a pair of scuffed boots, almost identical to Lily's, though one of his laces was a piece of twine. A nappy, quilted jacket was layered over a faded red t-shirt; the words, "Run, Forrest. Run." were just visible above a couple of large blotches where someone had obviously spilled bleach on it, back in the decade when it had actually been washed. To complete the ensemble, he wore a ball cap that was so filthy and grease-stained that I couldn't even read what it was advertising. It made my head itch just to look at it. I shuddered, trying to avoid wondering about the hat's previous owner. Jonas grinned like he knew what I was thinking.

I don't know how it happened so quickly. Jonas was ready to go. It had taken some finagling on his part, but he'd been able to drag Lily away from Raymond's side for a couple of hours in order to gather the right costume, as well as getting a few names and possible locations of some good street connections. I'm pretty sure there were two things that made her agree to do it. One...she wanted to stop Mark Spencer so badly she was willing to take a chance with Jonas' life, especially after what Spencer had done to her friend. And two...Raymond was still so out of it, he'd never realize she wasn't glued to his bedside.

At any rate, she and Jonas had obviously hit the mother-lode in the "homeless menswear department." Looking at him now, no one would ever suspect he was anything other than another of Savannah's bona fide down-and-outers—her words, not mine. Jonas would blend in effortlessly, and Spencer would be none-the-wiser. Now, was that a good or a bad thing? I wasn't sure.

Rolling my eyes, I said, "Okay, the first thing you need to remember is, whatever you do...*don't smile*. Teeth like yours will give you away in a heartbeat. People will *know* you're a fake. They're just too darned perfect." *They match the rest of you,* I silently added.

It was true. Even in this dumpster-worthy outfit; even with the scruff of a day-old beard beginning to shadow his face; even in that disgustingly filthy hat...he looked amazing.

His grin widened and he performed a clumsy pirouette, making sure I was able to see his outfit from all angles. "Thanks, I'll keep that in mind. So, what's the verdict? Do I pass?"

"Umm..." The question had to be rhetorical. I doubted he *really* wanted to know what I thought. If I believed, for an instant, that my opinion could possibly change his mind, then I'd let him have it with both barrels. What I thought was that even a blind person, and certainly anyone with even mediocre vision would know immediately that he was a fake; that this was all an act. But then, that was the opinion of someone who thought Jonas would look just as amazing if he were wearing a lawn and leaf bag. I took a deep breath and tried again, concentrating on seeing him through eyes unclouded by personal prejudice, and something else I wasn't ready to admit yet.

It was no use. It just wasn't possible for me to be *un*prejudiced where he was concerned. I hoped it was just me…that it wouldn't be so obvious to someone less smitten with him than I was. The idea of Spencer or his goons figuring out what Jonas was up to was too frightening to contemplate. But bringing that up right now wouldn't make any difference. No matter what I said, it wouldn't change Jonas' mind, so why bother arguing the point? "I think you and Lily did a good job with the clothing choices," I finished lamely. I couldn't seem to inject any enthusiasm into my words.

His grin slowly faded and was replaced by a look of utter seriousness. He stepped toward me and placed his hands on my shoulders, stooping down in order for his eyes to be level with mine. "It's going to be okay, Cleo."

"How can you say that? How can you be so sure?" I was desperate to believe him.

"Trust me. I know these things."

I gave him a derisive snort that was definitely unladylike. "Yeah? Well, I want to go on record as saying I voted *against* this idea."

"Have you come up with a better one, yet?" He waited a beat or two. "No? Well, then…it looks like those in favor of me disguising myself as a homeless man in order to nab Mark Spencer, wins."

"What do you mean *those* in favor? There's only us...me and you...two people. One, *for* and one, *against*. Lily doesn't count. All she's interested in is stopping Spencer. She's not thinking about the risks."

"Nope. I count three people who are for the plan...me, myself and I." He counted off the names on his fingers.

"Stop joking about it, Jonas. This is serious!"

"I know it is, but I believe it'll work. I believe it's the *only* way that will work. If I didn't, I wouldn't be doing it. Remember? I'm the seat-belt guy."

"I know...I know. I get it. Thank you for trying to make me feel better about this. I know *I* should be the one encouraging *you*, not the other way around. Here you are, willing to put your life on the line so we can catch these guys, and I'm acting like a prophet of doom. I'm sorry. It's just that..." I shrugged his hands off my shoulders and started pacing, hands gesturing wildly. "You're sort of sailing into unknown territory, Jonas. No one can predict what will happen. These guys are playing for keeps. I didn't want to believe it before—I kept telling myself there was another explanation, but after what happened tonight, I can't lie to myself anymore. They're *killers*. They've killed before and they'll do it again." I stopped in front of him and grabbed his arms. Tears stung my eyes, but I blinked them away. "I'm scared," I admitted, then drew in a shaky breath. "I just wish there was another way." *One that doesn't risk your life,* I silently added.

He reached for my hand and gave it a gentle squeeze. "Try not to worry, okay?"

Yeah, right. That was like turning on the faucet and then telling the water not to come out. I nodded once and muttered, "I'll try."

"Good girl."

Since Lily was otherwise occupied with Raymond and wasn't willing or able to help me with my art project, and Minnie was still giving me the silent treatment, I was on my own. Though Minnie had accepted, and even embraced, my decision to hang around with Lily, bringing a homeless man into the house in order to hide him from the cops was something altogether different; sort of like living out a real-life episode of Law & Order, a show she watched regularly and enjoyed. Apparently, *living* it—rather than merely *watching* it—were two altogether different things, in her eyes. The latter just wasn't her cup of tea. But then to her credit, she didn't know that the cop in question was the bad guy. Minnie's feathers had been severely ruffled, and I was paying for my transgression. I wondered just how long the cold shoulder would last this time.

****

After some half-hearted work on the sketches I'd already done, I was nearly frantic to get out of the house. I had to find something to occupy my mind or I'd go crazy. Grabbing my laptop and stuffing it into a messenger bag, I headed to the public library. I needed to do some research.

The library didn't have much on the subject of counterfeiting; a couple of dated tomes that droned on and on about such things as: optically variable inks, watermarks, holograms, and micro printing. I hated to sound crude, but the best way I could describe it was to use one of Minnie's colorful expressions: it was as boring as gray, dull as oatmeal, and dry as a popcorn fart.

Since I was about to nod off, I decided to fire up my laptop, typing "counterfeiting money" in the search box.

I was amazed at the pages of information I netted. One of the sites actually gave step-by-step instructions of how to do it! Unbelievable!

I learned that most modern currencies have anti-copy features...tiny designs that have the word "void" or "fake" embedded in them in such a way that they're visible if someone is dumb enough to try to use a copy machine to print money.

Along the same line, manufacturers of color copiers have implemented special features to keep people from using their equipment in counterfeiting. Most of the machines imbed a unique code, invisible in ordinary light, which can be traced back to a specific machine. They've also come up with the technology that will actually cause the machine to shut down if it detects the design elements of currency. I think it's a pretty sad state of affairs when companies have to spend big money in their R&D department just to stay ahead of the bad guys. I guess that's part of the reason those products cost so much.

I was surprised to discover that my scanty knowledge of counterfeiting wasn't how they did it anymore. You know the one I'm talking about...like from the Andy Griffith show and old black and white gangster movies. The heavy, Gutenberg-style press with the metal plate delicately carved out by some old craftsman was a thing of the past. Now, it involved producing a computer generated film negative. They burn the negatives onto a series of photosensitized aluminum plates; with each one showing different details from the bill. Those plates are then used on an offset printing press, so that each set of details are layered on top of the others, using different inks. Most successful counterfeiters opt for purchasing high-quality negatives rather than trying to make their own, since no matter how good the paper is, the finished product is useless if the photographic negative is shoddy. From the conversation we'd overheard in the alley, that was the option Spencer had chosen. Start up fees for something like that are pretty high, though. Those fancy negatives are expensive. A contracted set could cost over $2000, with the plates costing nearly that much, as well.

I sat back in my chair, staring at the computer screen, but not really seeing it. Mark Spencer had coughed up the big money so he could buy professional negatives and plates. Anything less couldn't have produced bills that looked and felt as real as the ones Lily had found in the trash. Aside from that slight misalignment, those hundreds had been perfect, and the tiny glitch was sure to have been remedied by now. Spencer would've seen to it. Since there'd been no rumblings in the news about counterfeit bills popping up in the Savannah area, I must not be the only one thinking they were real.

So…yeah, the start-up costs were pretty high, but when you're printing off hundred dollar bills by the sheet, it doesn't take long to recoup any losses. It was hard for me to wrap my head around the kind of money Mark Spencer was raking in. No wonder he seemed willing to do anything to keep the operation going. Even killing people…no matter how many it took.

Jonas was right. Spencer had to be stopped.

I just wished there was another way to do it.

****

In spite of being so tired I was nearly shaking, I couldn't relax enough to go to sleep. I sat up and turned my pillow over—*again*—punching it with much more force than was necessary. A beam of light streamed in from the street lamp outside, spotlighting Tut. He was staring at me with reproachful eyes.

"What?" I snapped. "My pillow was flat. You know I hate it when that happens."

I could tell by his look that he didn't buy my explanation. "Okay, you're right, that's not the real problem, although it *is* true. I *do* hate it when my pillow is flat."

Tut blinked patiently, waiting.

I rolled over to face him and sighed. "I can't sleep. I'm too worried about Jonas. He's planning to do something really stupid and really dangerous and he won't listen to reason! Yeah, I know Mark Spencer has got to be stopped, and I know we can't depend on the cops to help, but there's got to be a better way! Ugh! Why are guys so hardheaded? Oops, sorry," I apologized when he narrowed his eyes and flattened his ears. "Not *you*...and maybe not even most guys. Actually, there's only *one* man I'm sure about, the only one who really matters—present company excluded, of course—but he holds the title for the most stubborn of them all."

I reached out to rub my cat's head, and then moaned, "How'd he get to be so important to me so quickly, Tut? Am I really so pathetic that I fall head over heels for the first guy I ever really talked to? I've never felt this way until now…*never!* And frankly, I'm not sure I even like it. Caring about someone like this? I don't know…" I shook my head sadly. "It's like giving someone permission to reach in and rip your heart out. I've opened myself up to a world of pain…one that never existed for me before Jonas. What makes it even worse is this Jill person."

Tut's eyes widened at the mention of her name.

"Yeah, that's exactly how I feel. Who is she to Jonas? Somebody important? He hasn't said anything about her, but then again, we haven't had a real date—not in the normal sense of the word—so it's not like we know a great deal about each other. He knows a lot more about me than I know about him, but still…"

I sighed and scratched under Tut's chin, his familiar purr a comforting sound. "You know, I probably would've never even met him if not for Lily. Okay…I did run into him…*literally*, but I never would've *talked* to him. I'd have just blushed furiously, ducked my head down, and concentrated on walking away without tripping over my own feet."

He stopped purring and gave me a reproachful stare again. "That's the truth, and you know it!" I insisted. "But now I *have* met him and I think he likes me, but even if he doesn't, I've fallen for him, hook, line, and sinker, and I don't want to lose him. He's trying to catch a bad guy and I admire him for it, but if something happens to him, I'll—No! I can't let myself think about that. If I dwell on all the things that could go wrong, I'll never get any sleep. What am I going to do?"

Sometimes I wished Tut could talk; now was one of those times. As I stared into his eyes, I found myself thinking about children's church back when I was a little girl, before my parents died. The teacher, Miss Wendy, had assured the class regularly that God loved them and knew all about them—every little thing—even the number of hairs on their heads! I could remember giggling, thinking that it would be a lot easier for God to keep track of that number with someone like Miss Wendy's husband, who was almost bald. The class had also been encouraged to pray, which she explained was another word for talking to God. All they needed to do was bring any requests to Him, because nothing was too big or too hard for Him to accomplish. Nothing was impossible. She'd even taught the class a song about that…"My God is So Big." The melody returned, unbidden, and I found myself humming a tune I didn't remember knowing.

Where on earth had *that* come from? My wondering gaze met Tut's owlish one. His eyes were big and round…and wise. "You think I should pray? I know Miss Wendy told us that God wants his children to talk to him, no matter how big or small the problem is, and technically, I'm his child, even though I've kind of shut him out of my life for a while. What do you think?"

He just stared at me.

"Right. It couldn't hurt, and if that song is true, it could *help*. I'm going to try it."

I took a deep breath and paused. It'd been a long time since I'd done this, and I wasn't quite sure how to start. The thought made me feel guilty. "God, it's me, Cleo. Yeah, I know it's been a long, long time and I'm sorry about that. I know all churches aren't like Aunt Patricia's. The one I attended in North Carolina with my parents is proof of that. I was wrong to turn my back on you and I hope you can forgive me.

"Miss Wendy taught us in children's church, way back when, that nothing's too hard for you. Well, I have something pretty big weighing on me tonight; worrying me so much that I can't relax, and you know I need some sleep!

"Since you know everything, I'm sure you're aware of this Mark Spencer mess. He's killed people, God. Innocent people, whose only sin was desperation. Spencer's an evil man who deserves to be caught and punished, which is part of my request. The other part is: I'm begging you to keep Jonas safe. He's hatched this crazy plan of pretending to be homeless in hopes that Spencer will choose him as his next stooge. He says it's the only way to get on the inside, and maybe he's right, but I think it's a terrible plan. And because I can't think of a better one, I can't talk him out of it. So, God, will you *please*…take care of him?

"I guess that's it. I hope the song is right, and that there really is nothing impossible for you. In Jesus' name I pray all this…Amen."

I'd no sooner said the final word, when a huge yawn nearly cracked my jaw, and my eyes suddenly drooped halfway closed. My last thought was that I'd forgotten to pray anything about Jill.

Chapter Seventeen

Lily

"Mornin' Miz Lily," Raymond murmured when I walked into the bedroom.

He's awake! I gasped, nearly dropping the tray I was carrying. Hurriedly setting it on the small table near his bed, I grabbed his calloused hand and gave it a squeeze. "Raymond! You're okay!"

He started to grin, then winced as the movement stretched his split, swollen lip. He raised a hand, tentatively touching his mouth, before stretching a finger to trace his puffy eye, then the bandages on his head. "Yep, I guess I am." He shifted in bed and groaned. "But I feel like I been run over by a Mack truck."

I made a face and smiled. "Hate to say it, but you look like it, too, my friend."

His wheezy chuckle cut off abruptly, and his hands clutched his torso. "Ugh...don't make me laugh. Hurts too bad."

I retrieved a glass of water from the tray and gently pressed the straw to the less-injured side of his mouth. He gulped thirstily. "Mmmm...thank ya, ma'am. That shore helps. I's parched. Dry as a box of sodie crackers is what my granny'd say." He stared around the room, his good eye round with wonder. "Where *is* this place?"

"You don't remember? You've been a little out of it. We brought you here a couple of nights ago."

"We?"

"Jonas and Cleo and me. This is Cleo's house."

He wrinkled his brow, trying to remember, but gave up and shook his head. "Tell me."

"Here…take another drink. I haven't been able to get much in you since you've been here. I know you must be about dehydrated."

He took another long swallow. "Okay, that's enough. Now, tell me."

I hesitated, unsure of how much to say. I knew the power that a person's mind could wield in any healing process, and I sure didn't want to create a speed bump on his road to recovery by giving him more information than he could handle. His mental state was a little precarious already. His "lights" had been out for a while, yesterday—eyes open and staring—but nobody had been home. It'd been one of his "bad days."

"Well?" he demanded. "Whatcha waitin' for? Go ahead and tell me. Cain't be worse than wonderin'."

I wasn't so sure. "You were beaten up."

He rolled his good eye. "I think I figured that part out, Miz Lily. By who?"

"Mark Spencer's men." I didn't miss the flicker of some emotion in his eye at the mention of the name. *He remembers something.*

Raymond's jaw clenched, then he growled, "Go on."

"We followed Spencer's men, and when they stopped to get something to eat, we rescued you from their car trunk and brought you back here. We cleaned you up and bandaged you as good as we could. You've been sleeping ever since."

He stared at me in wonder. "You talk different. Don't think I ever heard you say that much regular talk before…without usin' one of them sayings of yours." Then he sighed, wincing again before closing his eye.

I panicked. Had I said too much? I'd tried to give him as little details as possible, but maybe it was still too much. I should've tried to stall him somehow, maybe even lie to him; whatever it took, but I should've waited. It was too much, too soon. He wasn't ready yet.

When he opened his eye again, it shimmered with a glaze of unshed tears. "I be so glad my granny's done passed on. I'd hate for her to know what I've done; it'd shame her, so."

"Do you need to talk about it? I'll listen if you do," I reminded him, softly.

He swallowed hard, his Adam's apple bobbing up and down beneath his gray-stubbled chin. A tear oozed from the slit of his bruised, puffy eye. "I thought it was my way out, my chance to be r'spectable. He say he gonna to teach me how to do it, and pay me good money, too. Alls I had to do was keep my big mouth shut." He shook his head, a mournful expression on his battered face. "I couldn't even do that. Easy as pie and I couldn't do it."

What could I say? Would I have acted differently, had I been in his shoes? I wanted to say yes, but my case was unlike the rest of Savannah's homeless. I'd *chosen* my route. The rest of them couldn't say that. They had no choice. Who could say whether my actions and reactions would be the same if this lifestyle had been forced on me, rather than something I'd chosen. But there was no sense dwelling on it. I couldn't, no…I *wouldn't* judge Raymond for the choice he'd made. Desperation had a way of leading people down paths they never thought they'd travel.

I squeezed his hand. "Never let success go to your head, or failure go to your heart."

The edge of his mouth tilted up the tiniest bit. "Thank ya, Miz Lily."

Now that Raymond was truly on the mend, it felt safe to take a break. I wasn't used to being stuck inside for this long, and cabin fever was about to get the best of me. Rose was probably wondering where I was too.

Rose…I needed to talk to my sister. The hours spent at Raymond's side had allowed me plenty of time to think. It was time for some straight answers…answers to questions that should've been asked many years ago. If I were honest with myself, I'd have to admit that I was a little scared, but I couldn't keep hiding behind those fears. I had to face them— head on—and Rose was where I needed to start.

But where to look? Probably north, toward the river. Rose frequented Factor's Walk and River Street, anywhere with the highest concentration of people and action. Even after her death, Rose was a "people person." She loved to mingle with the crowd—both ghosts and the living. When it was the latter, and it involved a handsome man, she'd even allow herself to become visible so she could flirt to her heart's content, laughing and basking in the limelight, just like she'd done when she was alive. Not much had changed in that respect.

Before I went anywhere, though, I needed to check in with Minnie; let her know I'd be taking a break. It had taken a lot of work…damage-control tactics by

Cleo, and vast amounts of schmoozing on my part, but we'd finally been able to smooth things over with Minnie. You could hardly see any rough places in the housekeeper's attitude, now. It hadn't started like that, though. That rocky, first meeting—the night we'd dragged Raymond in—was one I'd just as soon forget.

As soon as she'd seen the blood, Minnie panicked and snatched the phone from the wall, her shaking finger punching the numbers 9-1-1.

"No, Minnie!" Cleo shrieked when she saw what the woman was doing. "Put the phone down. You can't call the police!"

"What do you mean, I can't call the police?" her voice was just as shrill. "Nine-one-one is what you're supposed to call when there's an emergency. And if this ain't one, I don't know what is!"

My heart was racing. A call to the police would defeat the whole purpose of the rescue. It had to be avoided at all costs.

Cleo wrenched the phone out of Minnie's hand. "You *can't* call the police."

"The dickens you say! Give me that phone!" Minnie tried to grab it back.

I didn't know what to do, and Jonas *couldn't* do anything. He had his hands full with Raymond draped over his shoulder, dripping blood on the hard wood floor.

They tussled for several very long seconds. Minnie's weight gave her an advantage, but Cleo made up for it in desperation and youth.

"Minnie!" Cleo finally panted. "As your employer, I'm asking you to *let go of the phone!*"

The big woman froze. Her shocked expression was

almost comical; jaw dropped, eyes bugged out. Her hands dropped limply to her sides, she took two steps back.

"I'm sorry I—" Cleo began, but Minnie's hand snapped up, palm out, halting any other words she might have intended. The hurt, accusing look she gave the girl before she turned away made Cleo's shoulders droop. She'd obviously never played the "boss card" before.

That night had been a rough one. It was hard to know who'd been more shocked…Cleo or Minnie. Once everyone had calmed down, and Cleo had been able to explain—not everything, but *enough*—the housekeeper had finally lost some of her huffiness. It still felt like we were all walking on eggshells where she was concerned, so I didn't dare slip out without letting her know.

Minnie was on the phone and didn't hear me enter the kitchen.

"I don't know why you feel like you have to play "taxi driver" every day, Tobias. You know Miz Patricia would be rolling in her grave if she could see you driving her big ol' car around town, picking up every Tom, Dick, and Harry wanting a ride."

I cleared my throat just loud enough for her to know I was there. Minnie whirled around as quickly as her sizable girth allowed. She held up a finger, telling me to wait.

"Oh, go ahead. The more you're out there giving tourists the run-around, the less you're puttering around here getting in my way. Hope you're charging enough to pay for your gas, old man. Okay…bye."

"How's the patient?" Minnie wanted to know as

she hung up.

"I think he's reached a turning point. He'll get better quickly, now. Have you seen Cleo?"

"I think she's still in bed, and I didn't want to bother her. She hasn't been sleeping well, lately." The housekeeper's eyes moved to my hat and she arched a brow. "Heading somewhere?"

"I was hoping it would be all right if I got out of the house for a while. Raymond's taking a nap so he shouldn't be a bother. I've been cooped up inside for too long. I'm not used to living like this."

Minnie gave a fluttery wave of her hand. "Sure, sure...take yourself a good, long walk. You deserve it. You've barely left that room for days, and I'm sure you need a break. I'll check on Raymond in a little while. Go on with you, now."

"Thank you, Minnie. I'll just slip out the back way, if you don't mind. Don't want folks to see riff-raff like me using your fine front door. That might attract attention we don't want or need. Tell Cleo I'll be back as soon as I can."

****

I took a deep breath of the crisp December air. Ahhhh... It felt good to be outdoors again. Though it had been nice to not have to worry about being cold at night or where I'd get my next meal, I'd missed the freedom I'd grown so used to over the years.

A fleeting glance toward Forsyth Park was all I allowed myself. I'd love to visit The Fountain, but there wasn't enough time. River Street was all the way on the other end of town and I knew my old bones didn't move as quickly as they used to. There was no time to waste.

I turned onto Bull Street so I'd at least be able to walk through several squares on my way to the river. The first one was Monterey. To my left was the Mercer House, the place where that young man was tragically killed. Murder or self-defense? No one really knew, even after three trials. It was one of the city's biggest scandals as well as, biggest mysteries. Place was haunted too, and no wonder, with a history like that. Some fellow wrote a book about it, then Hollywood made the book into a movie, causing people to flock here in droves, even more than they had after that Forrest Gump movie.

I glanced around, self-consciously, hoping the ghosts would understand that I was limited on time, and that my regular glitter-sprinkling routine would have to wait. Maybe they wouldn't mind too much. The last thing I needed was to get a bunch of ghosts mad at me.

I hurried toward Madison Square. This was where the Green-Meldrim House was...one of my favorites. I loved wrought iron filigree, and this place had iron-work to spare. It was a shame that such a beautiful place had housed that hateful General Sherman during the Civil War. In order to save the city from Sherman's infamous "march to the sea," the civic leaders had surrendered in exchange for the general's promise not to burn the town. He agreed, so no shots had been fired. Sherman had written out his famous telegram to President Lincoln in that very house: "I beg to present you as a Christmas gift, the city of Savannah, with one hundred and fifty heavy guns and plenty of ammunition, also about twenty-five thousand bales of cotton..."

I had mixed feelings about that episode in the city's

history. If it hadn't happened like that, Savannah would've probably been listed with all the rest of Sherman's "burn towns," and all the beautiful, historic buildings would have ended up as piles of smoldering rubble. Even so, my Southern blood tended to boil a little at the idea of surrendering to that jack-dog, Sherman. Well, sometimes you had to do what you had to do, even if it went against the grain. Those leaders of long ago had sacrificed Southern pride for the greater good. My eyes swept around the square and I had to smile. I guess the trade had been worth it.

This city had a long list of "firsts" to boast about: the first Sunday school in America, the first orphanage, the first Black Baptist Church, the first golf course. John Wesley, the founder of the Methodist movement, wrote the first hymnal used in the Church of England while in Savannah. The Girl Scouts program was started here, and the first steamship ever to cross the Atlantic Ocean launched its maiden voyage from here, ending up in Liverpool, England in the early 1800's. It was a city to be proud of. I'd kind of forgotten that.

Maybe it was time…

No! Don't go there! It's too late for that. It's been too long.

I gently pushed my defenses away, opening my emotional door wider. Maybe…

Noooo!

My inner self turned savage, frantically clawing at the hand opening the door, seeking to slam it shut and bolt all the locks at any cost, but the swinging door gained momentum, hauling its unwilling passenger with it, despite the desperate clutching of the knob, the feet dragging against the floor trying to slow the process.

213

Maybe...

I nodded with a smile. Meeting Cleo and Jonas, the close call with Raymond...these things had opened my eyes. Now I needed to hear the truth from my sister. Once I did, perhaps I'd be ready to drop my homeless façade and try weaving myself back into the fabric of society.

But I needed to talk to Rose, first.

****

By the time I crossed Bay Street and started down the sidewalk bordering Emmet Park, I could feel the beginnings of a blister on my heel. Now, if I'd had my cart, that wouldn't be a problem. I'd just find my roll of duct tape and fix it right up. Unfortunately, my cart wasn't with me. It was where it'd been ever since the day Raymond had disappeared; the same place Raymond's cart was put, after we'd gone back and retrieved it from his bench so it wouldn't get stolen...in the trunk of Jonas' car, and I had no idea of where that car was. I'd just have to tough it out.

Steep stairs took me down to River Street's bumpy cobblestone surface. The stones had once been used as ballasts, for weight and stability in the hulls of huge sailing ships that had brought the first colonists over. Before heavy cargo was loaded onboard, these stones were taken out of the ships and left behind. They made a quaint, but extremely uneven road surface that was difficult to walk on in the best of circumstances. The flopping tendency of my oversized boots compounded the problem, forcing me to be very careful how and where I stepped.

"Lily!"

The masculine voice startled me, causing me to

stumble and nearly fall on the treacherous surface. My arms waved wildly as I tried to regain my balance.

"Whoa! Careful!" A pair of hands caught and steadied me, keeping me from a painful fall. Warm brown eyes peered at me from under a disgustingly filthy ball cap.

"Jonas! Thank goodness it's you." I straightened my hat and adjusted my coat, my heart still racing from my near-spill. "Anybody else would've probably just let an old woman fall."

He laughed. "I think you might be underestimating humanity a little. Do think you could cut it some slack?"

"Cut it some sla—" I broke off, laughing, then shrugged. "Maybe you're right; maybe you're right." I gave him a head to foot appraisal, and then nodded. "I have to say, your disguise is definitely a success. You fit right in. No one would ever be able to tell that you're anything other than a genuine, bona fide homeless man. I'm sure that's a title you've always aspired to. So…what are you doing down here?" I gestured to the waterfront.

He didn't answer for the longest moment, but rather studied me through narrowed eyes. "There's more to you than meets the eye, isn't there, Lily?" he finally asked.

"I-I'm sure I don't know what you mean," I hedged, picking a piece of lint off my sleeve, and avoiding the eyes I could feel still staring at me. I needed to be more careful. Jonas was more astute than I'd realized.

"Ahhh, but I think you know *exactly* what I mean. I guess I can let you slide for now, though. You can fill me in later."

I couldn't hold back my small sigh of relief before prompting him, "You were about to tell me what you were doing here…?"

"Right!" He looked around before lowering his voice. "I overheard a couple of guys say this is the place to be. I saw someone earlier who might've been one of Spencer's guys. He was being unobtrusive, but I'm pretty sure he was watching me. Hey, where's Cleo?"

"She was still in the bed when I left. According to Minnie, the poor thing's had some trouble sleeping lately." I gave him a stern look, cocking an eyebrow. "I wonder why *that* is?"

"Now, wait just a minute! You helped me with the disguise. I thought you were on *my* side."

"I *was*, until you told me you thought one of Spencer's men had his eye on you. I'm afraid for you, Jonas. Cleo would never forgive me if something happened to you. She already blames me for encouraging you with this crazy plan of yours."

"I'll tell you the same thing I told her. Nothing's going to happen to me. I'm not some desperate homeless pers—" He winced. "Sorry, no offense."

I chuckled. "None taken."

"Anyway, I'm not desperate, and I *am* going into this thing with my eyes wide open. I promise to always stay one step ahead of them. Okay?"

I nodded slowly, reluctantly. "I'm counting on it, but more importantly…*Cleo* is counting on it. And young man…?"

He snapped to attention at my tone. "Yes, ma'am?"

"You better not be toying with that child!"

His grin stretched from ear to ear. "I wouldn't dream of it."

"Stop it!" I growled, trying to keep the corners of my mouth turned down, but failing. "Remember what Cleo said about that smile."

Though his face was an immediate mask of somberness, traces of humor and a bit of devilment sparkled in his eyes as he gave me a nod. "Yes, ma'am!" Then he turned and sauntered away.

As I watched him until I lost him in the crowd, an uneasy feeling settled in the pit of my stomach.

****

"There you are!" I cried when I spotted Rose's fiery red hair in the middle of a group of tourists that had just gotten off one of the river taxis. "I've been looking all over for you."

Rose's expression cooled as soon as she saw me. My heart sank. My sister was still mad at me for not taking her advice about Cleo. That was going to make this conversation even tougher.

"What do you want?" Rose spoke ventriloquist-style, behind a brilliant smile she was flashing at the gorgeous hunk waving at her from a passing boat. She fluttered her fingers in response, trying to look like she wasn't connected in any way with a crazy old woman wearing a flamboyant court jester hat.

I was used to it. It was the way she always treated me. Then I stopped, stunned at that sudden realization. I replayed the scene in my mind, focusing on the fact that my sister had tried to pretend she didn't know me. Similar memories flashed through my mind. Scene after scene, time after time. Others followed...more painful ones, this time: Rose laughing when I failed at something, Rose belittling me—both publically and privately, Rose discouraging any attempt at anything new, demanding all my attention and pouting when she didn't think she got it.

I'd spent my entire life idolizing Rose, putting her on a pedestal, giving her the devotion she thrived on, squashing my own wants in order to give in to my sister. How could I have been so blind? How could I have missed seeing how utterly self-absorbed and egocentric she really was?

Had it always been this bad?

I thought back to my early childhood: favorite dolls and toys that somehow ended up in Rose's room; the shows on television…always Rose's choice; Rose was afraid of clowns and hated the circus, so we'd never gone; my favorite outfit that had gotten ruined with bleach when Rose had helped with the laundry.

My thoughts ranged forward a few years, seeing it through new eyes, observing a pattern that I'd never noticed before. I'd never been allowed to wear anything royal blue even though I loved the color, and everyone thought it looked good on me…everyone, but Rose. My big sister had told me that blue didn't suit me, so I hadn't worn blue; hairstyles that Rose recommended always turned out disastrous; the perm Rose had once given me that burned my hair so badly, I'd had to get a pixie cut to get rid of the damage.

I looked down at my clothes; the mismatched patterns, the scuffed boots. Rose had encouraged my transformation into a crazy, homeless woman, too. I shook my head in amazement, having a hard time absorbing this new insight. My sister had been sabotaging me for years, always trying to make me look bad.

I reached up and pulled off my hat, stuffing it into my pocket, then straightened my spine, and drew back my shoulders. It was time for the abuse and ridicule to stop. It was time for the truth.

"There was never an affair, was there?"

My words grabbed her full attention. Her million-dollar smile faded like it was on a dimmer switch.

"I'm sorry, what?"

My lips felt stiff. The words had to be pushed from my mouth. "Michael...all those years ago. There was never an affair."

She blinked as if I'd flicked water in her eyes. Then a whole range of emotions travelled across her face. It was like looking through one of those old Viewmaster toys, pushing down the little plastic handle to see the next scene: shock... anger... denial... cunning...

Finally, her acting skills kicked in and she pasted her smile back on. "Of course, he had an affair, Lily. Why else would you break things off?" The line was delivered flawlessly...except for the way her voice cracked on the word, "off."

But before I could say anything, she blurted, "I found out why that girl's aunt hated her so much."

The abrupt change of subject was unexpected, and struck me speechless.

She took advantage of it. "Apparently Julie Davenport—that's the girl's mother—was a bit of a handful and got herself barred from the private school Patricia had pulled strings to get her into, so Patricia hired a live-in tutor—a Mr. Jake Davis—and the problem appeared to be solved. Julie excelled under his

219

tutelage, and everything seemed fine for a time." Rose paused to make sure I was paying attention, then nodded. "Now, here's where it gets good…

"…As time went on, ol' Patricia ended up developing soft feelings for Jake, even though she was several years older than he was. She kept her feelings to herself, thinking it would be unseemly to entertain such ideas. After all, the man was living under her roof, in her employ. She refused to give her acquaintances food for gossip, so she held her peace, opting to wait until Julie graduated and wouldn't need him as a teacher anymore, before revealing her true feelings. She'd already introduced her niece to the respectable young man whom she expected Julie marry, a man with good connections and fine parentage…a good match, as far as she was concerned. She was biding her time, but Julie had other ideas…"

Rose glanced at me and raised her eyebrows. "Ready?"

"Oh, just tell me and stop being so dramatic!"

You'd have thought I stuck her with a pin the way she flinched. My outburst was definitely not my usual reaction to her theatrics, and it threw her off. It took her a couple of seconds to recover.

"Okay, well…um…this is the part that frosted Patricia's—um…I mean…what made her so angry that she took it out on Cleo. Unknown to her aunt, Julie had fallen for Jake, and it was more than just a crush. Even though he was almost ten years her senior, and he tried to discourage such feelings, soon he was as smitten with her as she was with him. The night after she'd officially graduated, they eloped, left Savannah, moved to the mountains of North Carolina, and about nine months later—some say less—Cleo was born." She arched her eyebrow suggestively, waiting for some kind of response.

I knew what she wanted, and I was determined not to give it to her. It took conscious effort, but I kept my expression cool and detached; looking completely unfazed by her innuendo. The briefest of brief creases appeared between her brows for a split second. Nobody else would've even noticed it, but I did.

After a pause, she continued, but was now wearing a forced smile, "Patricia never got over it. After the accident that killed Julie and Jake, Cleo showed up on her aunt's doorstep, the spitting image of her mother, only with her father's remarkable eyes. It was more than Patricia could take. The resentment she'd felt at Julie's betrayal, all the bitter feelings she'd kept bottled up inside, building for years, everything came gushing out the day the little Cleo arrived."

When Rose finished, I was quiet for a long minute. If I allowed myself to think too deeply, my resolve would slip, so I steeled my spine. "Thank you for finding out for me, but if you think that changing the subject will make me forget about what you've done, you're very much mistaken."

I gave my sister a long, hard look, felt the sting of tears in spite of iron-fisting my emotions. "Goodbye, Rose," I whispered.

Then I turned and limped away.

****

I'd taken no more than a half dozen steps, when someone grabbed my arm and spun me around. "There you are!" Cleo exclaimed. "I've been looking for you everywhere! No wonder I couldn't find you...you aren't wearing your hat." She gave me an impulsive hug before demanding, "Are you okay?"

I nodded, my heavy heart already lightening a bit in the face of Cleo's exuberance.

"Why didn't you wake me up? I could've walked with you, done some more sketches."

"A good laugh and a long sleep are the two best cures for anything."

Cleo laughed. "Yay! I never thought I'd say this, but I've been missing your little sayings lately. What are you doing way up here?"

"I had to ask my sister something."

Cleo's eyes went wide, darting in every direction. "Rose? Rose is here?"

I stared over Cleo's shoulder. Rose was still standing there, statue-like, in the same position, an unreadable expression on her face. "No, she's not here," I replied firmly, my eyes locked with my sister's. Then I added, "Never make someone a priority, when you're just their option." At my words, Rose disappeared.

"Uh…okay," Cleo replied, a confused look on her face. I was sure she was trying to figure out what relevance my comment had to the situation, but then she shrugged and asked, "Where are you going now?"

"Back to your house to check on Raymond, and to find a band-aid."

"Band-aid? Are you hurt?"

"Just a blister."

"Oh, wait! I think I have one in my backpack. Let me look." She unzipped a couple of pockets, scrambled a few seconds and then exclaimed, "Voilà! Success! Here you go."

I limped to a nearby step and sat down, unlacing my boot. "Thank you, thank you, thank you!"

"Better?" Cleo asked brightly, once I had retied my bootlace.

I groaned with relief. "Much! But I still need to check on Raymond."

"Okay, but can I draw while we walk?"

"Life is about using the whole box of crayons."

Cleo's giggle made me smile.

Chapter Eighteen

Cleo

"You saw Jonas?" My voice sort of squeaked his name. "Why didn't you say something? Where? How'd he look? Any bad-guy contact yet? Is he doing okay? How long—"

"Whoa! One question at a time!" Lily held up her hand, interrupting me. "I thought you wanted to sketch on the walk home. So, start sketching!"

"Okay, okay, but give me all the details, while I do."

Before she could answer, a pimped-out, poison green Cadillac with sparkling chrome spinners on its wheels, and windows tinted so black I wondered if the driver could even *see* through them, rumbled around the corner toward us. The bass was turned up loud enough to make the ground tremble and my teeth vibrate.

"Jeez!" I complained. "And their windows are rolled up! Imagine how it sounds *inside* that car!"

"Rap is to music what etch-a-sketch is to art." Lily shouted to be heard.

I burst out laughing and yelled back, "I'll have to remember to tell that one to Professor Hudson. He absolutely abhors rap."

"Oh, yeah? Well, here's another one for him, then. You know what rap is?"

The car paused at a stop sign, then crept forward. It was as if the driver knew he was annoying us and was trying to drag it out as long as he could.

I shook my head and screamed, "You mean, besides being an insult to music?"

"R-A-P," she spelled loudly. "Retards Attempting Poetry!"

I giggled, quickly scrawling both sayings on my sketchpad so I wouldn't forget them. The car finally moved out of earshot, making the street seem extra quiet in comparison. "Now, you were talking about Jonas…?"

"He's fine. He looks like a homeless person. He thinks one of Spencer's men was watching him. He asked about you." She counted off on her fingers.

My heart had screeched to a stop at the mention of Mark Spencer's goon, only to jolt back into action upon hearing her final point. My fingers went numb. I didn't even notice that I'd dropped my pencil. It rolled to the edge of the sidewalk, and Lily bent to pick it up.

"Cleo? Yoo hoo…" She waved it in front of my face, then snapped her fingers. "Earth to Cleo. Come in, Cleo. Houston…we have a problem."

I shook my head, clearing the stars away and gave her a beatific smile. "He asked about me? He *really* asked about me?"

Lily rolled her eyes and handed my pencil back to me. "The human brain is the most amazing organ. It works twenty-four hours a day, seven days a week, from birth until the moment you fall in love."

I ignored her, hugging my sketchpad to my chest, still wearing a thousand kilowatt smile, and dreamed of Jonas a couple more seconds, before sighing. "So what did he say…*exactly?*"

She chuckled. "He said—and I quote—"where's Cleo?""

I felt like she'd punched me in the stomach. "Is that all?" I pouted.

Her gray eyes gleamed mischievously. "That's all I'm saying for now."

"There *was* more!"

Lily kept her face deadpan. "Life is between the trapeze bars."

"Ugh! You're killing me, Lily! I can't believe I said I missed hearing those quotes." I reluctantly turned my attention to the pad I held. "Fine!" I groused. "I need you to put your hat back on so I can get a few more sketches, and I wish we had your cart."

****

I called Minnie to check on Raymond. She'd just taken him some lunch and he was napping again. Since we didn't have to hurry, we decided to rest for a few minutes at one of the little tables on the sidewalk in front of the Mellow Mushroom. Well, Lily was resting; thoroughly enjoying a glass of sweet tea, from the looks of it. My glass was pushed to the side, untouched and getting watery, while I drew like a maniac. It was a close-up of her face.

Suddenly she gasped, "Oh, no!"

I was instantly alert, searching around in a panic. "What?"

"Don't turn around," she murmured in a deceptively calm manner through lips that barely moved. "Be as inconspicuous as possible. Mark Spencer is just inside the restaurant."

I tried to keep my eyes from bulging and my heart

from galloping out of my chest. Casually picking up my glass of tea, I took a sip, using the process as a chance to turn my head and peer through the window, without looking obvious. And there he was.

He definitely looked better in his airbrushed campaign posters or heavily made up on TV. In real life, he couldn't hide the bags under his eyes that made him look permanently hung over. His hair usually had that carefully manicured, but very hard-hattish look, a sure indication that it'd been hair sprayed and gelled to within an inch of its life, but right now it appeared shaggy and unkempt, and his stretchy golf shirt couldn't hide the paunch that a sports jacket usually covered up. Seeing him now and remembering the end he'd intended for Raymond, was enough to make me sick to my stomach.

Then I saw who was with him.

"Ellie," I whispered, numbly. "You've *got* to be kidding me." I started throwing my gear into my backpack. "Lily, we need to leave…*now!*" Out of the corner of my eye, I could see Mark and Ellie moving toward the door. I did *not* want her to see me. She couldn't see me…*no, no, no!*

"Well, well…look who it is!" The familiar voice sang out behind me.

I squeezed my eyes shut and ground my teeth together. *Too late!* I glanced toward Lily's chair and wasn't even surprised to discover it empty. She was an expert at her disappearing act. Taking a deep breath and pasting on a smile, I turned to face my enemy. Thank goodness Jonas wasn't here.

"Ellie! What a surprise!"

Her jaw tightened, and she struggled not to correct

me. "Yes, isn't it?" She trilled, linking her arm through Mark's, leaning into him while giving me a "drop dead" look. She was barely wearing a little black dress—emphasis on *little*—and on a side note...wasn't lunchtime a bit early for that kind of attire? It sure didn't leave a lot to the imagination, no matter what time of day it was. "I'm sure you recognize Mark...or *you* probably know him by the title Commissioner Spencer. Mark...meet Cleo Davis. Her great-aunt was the late Patricia Davenport. You remember her, right? She owned the Brantley house, faces Forsyth Park? Now our little Cleo owns it." Ellie wrinkled her nose, smiling in a cutesy, pouting sort of way.

I clenched my teeth tighter and smiled. I hoped it didn't look as sickly as it felt. I reached out to grasp the hand Mark held out, wishing I had some hand sanitizer with me.

"Glad to meet you," he boomed, ever the politician, giving my hand a brisk shake. "Knew your aunt well. Quite a lady. Pillar of Savannah society."

It took some effort, but I kept from rolling my eyes. He knew Aunt Patricia "well," according to him. Why didn't that surprise me? I forced my mouth to say the expected words. "Nice to meet you, Commissioner Spencer."

Saying it, almost made me gag.

"Oh, please, call me Mark," he replied a little too jovial for my taste. "Any friend of Elle's is a friend of mine."

Not in this lifetime, buster, I thought to myself, while forcing my lips to stay curved upward.

Ellie glanced at the table where I'd been sitting, and her eyes narrowed when she saw the extra glass of tea. "Where's your date? Did we interrupt something? Maybe someone you weren't supposed to be with?" she asked suggestively, and actually gave me a wink.

I sent her my "death stare." I wanted to grab a fork from the neighboring table and stab her in that winking eye. Probably not a good idea, right in front of the Police Commissioner. "No," I answered as calmly as I could. "Just a good friend. She had another appointment and had to run."

Ellie pursed her lips, clearly disappointed that I hadn't given her some juicy bit of gossip to gnaw on. "Oh...well, it was good to see you again. We've got to run. Things to do, people to see, you know. Take care, now." She tilted her face up to Mark and dimpled. "Ready, babe?"

He squeezed her waist, then nodded my direction. "Cleo."

My return nod was a little stiff. "Mark."

They turned right, hurrying toward the DeSoto Hilton. Not much of a surprise, there.

I waited...I knew it was coming, and she didn't disappoint. Ellie half-turned and called back airily, "Next time you see Jonas...*if* you see him again...tell him to call me. He has my number. TTFN!"

I was breathing heavily, gripping the back of my chair so hard, that the edge of it dug into my palm, nearly cutting me. I ignored the pain, almost welcoming it, so angry my blood was boiling. *TTFN? As in ta-ta for now? Really? Did people still even use that acronym? Well, obviously one person did.*

A familiar, gravelly voice spoke behind me, "Holding on to anger is like grasping a hot coal with the intent of throwing it at someone else. You are the only

229

one who gets burned."

"Thanks," I growled through clenched teeth before turning. "Nice vanishing act."

Lily lifted her chin toward Ellie and Mark who were just entering the hotel's doors. "Didn't want him to see me with you. Guess I was afraid he'd somehow know I saw him shoot that man in the alley...that he'd be able to read it on my face. If he knew...if he had any idea, it wouldn't be safe for you to associate with me."

I waved my hand impatiently, like I was shooing a fly, exclaiming without thinking, "He doesn't know you saw him. If he did, you'd probably already be in the river." As soon as the words were out of my mouth, I regretted them. "Sorry, Lily," I winced. "I need to work on my tact."

She shrugged. "Here's a quote your floozy friend should remember."

"She's *not* my friend!" I snapped.

"Even so..." Lily patted me on the arm in a soothing manner. "It's something I remember my mother telling me: "your dresses should be tight enough to show you're a woman and loose enough to show you're a lady."" She pointed toward the Hilton. "*She's* no lady!"

"Agreed." I drew a deep breath, my blood pressure working its way back to the normal range. "Let's go home."

****

Everyone, but me, was tucked into bed, probably taking a long winter's nap, but I couldn't sleep.

I couldn't stop thinking about something Lily had shared with me after we left Mellow Mushroom. She'd been engaged once! Back when she was about my age.

His name was Michael, and he'd broken her heart with another woman, at least that's what she'd thought at the time. Apparently, her ghost sister, Rose, was a real piece of work. She'd told Lily back then, about Michael having an affair—that she'd actually *seen* him with the other woman—and poor Lily had believed her. She'd broken things off with Michael, never giving him a chance to tell his side, and had transformed herself into a homeless woman, effectively shutting herself off from another chance at love. The real heartbreak, though, was that Rose had lied about the whole thing. Lily had just found out about it, almost fifty years too late.

I wasn't sure why she'd shared this tragic tale with me. Maybe she just needed to get it off her chest, but I couldn't shake the sad image of a much younger Lily giving up on true love all because of a lie. It was such a waste. If Rose hadn't already been dead, I'd scratch her eyes out.

And if all that drama wasn't enough, I couldn't seem to shake a strange sense of foreboding, some sort of ominous undercurrent lurking just beneath the surface. It was how wild animals must feel right before a bad storm or an earthquake...like nature was holding its breath, a waiting period right before everything hit the fan.

Whatever it was, it had me wired and I couldn't relax. I sketched some more, read for a while, soaked in a warm bath, tried some deep breathing...nothing worked. As a very *last* resort, I headed downstairs to the exercise room. To my knowledge, I was the only one who ever used it. Which begs the question...*why?* Why did we have it? Why did Aunt Patricia go to the considerable expense of having a room full of state-of-the-art equipment put in? Had there been a man in her past? Someone who'd been really into exercise?

Ha! Yeah, right!

Re-sale value?

Hardly! I could never sell this place. Who could afford to buy it? And if I ever tried to sell, she'd probably come back and haunt me.

From any angle, it made no sense to me. It certainly wasn't for *my* benefit. I generally tried to avoid exercise, the same way I would the Bubonic plague, and of course, Minnie and Tobias never darkened its doors. That left...*nobody.*

I gazed around pensively while I jogged on the treadmill. Well, maybe calling it a jog was a stretch, but I was doing my best. There was a lot of interesting stuff in here...if someone happened to like working out. It was sort of a shame that it never got used.

Slowing to a stop, I grabbed my towel and wiped my face. Enough! That was all the exercise my poor, non-athletic body could stand.

After a quick shower to get rid of the sweat, I was back at square one: lying in the bed, staring at the ceiling and worrying. I flung an arm across my eyes, trying to squelch the feeling of doom that swirled around all the people in my life. Jonas, Lily, Raymond, and...Ellie. Ellie? Why was she included? The thought was appalling. After all the things she'd said and done to me over the years...? Why was I worrying about *her?*

The truth was, as much as I disliked her, the fact that she was keeping company with a sleaze-ball like Mark Spencer scared me. I realized that she was probably just adding another notch on her bedpost with him—maybe his position of power gave her a rush or something—but she couldn't possibly *care* for the guy. No way! That was too low, even for *her*. Maybe, I should try to warn her, hint at what kind of a person he was without giving too much away. Would she believe me? Maybe not, but I had to try. Even Ellie didn't deserve someone evil.

****

The decision to warn my nemesis must've been the sleeping potion I needed, because when I opened my eyes again, the morning sun was shooting pale, yellow stripes through the slats of the window shutters. I reached for Tut, but ended up patting a cool pillow. Hmmm. No Tut. He was probably with Raymond. For whatever reason, my cat had taken a liking to sleeping upstairs at the foot of Raymond's bed. Who knew why?

Some slight movement caught my eye and I jerked my head to see what it was. Tut was sitting at attention, right by the door, staring at me.

That was weird.

I sat up and studied him, holding out my hand and calling, "C'mere, Tut. Come see me, boy."

He was as still as a sphinx, eyes unblinking. I frowned. Something was wrong. "What is it, boy?"

He just stared, his eyes fixed on mine, like he was trying to drill something into my head.

I scrambled from bed and took a step toward him. He turned quickly and squeezed himself through the door.

Was I supposed to follow him?

I yanked the door open and looked both directions. He'd stopped at the foot of the stairs to the third floor, glancing back over his shoulder at me. As soon as we made eye contact, he zipped up the stairs. My stomach dropped.

Raymond. Something was wrong with Raymond!

****

I was out of breath when I burst into his room, crashing into Lily who stood just inside the door.

"Ooof...sorry. I just wanted to check on Ray—" I broke off when I saw that Tut was the only one on the bed. He sat by the empty pillow, and turned wild eyes toward me. "Lily, where is he? In the bathroom? Does he need some help? Is he hurt? Tut—"

I broke off when she wordlessly handed me a piece of paper, and I knew he was gone without looking at it.

I sank to the floor, clutching the note. "Why? Doesn't he know he's not safe out there? If Spencer or his men see him, he's toast. If they catch him again, he won't be so lucky. We won't be able to help him! What is he thinking?"

Lily's voice was filled with ultimate sadness. "Read his note, Cleo, just read the note. You'll understand."

I unclenched my fist, smoothing the wrinkles out of the paper as best I could, and slowly unfolded it. Tears filled my eyes. "No!" I threw my head back and cried, "No, no, no!"

The page was completely filled with curlicues.

Chapter Nineteen

Cleo

"I don't know what kind of mess you've gone and stepped in, child, but I'm afraid it's a lot deeper and a lot more foul-smellin' than you ever let on to me," Minnie fumed.

I winced when I saw the ferocious way she was scrubbing the clean pot. How did the thing still have a bottom?

I needed Minnie's help. I wanted to fill her in on everything in hopes that we'd be able to put our three heads together and come up with a plan, since so far, two heads weren't working so well. My gaze strayed to Lily and silently asked the question, *Can we tell her?*

When she nodded, I took a deep breath. This wasn't going to be pretty.

"You're right, Minnie. I've kind of left some stuff out."

Her wide shoulders stilled and then tensed up like she was waiting for a blow.

"Maybe you should sit down," I suggested.

"I'll stand," she snapped.

"O-kay…" I mouthed silently. The best way was probably just to jump in and get it over with. Taking a deep breath, I blurted, "We-rescued-Raymond-from-the-trunk-of-some-bad-men-who-were-going-to-shoot-him-and-then-dump-him-in-the-river." The whole sentence ran together like it was one long word, then I tagged on, "He was supposed to be the fourth one."

Minnie turned to face me. Her normally caramel colored skin had turned a sickly shade of washed-out khaki. "Uh, maybe I *will* sit, after all."

I moved over to make room. "Good idea." Once she got settled, I continued, "The way these guys work, is they offer a job to desperate homeless men, with nothing to lose—men like Raymond. This job is too good to be true, one they couldn't possibly refuse, but there's a catch. If they say a single word about the job—to anyone—even a hint, they're killed and thrown in the river."

Minnie's eyes were wide; her mouth formed a perfect circle. "What's the job?"

"Printing hundred dollar bills."

"Counterfeiting," she breathed. After a long moment, she closed her mouth and pressed her lips together until they made a thin straight line.

Wow! She was handling this better than I thought she would.

"And Raymond was offered this job?" she asked, quietly.

"Yes."

"And he talked about it to someone?"

I glanced at Lily before repeating my answer. "Yes."

"But you all rescued him...from a trunk of a car, you said."

I started feeling a little uneasy. She was acting too calm. "Y-yes."

She stared at me another second or two, then

narrowed her eyes. "How, exactly?"

Uh-oh. Looking at Lily was no help. She was rubbing her temples like she had a headache. "Well, it started out with us hiding in the alley behind the building where the counterfeiting is done."

Minnie opened her mouth, then closed it and shook her head. "I suppose you'll be telling me just how you knew it was *that* building, later?"

Oh, jeez, now Lily was holding her head like she was afraid it was going to fall off. "Um, sure…later. Anyway, we overheard enough to figure out what the plan was, and followed them in Jonas' car." I didn't like the way Minnie's nostrils sort of flared when I said that part, so I hurried on. "We followed them until they stopped at a truck stop and they went inside to get something to eat. I kept a lookout and Jonas jimmied the trunk lock with a screwdriver so he could get Raymond out. Then we stuffed him in the back seat of Jonas' car, and tore out of there."

"And came here."

"Yeah, we came straight here." Guessing where she was going with that, I rushed to explain. "Don't worry! They couldn't follow us. Jonas used the screwdriver to puncture two of their tires before we left. No one has two spares in their car, you know. They were stuck. It was brilliant, actually."

Too late. I should've kept my editorial comment to myself.

"Brilliant!" she almost snarled the word. "You say it's brilliant? Chasin' after men who are *murderers*, who were on the way to *kill* another person, and who are also involved in a *counterfeiting* ring? You call that *brilliant?* Your boyfriend vandalizes their car, and he's *brilliant*? Are you out of your cotton-pickin' mind?"

Call me crazy, but I sort of zoned out after she referred to Jonas as my boyfriend.

But Minnie wasn't done. "When did you turn vigilante on me? We *do* have a police force, and they're paid to handle situations like this. It's their job. Why didn't you pull out your phone and dial 9-1-1?"

"Because Mark Spencer...you know, *Police Commissioner* Mark Spencer? He's the head of the whole thing."

"What? He can't be!"

"Well, he is," I retorted. "And that's *why* we couldn't contact the police. The good guys are the *bad* guys in this situation!" I was losing my patience, tired of her interrogation. I needed help, not a pointing finger. "Look...you can rest assured we went through all this before going after Raymond. We're trying to nail Spencer, which is why Jonas is out there somewhere, right now, disguised as a homeless man. He's trying to be the next guy Spencer picks, and I'm scared to death. He has no idea Raymond's back out there and I don't know how to let him know."

"Doesn't he have a phone?" she asked in a more subdued tone.

Well, duh! I exchanged a look with Lily, thankful to see that apparently, she hadn't thought of that either. "Um...yeah."

Minnie rolled her eyes. "What's the problem, then?" Her question followed me up the stairs. I was already halfway to my room to look for the business card he'd given me the day we met.

It only took a second to find it in my backpack, then my trembling finger was punching numbers on my phone as fast as I could go. After two interminably long rings, he answered.

"Holmes."

"Jonas?"

"Cleo? What's wrong? Are you all right?"

"Yeah, listen…I don't want to blow your cover or anything, but Raymond is gone."

"What do you mean, gone?"

"I mean, this morning, when I went upstairs to check on him, his bed was empty." I didn't think it was important to tell him about the note full of scribbles.

There was an exasperated sounding groan from the other end, and then, "We can't save him this time. If they find him, they'll kill him quickly, then dump him; they won't make the same mistake twice." He sighed. "How's Lily?"

"Worried."

"How are *you?*" His voice went soft, smooth like velvet, and I sort of melted.

"I'm worried too, but mostly about you."

"I'm fine, babe."

Babe? Did he just call me, babe? My heart stuttered a couple of times. My throat went dry. I knew better than to try to speak.

He cleared his throat, then continued as if the world hadn't just stopped spinning. "Listen, I'm going to poke around some, keep my ears open, see if anything comes up. Then I'm going to break cover and run home to get my car about dusk. I'll come by and pick you up, and we can go sit at the truck stop and see if we spot their car. They may not retrace their steps, but then again, they might. They don't strike me as being highly intelligent, more like trained monkeys on steroids."

"I don't even remember what their car looks like!"

"I do. Got the tag number too, so we're set."

"Right. Okay." I took a deep breath, trying to calm my inner trembling. "I'll see you this evening, then."

"Bye, b—...Cleo."

Had he started to say "babe," again? Why'd he stop? How could I know for sure? Ugh! How...*infuriating!*

"Bye," I whispered.

****

I went downstairs to tell Minnie and Lily the plan for this evening, then turned around and left. Unbelievably, Minnie spared me the third degree. Maybe she realized I was nearly at my breaking point and she didn't want to be the "last straw." Never stopped her before, but that's the only explanation I could come up with, unless Lily had been bearing the brunt of a Minnie-style inquisition, and had managed to fill in enough blanks to satisfy her for the time being. Just to be on the safe side, though, I took the stairs two at a time and locked the door to my room. No sense in taking any chances, right?

I thought briefly about the expression Lily wore just seconds before. She seemed very deep in thought, her face sort of closed down, unreadable. Minnie was back at the sink, scrubbing the heck out of clean pots.

Seems we all had plenty to think about.

One thing for sure, if I wanted to keep from going crazy, I needed to get busy, and *stay* busy. If I just sat around and waited until Jonas finally got here, every single minute, between now then, would seem at least a month long, maybe a year.

The best way for me to lose track of time was to paint, so it was the perfect time to get started on that part of my illustration project. Setting up my easel and equipment, I donned my painting smock—which was really a man's denim shirt I'd gotten from the Goodwill store years ago. I'd tried to girl-y it up a little by embroidering my initials and a few flowers here and there, added some lace to the cuffs. It helped some, but you didn't really notice my decorations much anymore amid all the splotches and streaks of paint.

Grabbing a large canvas from my supply in the closet, I secured it to the easel, quickly prepared my palette, and immediately started blocking in color. I'd decided this first painting would be composed of Lily sprinkling glitter around a parking meter. Its purpose? Well, basically, I wanted to capture her essence two-dimensionally and introduce the viewer to her colorful personality. I wanted to make her real enough, so that everyone could experience the same magical pull I'd felt the minute I saw her. It was a tall order, but I was anxious to try.

It didn't take me long to get lost in my work.

****

When I stepped back and glanced at my watch, I did a double-take. Wow! After five, already. I glanced at the window, noting the fading light with a mixture of emotions. I didn't know how I was supposed to feel. Excitement and anticipation were walking hand in hand with fear and worry…a veritable smorgasbord of emotional contradictions.

Tut opened one eye at me from his usual place on his pillow and yawned big enough I think I might've seen his small intestine. "Ugh! Thanks for sharing, Tut.

Just what I wanted…a personal tour of a feline gastrological system."

He ignored me and settled back down, pulling one of his front legs up over his face, like the big, bad light was hurting his poor, wittle eyes. Oh, brother!

Turning my attention back to the painting, I tried to study it "clinically," in other words, to separate myself from my emotions—an admonition repeated by every SCAD professor when they critiqued our work. That was actually harder than it sounded. It's the nature of the beast, really. We, artists get emotionally attached to our work, because we put a little piece of ourselves in everything we do. After a few minutes I nodded, and finally smiled. Not bad. Once it dried some, I'd add a few details here and there, and it could work. It could definitely work.

Hanging up my smock, I caught my reflection in the closet's full-length mirror, and gave my appearance a critique, too. No stray paint splotches on my face…that was good, but was my outfit right for a stake-out? What did one wear to something like that? Was there some sort of protocol? Probably something dark, preferably black. I grimaced. Not really my color, so I don't have too much to choose from. Decisions, decisions…Of course, the romantic side of me wanted to wear something pretty and feminine, something that'd knock Jonas' socks off, but the practical side had a big mouth, and more volume.

Practicality won.

Heaving a sigh, I snagged a pair of black jeans from a hanger, before turning to the chest of drawers. The deep bottom one was full of sweaters that I rarely used since Savannah had such mild winters. The one I was looking for was underneath all the others; a black turtleneck that'd never been worn. Aunt Patricia had given it to me two Christmases ago and it still had the tags on it. I'd planned on exchanging it for something I'd be more likely to use, but had never gotten around to it. Staring at it, I wrinkled my nose.

Minutes later, I stared at the slim, boyish figure who gazed back at me from the mirror. The form-fitting black did nothing but emphasize my lack of "form." I turned in order to get a side view and groaned. That was even worse! And I looked like a cat-burglar. All I needed was black knit cap and a mask. Maybe this wearing solid-black idea was overkill. Surely I had something both dark colored and frilly somewhere.

All of my clothes-changing activity had finally roused Tut, and he now sat at the end of my bed, staring at me.

"So…what do you think, boy? Do I look too much like Cat Woman?"

The expression he gave me was the feline equivalent of an eye roll.

I snorted. "Yeah, I know, I know…you're saying, "You *wish!* Anne Hathaway, you're *not*." She might be able to make that look work, but…" I chewed my bottom lip, undecided. This was harder than it ought to be.

Minnie made the decision for me when she hollered upstairs. "Cleo, your date's here!"

Date? Oh, no! I leaned my back against the door, head in my hands, embarrassed beyond belief. I felt like strangling her. This *wasn't* a date, and Minnie knew it. I could almost picture the sly look she was more than likely wearing. What must Jonas be thinking? Probably wondering what I'd been telling her. My groan was filled with despair. If only the floor would supply a hole that would swallow me.

Okay, stop! Get a grip! You are *not* going to cringe back into the old Cleo...the pre-Lily Cleo. Jonas is downstairs, you idiot! What are you waiting for? Plus, you have no way of knowing what else Minnie might be saying to him at this very moment. She might refer to him as your boyfriend again...or worse. Get a move on!

Chapter Twenty

Jonas

I knew I was taking a big chance by breaking my "cover," but if there was the slightest possibility that we could save Raymond again, it was a chance I was willing to take. Maybe it was the fact that I'd risked my life for him once already, but I felt like I had a lot invested in the guy.

I had to be careful, though. Spencer had connections. I didn't know how many people were actually on his payroll, how many "eyes" might be watching me and would report back to him.

I hadn't told Cleo yet, but my disguise had worked better than I'd expected. One of Spencer's muscle-bound gorillas had approached me just after Cleo's panicked call about Raymond.

"Haven't seen you around here before."

I glanced over at the man in a black leather jacket who was seated at the other end of the bench. The pea-sized diamond stud in his right ear caught the sun and sprayed a shimmering rainbow across his thick shoulder. The spectrum struck me as odd, out of place, the right prop on the wrong stage. He also had a tattoo on his neck. Some kind of a Chinese symbol. One that was supposed to mean "eat hot death" or "kitten torturer," or some other sadistic line, but probably meant "I love butterflies." I mean, besides the tattoo artist, who'd know? Someone fluent in Chinese, yeah, but there weren't a lot of them around. It was the perfect joke to play on someone.

"Just got here this morning," I drawled. That was one thing I hadn't asked Lily...how I should speak while in this disguise.

"Where from?" He turned his head toward me for the briefest of seconds, and I caught a glimpse of his eyes, so pale blue, they were almost devoid of color. Their coldness was like an icy finger running up my spine, and it was all I could do to keep from shuddering.

"Charleston. Thumbed my way down."

His only answer was a sort of low hum, then he was quiet. I listened to the everyday sounds of the city while I waited for him to speak, trying to pretend I didn't care whether he had anything more to say to me or not. The *beep-beep-beep* of a UPS truck backing up; the high-pitched whine of a mo-ped; the unmistakable sound of Beach Boys music wafting from someone's car window; a jogger panting past us, dragging an overweight Pomeranian on a leash behind him. The poor dog looked like a furry balloon on a string.

"You looking for work?" he finally asked.

This is it! "Uh...yeah, guess I could use the money. What kind of job we talking about? I don't have a lot of experience."

"Oh, we train you. That ain't a problem, but it's a real special kind of job...delicate, if you know what I mean...the main requirement is having the ability to keep your mouth shut. You got that kind of skill-set?"

"You mean can I keep my eyes and ears open and

my mouth closed? Yeah, I got plenty of practice at that kind of job. I'm your man."

Gorilla-neck nodded. "Glad to hear it. We work nights. I'll meet you here at midnight."

I nodded. "I'll be here."

****

He'd no sooner lumbered off, when my phone buzzed. I answered without checking the screen, thinking it was Cleo again.

"What's up?"

"Jonas?"

My stomach flopped. It wasn't the voice I was expecting.

"Oh, God! Jonas! I've been calling and calling. Didn't you get my voice mails? Why haven't you called me back?" She sounded breathless, excited.

"Hello, Jill."

"Well?"

"Well, what?"

"Why haven't you called me back?" Had she always sounded this whiney?

"I'd have thought that was pretty obvious, wouldn't you? You're pretty dense for a smart girl."

"Don't be mean, Jonas."

What? "Please tell me you didn't just say that. You *can't* be serious. You dump me the night before our wedding; I don't hear a word from you for *three years*, and now you're telling me not to be "mean"? Give me a break!"

"I just needed to talk to you," she whined again. I could almost see her famous pout. She wielded that tool like a pro, always managing to get what she wanted, but doing it in such a cute way that I'd never minded being maneuvered before. That is, until now.

"Everything was said three years ago."

"No, Jonas. It wasn't. I was wrong. I know that now. I—can we meet somewhere? To talk? I'm here…in Savannah. Didn't your mom tell you?"

Jill was here? "No, I haven't talked to her lately."

"Yeah, well…I'm looking for an apartment now. I thought we might—"

"Might what? No, don't tell me. I don't want to know." I yanked off my cap and raked an angry hand through my hair. "You can't possibly think that you can waltz back into my life after all this time, that we'll just pick up where we left off. It doesn't work that way, Jill."

"But—"

"No! If that's what you came down here thinking, then you've wasted your time, and you might as well turn around and go right back the way you came. It's over. It's *been* over. There's someone else in my life, now…someone very important to me." Though I was surprised to hear myself saying those words aloud, I realized they were true. "And besides that, I'm in the middle of a big story. There's no time to see you even if I *wanted* to—which I *don't*—by the way. I've just got too much going on right now."

After a long silence, she asked, "What's her name? She must be pretty special if she's captured your heart."

"Her name's Cleo…Cleo Davis…and yes, she is special."

I heard her sigh. "Well…okay then. I'll let you go. I know you're busy. Maybe I'll see you around."

"Goodbye, Jill."

****

I pulled my cap back on, yanking it low, staring at nothing through narrowed eyes. That was weird...very un-Jill-like. She'd acquiesced too easily. Made me suspicious. What was she up to? And what had caused her decision to move to Savannah? There had to be more to it. She wouldn't have up and moved like this just to be closer to me. Last I'd heard, she'd married some rich old guy, about three times her age. Had he kicked the bucket or kicked her out? Maybe it was time to call Mom. I was sure she could shed some light on the subject. But not now. It wasn't a good idea to stay on the phone for too long. I didn't know who might be watching me. It was time to head to my apartment, anyway. Time to take a shower and change so I could meet Cleo.

Cleo...

Thinking about her made me smile. No teeth showing, though; I remembered her warning. The circumstances were far from ideal, we were mired up in some pretty serious stuff, and Raymond could be in grave danger again—maybe even dead this time. In spite of it all, I couldn't wait to see her.

****

My apartment phone rang as I was heading out my front door, but I ignored it. I'd taken enough time to shower and change out of my hobo clothes into something more conducive to nighttime surveillance, but there was no time for chit-chat. If it was important, they'd leave a message or call back.

Before the fourth ring had even finished, my cell phone started vibrating. Wow! Someone was sure being persistent. I glanced at the screen. Mom. *Better late than never, I guess.* I unlocked my car door and slid inside before answering. "You're late." I scolded as I wheeled out of my parking space.

"You already know." She sounded deflated.

"Mm-hmm. What took you so long?"

Silence crackled on the other end of the line before she finally asked, "Are you okay?"

"Yup."

"You *sound* okay."

"That's because I am, Mom." I laughed.

Another silence crackled. "You've met someone."

How did she *do* that? Were all mothers equipped with special radar when it came to their kids? Some sort of device that was able to read mood variations via voice over the telephone? Or maybe it was just *my* mother. "I guess there's no sense in my denying it. You'd see right through me. Yes, I've met someone, but it's complicated."

"Complicated? How?"

"I met her as a result of the story I'm working on for the paper, and it's just taken an unexpected turn."

"The story or the relationship?" She laughed.

"The story. She doesn't know about the relationship, yet."

"But you're going to tell her, right?"

"Yes, Mom, but not yet. Like I said…it's complicated."

"Can I give you a piece of advice, Jonas?"

"If I said no, would it stop you?"

"Has it ever stopped me before?" she laughed.

"Exactly. Go ahead, before you burst."

"It's just this…tell her soon, son."

"Right."

"And Jonas…?"

"Yeah?"

"This story you're working on? The one for the paper? I don't know, but I've got a feeling that there's danger involved?"

"No fishing, Mom."

"You just answered my question. I don't want to know any details. It's easier for me *not* to know. Just please…do me a favor and be careful. I told you, I need more grandbabies, and you can't give them to me if you're not around."

"Right. I got it. Gotta go."

Chapter Twenty-One

Cleo

When I saw what he was wearing I couldn't help grinning. We were identical! Well...what we *wore* was identical. He looked *so* much better than I could ever hope to, but it was nice to know I'd chosen the right outfit.

I managed the stairs without stumbling over my feet, but when I reached the bottom and looked up into his eyes, my bones sort of jellied. He seemed even better looking than the last time I'd seen him, even with the two-day growth of beard darkening his face. He'd be returning undercover later tonight, and that'd kept him from shaving. My fingertips were tingling with the desire to stroke along his jaw, across his chin, over his lips...

I fisted my hands. Whoa... I needed to keep those kinds of thoughts under a tighter rein. My eyes went back to his and locked in place. His gaze was warm...like melted chocolate. Too warm! I fought off the sudden desire to fling myself at him. What was happening to me? I'd never felt like this before. I pulled at the neck of my sweater, feeling a trickle of sweat slide down my back, between my shoulder blades. Had Minnie been messing with the thermostat again?

Minnie!

I whipped around and there she stood in the kitchen doorway, arms crossed under her quadruple-D chest, brows raised over eyes that missed nothing, wearing an "it's about time you got yourself a man" smirk. I felt my cheeks grow hot under her scrutiny. "Where's Lily," I asked in a panic, afraid she'd say something else mortifying, and hoping my question would throw her off-track.

"Upstairs. Said she was tired...something about walking around too much today."

My diversion tactic seemed to have worked, and I breathed a little easier. "Oh, yeah, she did...all the way to the river and back. Ended up with a blister. I hope she didn't over-do it."

"She'll be fine. Just needs a little rest before dinner. She's one tough lady." Minnie's gesture included Jonas. "When you two gonna be back?"

I shrugged, but he answered before I could open my mouth. "We shouldn't be too late. This is probably pointless anyway, but I can't think of a better idea, so we'll try it and see what happens."

She beetled her brow at him. "I 'spect you to make sure nothing happens to Miz Cleo. You understand what I'm saying to you, son?"

He grinned. "Yes, ma'am, I do."

"Well, all right then. C'mere, youngun." She motioned me over.

Wrapping me in a bone-crushing hug, she whispered in my ear, "Please be careful, child. I got a bad feeling 'bout this."

Her lapse into her old way of speaking showed me how distressed she really was. Though both of my arms were mostly pinned, I managed to pat her clumsily on the back. "It'll be okay, Minnie. Don't worry."

****

"I've been thinking…" Jonas began, as soon as we were in his car. "…what do you say to us checking out the alley again before heading out to the truck stop? I know we probably have a better chance of winning the lottery…twice…than we do of something actually happening there again, but my gut is telling me to go there first. What do you think?"

What did he expect me to say? His idea would provide me with the perfect excuse to sit all squashed up next to him for as long as we were there. It was a no-brainer. "Sounds like a plan!" I agreed, feeling very much like a half-grown puppy, eagerly prancing back and forth; waiting for the ball or Frisbee to be thrown. It's how I *felt*. I hoped I didn't *look* like that.

"Okay, then…let's roll."

****

Just minutes later, we were pulling into the same spot behind the real estate office we'd parked the night of Raymond's rescue. Had it really been two nights ago? In one way, it seemed like last night, but then again, so much had happened in the past couple of days, it seemed much longer. The engine went silent.

"Sit still," he ordered and then got out of the car.

I was confused, but I did as I was told. As soon as his door shut, his dark clothes camouflaged him completely, blending him so perfectly into the pitch blackness of the alley that he seemed to disappear, making me jump when he tapped on my window. I scrambled for the unlock button, and he swung my door open, reaching for my hand and pulling me out. He didn't let go.

"I can't see you." His low voice rumbled near my ear once the door closed and we were enveloped in darkness thick enough to be felt. He squeezed my fingers. "I don't want to take a chance that we'll get separated, so I'll just hold onto you, if you don't mind."

"Okay." I was glad I had an excuse for whispering. My voice would probably have cracked like an adolescent boy's. My fingers slid between his. Perfect fit.

"Instead of behind the trashcans, let's try hiding between the buildings this time…you know, beside the window? I think we'll be able to see and hear better from there, and we can avoid the smell of the garbage. C'mon."

I stumbled along beside him, trusting that he knew how to get to that walkway, because I sure didn't. How in the world could he see anything? Did he have a pair of night-vision goggles I didn't know about? Or was he part cat? Whatever the case, we were soon settled in the narrow strip of space between Lily's building and the next. It felt safe here, in spite of what had occurred during our previous visits. I was sure that part of it was just because I was with Jonas, but another part was because I didn't think Spencer or his goons could even fit between these buildings.

I shivered. It was chillier tonight, and I sidled up to him as closely as I dared, soaking up his radiant heat.

"Are you cold?" he whispered. "Here, scoot this way." He pulled me in front of him, between his knees, his chest pressed against my back, then wrapped his arms around me.

Instant warmth. Mmm…this was nice. I leaned the side of my head against his neck, and breathed in his delectable smell. The desire to press my lips to his skin was nearly overwhelming, but I somehow managed to squelch it. Sparks skipped along all my nerve endings.

He dipped his head, his mouth brushing against my ear, and I gasped. "Better?" he murmured. His deep voice sent shivers that had nothing to do with the cold, up and down my spine.

I couldn't speak, but nodded, trusting that he'd feel the movement.

I was still trying to get my breathing into a somewhat normal rhythm when I felt his chin start rubbing back and forth against my hair. So much for a normal breathing pattern. When he leaned down and pressed his face against the top of my head, I stopped breathing altogether.

"Mmm, you smell so good," he groaned.

My heart was going to explode! It hammered against my throat, like a wild animal trying to escape.

Whether it was his words or his groan, or maybe both together—I didn't know—but somewhere, deep in my belly, it was if a switch got flipped to the "on" position, and my bones started melting. My head turned toward him—I couldn't help it, I swear—and I finally got to do what I'd wanted to do since that first night in the alley. My lips touched his skin, scorching just above his turtleneck, and I breathed in his scent...wild, raw...masculine.

He groaned again.

My heart was suddenly thundering in my chest like a thousand wild horses. His hand tilted my face up, softly stroking my cheek.

"Cleo." His breath was warm and delicious against my lips, thrilling me with anticipation.

I closed my eyes...*oh, sweet agony*...

Then Jonas froze and lifted his head.

No! "What—?"

He pressed a finger to my lips. "Shhhh," he warned.

It was all I could do not to touch my tongue to that finger. At that particular moment, I didn't even care that we might be in danger. Then I heard it too, though how I could hear *anything* over the booming of my heart was beyond me, but that sound was the equivalent of a bucket of ice water being dumped over my head.

I listened so hard, I thought my eardrums might burst; sifting through the other nighttime sounds to pinpoint something that didn't belong.

There it was again—a faint *pop*—the sound of tiny piece of glass being crushed between the heel of a shoe and the sidewalk. There was someone there! Whoever it was, was trying to step quietly, but that almost imperceptible noise had given them away.

Fear congealed around my heart. My breaths were coming in short, frantic gasps, making me a little lightheaded. Not enough oxygen was getting to my brain.

The measured footsteps came nearer, moving slowly, pausing often, as if they were listening too. Did the person know we were there? Had he heard us? We were sitting ducks, unable to move without giving ourselves away.

Now, I couldn't breathe at all.

Then suddenly, a voice spoke out of the darkness. "Who's there?"

A woman's voice? That surprised me. And it sounded familiar.

"I know you're there…I *heard* you."

My mouth dropped open. I recognized that voice! But what was *she* doing *here?*

I reached a hand up behind Jonas' neck, pulling his head down, and putting my mouth against his ear. "It's Ellie," I whispered.

"Who?" he whispered back.

"Ellie…you met her at Moon River."

"Ohhh…" I could feel him smile, and I narrowed my eyes. I wanted to slap him.

"I can hear you whispering," Ellie snapped, her voice sort of echoing between the buildings. She sounded as irritated as I felt. Almost. "Just so you know…I have a can of pepper spray and I'm not afraid to use it."

I rolled my eyes, even though no one could see it. Good grief! If Mark Spencer and his men came back now, she'd get us all killed. "Oh, just chillax, Ellie. It's me."

"Cleo?"

Ugh! How had everything gone so wrong so fast when it'd started out so nicely? Things had just taken a sharp turn south. I sighed, "Yeah, it's me."

"What are *you* doing here?"

"I could ask you the same thing."

"Long story."

"I'm all ears."

There was suddenly a solid *thunk*; followed by enough R-rated words, I'm sure sailors all the way to Charleston were blushing to the roots of their buzz-cut hair. I know *I* sure was. "Arrg! Who *lives* in these houses, anyway?" Ellie nearly shrieked. "Don't they believe in any lights?"

I had to bite my lip to keep from giggling. She must've run into those electric meters I'd nearly hit when we'd escaped through here the other night. I could feel Jonas shaking. Was he *laughing*? I elbowed him, eliciting an *ooof*, which made me grin.

"What was that noise?" Ellie asked, her voice nearer, now.

Might as well 'fess up.' "Um…I'm not here by myself." I gasped when I felt his finger run along my jaw line and then trace gently around my ear. The sensation had me fighting the urge to lean into his touch. He definitely wasn't playing fair. "Jonas is with me," I choked out, my pulse racing as his nose stroked against my neck.

"Hi, Ellie," Jonas called.

Any sound of movement abruptly ceased. She was surprised, which was something that rarely happened, I'm sure. "Are you all right," I called out, not really caring, when she didn't answer. How could I be concerned about something like that, with Jonas nuzzling just below my ear? "Be nice," I whispered to him.

"I'm trying to be," he growled. "But I could be a lot nicer."

Holy smokes!

Ellie would be there any second, now. I grabbed both of his hands and held them tightly in front of me, stifling another giggle when he whispered, "Party-pooper" in my ear.

Oh, no, I thought. *The party-pooper is definitely our uninvited guest.*

Then Ellie's shoe hit my leg, and one of her flailing hands caught me in the side of the head. "Oh, sorry!"

I'll bet! "You're here," I informed her, dryly. "Have a seat."

"Well, well, well, Cleo...I'll have to say this is a surprise." Her voice held a smirk as she settled herself beside us. "Who'd have ever thunk it? Guess you were just waiting for the right guy, huh?"

I squeezed Jonas' hands in a death grip, praying for that hole in the ground again and parlayed her question with one of my own. "What are you *doing* here, Ellie?" I snapped.

The fact that she didn't correct my pronunciation of her name should've told me that something was wrong. She didn't answer for a long time, and when she finally spoke, her voice was a bit shaky. "I didn't know where else to go."

She sounded almost...scared. That couldn't be right. As far as I knew, *nothing* scared Ellie. It struck me as "off," and I couldn't help being a little suspicious. "What's wrong?"

"I don't know if I should tell you, but I need some advice. I don't think I can take it if anyone else gets hurt."

Was she faking it? Was this all an elaborate act? Probably. She was a very good actress. I'd had a lot of practice watching her act through the years, and could spot any fakery in an instant, but it was hard to do that in the dark. I wished I could see her face. She *sounded* genuine...totally out of character, of course, but genuine, nonetheless. I could almost hear tears in her voice. Then again...good actresses knew how to turn on the waterworks. If the script said "cry," they'd flip that internal switch and the tears would flow. But what if it was real this time? Without thinking, I blurted, "If it's about Mark, I already know more than you think."

She gasped, "What? How could you—? What do you think you know?"

The last question sounded suspicious.

"Tell us what happened, first," Jonas finally spoke up, his voice demanding obedience.

Ellie drew a ragged breath. "I came by here earlier to see Mark."

I bit my lip to keep from speaking. If she knew about this place, then she must know about the counterfeiting. *That* sounded typical, more like the Ellie I knew.

"I was about to open the door when I heard someone groan. It scared me to death."

My heart sank. *Raymond!*

"I was afraid to just walk in, and I thought about calling the police, but…well…Mark *is* the police, so I just stood outside the door and listened."

Even though Jonas' arms were still around me, I suddenly felt cold…chilled to the bone; afraid I'd never get warm again.

"What did you hear, Ellie?" I asked, hardly recognizing my voice.

"I don't know who it was, but I think they might've been torturing him," she cried. "I don't know, but whatever they were doing, it was horrible. He kept moaning and groaning, crying and begging them to stop, but they wanted a name, a description, a location…"

I was hardly aware of the tears streaming down my face. I could practically hear Raymond's cries in my head, and it made me want to throw up. Poor Raymond…if he'd only been able to escape to his world of curlicues.

"Did he give them what they wanted?" Jonas asked, and something in his voice got my attention.

"Yes, finally."

"What was it?" he asked.

"I...I..."

"Tell us!" he insisted.

"They kept asking about a bag. "Who found the bag?" they wanted to know. Give us a name! A name!"

My heart stopped! The bag! The bag of money! Did Raymond know? Had Lily told him? No...not Raymond! She wouldn't have told him...not knowing how he was...with his notebook filled with scribbles. She wouldn't have done that! She *couldn't* have!

"She wears a hat," Ellie whispered. "He told them she wears a pink and green hat...one with little silver bells."

I heard Jonas take a sharp breath. This couldn't be happening...

"I was so scared, I can't remember the name he said," Ellie continued. "But I'm pretty sure it was the name of a flower..."

Lily.

****

My cell phone rang, just as I was hitting the speed dial to call Minnie. I looked at the number...*home!*

"Cleo!" Minnie's voice was in a panic. "Lily's gone! I just went up to check on her, let her know supper was ready, and she wasn't in her room!"

I couldn't speak. My fingers were numb. Jonas grabbed the phone from my hand.

"Minnie! Don't do anything. Stay there and whatever you do, don't call the police! The message will go straight to Mark. If he hasn't found her yet, we don't want to let him know she's out on the streets somewhere for easy picking. We'll look for her. Don't worry. Stay by the phone."

He grabbed my icy hands, rubbing them vigorously between his warm ones. "Cleo? Baby? Don't shut down on me. We've got to go. We've got to try to find Lily before they do. C'mon, baby...I need you to stay with me."

He stood, dragging me up with him, and barking toward the darkness that was Ellie. "You got a friend you can stay with?" He didn't wait for her answer. "It would probably be a good idea for you to go there until this is over. Be careful."

"You're not leaving me here by myself. I'm coming with you!"

"Then come on! We're leaving."

Then he stooped and slung me over his shoulder like a bag of feed and practically ran with me to his car.

Chapter Twenty-Two

Cleo

"Where are we going?" My voice sounded dull and lifeless. I watched as we roared out of the alley, taking the turn practically on two wheels.

"To find somewhere inconspicuous to wait out on Highway 80."

His words didn't make sense. We should be driving around, looking for Lily, not sitting on the side of the road, unless he thought...

No! Don't even think it!

He came to a rolling stop at the next intersection, then surged forward, pinning my head back against the headrest. I could see the light at the next crossroad turn yellow and he sped up, zooming through on pink-tinted pavement. His aggressive driving was bringing me back to the land of the living. I reached down beside me, fumbling for the end of my seatbelt, pulling it across my hips, snapping it into place.

"Um...Jonas...?"

"What?" he barked.

"You think we might be able to slow down, just a tad?"

"We're in a hurry, Cleo."

I tried again. "Probably not a good idea to get pulled over by the cops tonight."

"My driving is fine!" he growled.

*If you say so…*My hand clutched the dashboard when we screeched to a stop at the next light. When it turned green, we roared off again. There was a thud from the back seat, followed by a string of obscenities, then the *click* of a seatbelt. I smirked a little.

"Um…maybe you'd better put your seatbelt on, too," I urged Jonas. "You know…it's the law."

He muttered something under his breath about back seat drivers being a pain in the neck—at least I *think* he said neck.

"I'm not *in* the back seat," I retorted, but I was glad to see that he did what I asked. After another few seconds, the car slowed down perceptibly, coming to a sedate stop at the next light. "Better?" he asked with a tinge of sarcasm.

I gave him my best smile. "Very much, thank you!"

He grinned, then reached over and took my hand, giving it a squeeze. "Are you all right now?"

"Are you?"

"I'm not worried about me."

"Let's just concentrate on finding Lily. I can fall apart later."

"We'll find her, Cleo."

It sounded like a promise, and even though I knew there was no way he could be sure about it, I clung to it like a drowning person would a life raft.

****

We were positioned where we could clearly see each car zoom past us on Highway 80, but were hidden in the deep shadows provided by a convenient row of pine trees. My heart rate skyrocketed with each dark car we saw. It seemed to me that Savannah's ratio of dark to light cars was inordinately weighted on the dark side. Or maybe only people driving dark cars lived out here. Whatever the case, I'd probably end up having a stroke before the night was over.

As the evening dragged on, there were fewer and fewer cars whizzing by. I was trying not to panic, but was really beginning to think that just sitting here was a waste of time. We should be *doing* something…something proactive. Not just sitting on our butts. We should head back to town and start looking for Lily block by block, street by street. Anything was better than this! Not to mention the fact that Ellie was *really* getting on my nerves. If she made one more sexual innuendo toward Jonas, I would lose it. As it was, I felt like dragging her out of that back seat by her Miss Clairol tinted-hair and treating Jonas to a cat-fight the like of which he'd never seen before…one that he'd not soon forget.

Just as I opened my mouth to suggest heading back to town, Jonas sat up straighter, his attention focused on the dark car just passing us. Its brake lights glowed a couple of times, as if considering whether or not to use the truck stop exit. Obviously deciding against it, the car sped up and continued down the highway.

Usually, one sedan-type car looked like any other sedan-type car to me, but as I stared at this one, I felt hair stand up on the back of my neck.

"That's it," Jonas said, as he turned the key in the ignition and slowly pulled out of the shadows, never taking his eyes off that car. I re-buckled my seatbelt, my heart racing.

He allowed two cars to go by before he pulled out,

then kept a measured distance between his car and the one we were following. I wasn't sure what the plan was when these other two cars turned off and we were left on our own. I was pretty sure that Jonas had no idea either; that he was adlibbing again, making up a script as he went.

One of the decoys in front of us slowed, pulling into the turn lane with its left signal on. My mouth was so dry; I couldn't work up enough spit to swallow. Once they turned, Jonas stepped on the gas to catch back up. We sped down the long, narrow two-lane causeway that led out to Tybee Island, surrounded by nothing but marshland. I stared, unblinking, focused intently on the first set of taillights, not seeing anything else.

"Why'd the turtle cross the road?" Ellie quipped from the back seat.

My mouth dropped open in disbelief and I shot a glare over my shoulder. She's telling a *joke? Now?*

"What?" she snapped. "I just saw one of those turtle crossing signs and thought I'd try to lighten the moment a little. Sue me! So...?"

"So, what?" I asked.

"So why did the turtle cross the road?"

"I don't know," I ground out through clenched teeth, keeping my eyes trained on the taillights ahead.

"To get to the other tide...get it? You know, like the chicken getting to the other side?"

Jonas came to my rescue again. "You know, Ellie, it's not really much of a joke if you have to explain it, but maybe it would've been funnier in another situation."

We drove in silence for a couple of minutes until

267

we met a car, coming from the opposite direction. It had both its high beams and fog lights on; blazing brighter and brighter the closer it got to us.

"Oh, my god!" Ellie screeched from the back seat. "Dim your lights, you moron!"

Though my left ear was ringing, I had to agree with her. The glare was blinding, and it forced me to look away until it passed us. I blinked to get rid of the black spots in my vision. When I looked again, we were driving across the Bull Creek Bridge and there was only one set of red lights in front of us.

What? I looked around in a panic. "Where's the other car? Which one is that one? How'd we lose them?"

"Our guys just turned on a dirt road back there, just before the bridge. I can see their lights in my rearview."

I twisted in my seat in order to see. Sure enough, I could see the glow of headlights inching off at a forty-five degree angle from the road. "What are you going to do now?"

"I'm going to drive up here past the curve so they can't see me, whip this thing around at the entrance of Fort Pulaski, and head back."

I didn't ask him anything else, just clamped my icy hands tightly between trembling knees. Once we were out of their sight, he made a tight u-turn, then sped back to the curve in the road, before slowing down once again. The dark sedan was already pulling back out onto the road.

Ellie cursed, "They're done? That was fast!"

She took the words out of my mouth, minus the cussing, though I might've been *thinking* some of those words. Surely, in that short amount of time, they'd only had time to dump one body, and not *two*.

I clapped my hand over my mouth to keep from crying out. Tears stung my eyes, and I turned and stared at Jonas as we crossed the bridge and drove past the dirt road, following the car back the way we'd come.

"We can't do anything there," he answered my unasked question. "If we follow them, maybe they'll lead us to Spencer."

I nodded, thinking about that creek we'd just crossed over…a creek whose waters would eventually flow into the Atlantic Ocean. Maybe the authorities would discover it before the sea creatures staked their claim; maybe they wouldn't. In either case, we hadn't been able to cheat death after all.

I stared out my window at the scattered jewelry blurring against the dark velvet sky, barely registering that there seemed to be a lot more "diamonds" showing up out here away from the city lights. I didn't bother to wipe the tears that streamed down my cheeks. Raymond deserved to have someone to sorrow over him. It was the least I could do for the creative man who would never make roses out of palmetto leaves again.

****

The dark sedan pulled into the parking lot of the Pirate's House Restaurant. Twenty seconds later Jonas rolled past the building, and whipped around the corner to park behind a large construction dumpster sitting in front of one of the city's renovation projects. He cut the engine, then turned to me, thrusting his phone into my hand. "Call my boss…Joel McMillan. Speed dial nine. He knows I'm working on this story, but he doesn't know everything. Tell him. Be sure to explain the police involvement. He'll know what to do."

I stared at him, mouth hanging open, unable to say anything.

"I've got a hunch that they're heading for the tunnel. There's supposed to be an entrance under that restaurant. I'm going to try to follow them. They're probably meeting Spencer here. Cleo, I want you to stay in the car. It's too dangerous for you to come too. I can only look out for one person, and if you were with me, that person would be you; then we'd both be in danger. Please try to understand."

My mouth snapped shut and I finally found my voice. "It's too dangerous for *me*, but not for *you?* You're crazy! They have *guns!* What do *you* have?"

"Cleo, please...I don't want you to get hurt. I couldn't stand it if something happened to you."

"How do you think *I'd* feel if something happens to *you?* You big idiot!"

He grabbed my face, kissing me, hard, then he whispered. "Please..."

I was in a daze from his kiss, something he'd probably counted on. "Fine! Just *go!*"

Ellie opened her door the same time he did.

"What the heck do you think you're doing?" he snapped.

"Coming with you."

"Weren't you listening? It's too dangerous!"

"How chivalrous of you! Yes, I was listening, and although your declaration of love was touching, I can take care of myself."

"You're going to get us both killed!" he growled.

"Nah! I can handle Mark. I'm an expert at it. The handling part." She winked at him. "You know what I mean?"

Jonas muttered angrily under his breath as he reached down to pop his trunk, then disappeared behind his car. He was back in a moment, carrying a small canvas duffle bag. He rummaged in it a minute, finally finding what he was looking for. With lightning speed, he spun Ellie around, grabbed both of her hands in one of his, and noosed them tightly with the length of rope he'd retrieved. Her mouth gaped open in surprise as he quickly knotted its end. Not giving her a chance to gather her wits, he pulled a bandana out of his pocket and stuffed it into her mouth, stifling her cries before she uttered them. He whirled her back to face him, his nose almost touching hers, and snarled a whisper, "There! Something I've wanted to do ever since you showed up in that alley tonight. Consider it pay-back!" Then he pushed her into the car and leaned down to grin at me.

"I'll be bahhk," he growled in a pretty good Arnold Schwarzenegger imitation, and quietly closed the door. Before turning to leave, he shrugged on his ratty flannel shirt, buttoning it over his turtleneck, then pulled on his filthy ball cap, turning it around backward so it wouldn't shade his face.

I watched him sprint across the street and disappear into the shadows while Ellie thumped and grunted from the back seat.

"Do you mind?" I snapped over my shoulder. "I've got to make a call and I can't hear myself think with all your noise."

"Mmmuf-ffoo!"

It wasn't hard to figure out what *that* meant. I made a face that she couldn't see, pressed the number nine on

Jonas' phone, and then "Send." It rang five times before a sleepy voice answered, "Hello?"

"Joel? Joel McMillan?"

"Who is this?"

"Cleo Davis. You don't know me, but Jonas Holmes asked me to call you…"

Chapter Twenty-Three

Lily

I tiptoed downstairs, cringing at each creak, praying they wouldn't give me away. Over my shoulder, I could hear Minnie talking to someone. I paused, listening. It only took a few seconds to figure out she was talking to that crazy husband of hers again. He was probably out in that big car, playing taxi. Cleo was in her room. I'd heard music playing earlier when I'd crept by her door.

I eyed the front door and made a face. I'd rather go out the back. That was the safer exit for someone looking like me—less conspicuous—but in order to get there, I'd have to go through the kitchen, and that would sort of defeat the purpose of sneaking out. Cocking my head, I listened for Minnie again. She was still talking...good. The coast was clear.

I scurried across the foyer to the door, grabbing the knob, turning it. The door swung open silently, and I breathed a sigh of relief. Thank goodness for quiet hinges. Slipping out, I closed the door without a sound, then fled down the front stairs, opening and shutting the iron gate behind me.

I paused, listening for a shout of alarm, something to indicate I'd been discovered. Still clear. I turned to the right, hurried to the corner, and made another right, onto Whitaker. Though I was out of sight of the house, I needed to put a little distance between us before I would feel safe.

Safe? Was it safe for me on the streets? Maybe, maybe not; but that didn't matter. Raymond was out here somewhere, and he was my friend. I needed to find him before Spencer's men did. I had to try. It was too late now, but I really wished I hadn't told him about the bag of money I'd found in the trash. If Spencer's men found him first...if he happened to tell them about it...well, it wouldn't bode well for me.

I quickened my pace. I needed to find Raymond.

****

I was waiting for the little green man to show up on the crosswalk sign when a low voice drawled, "Nice hat."

I glanced up and froze, staring into the cold eyes of a snake: Mark Spencer.

His smile was just as cold as his eyes. "You must be Lily. Raymond told me how to find you." His eyes flicked toward my hat. "You're hard to miss...that thing makes you stick out like a sore thumb."

My heart was thudding in my chest. I looked around at the throngs of passersby, pleading with my eyes, praying that someone...*anyone* would notice my distress, but except for a few snickers at my appearance, I was ignored. Not a single person bothered to look me in the eye.

"I wouldn't try that if I were you," he murmured, low enough that I was the only one who could hear him. "I have a gun, and I can make it look like you're resisting arrest. No one would question me; no one would blame me if I shot you. After all, you're just another of the many homeless people. They'd probably thank me for getting you off the streets." He motioned with his chin. "My car's over there. The black Lincoln. Get moving. We need to talk…somewhere private."

****

"Do one thing every day that scares you."

"Yeah, yeah, yeah…" Spencer muttered as he tied my hands behind my back. "I've heard that one before. Eleanor Roosevelt, right?"

I nodded.

"Good. Now shut up. I need to think."

We were in a tunnel, somewhere under the Pirate House restaurant and I was using the only weapon I had: my quotes. My aim was two-fold. One…to convince Spencer I was, indeed, a crazy woman, not a threat to him, and two…to irritate the living daylights out of him so he couldn't think. The second part was dangerous, though. I had to balance the irritation. I didn't want to go too far. After all he had a gun, and even if he didn't use it, he could use his fist. It was a fine line I was walking. I had to be careful.

"If God can make a firefly's butt light up, I believe He can do anything."

He groaned. "I told you to shut up, old woman."

"Trying to have a conversation with you is like playing Scrabble with M&M's."

"That's it!" he roared and jumped to his feet. "Enough! I need to think!" And he slapped me across the face, snapping my head to the right.

The pain stunned me. Pulsing waves of it radiated from my jaw and mouth, stars circled my head. I touched my tongue to my lip, tasted blood. Okay…so much for my balancing act. Maybe I should be quiet for a little while.

"That should teach you. Now, I need to make a call and take a leak, but I'll be back, and we'll talk more then. Don't go anywhere." His mocking laugh echoed down the tunnel.

I studied my surroundings. There wasn't much to see. Dim, yellow lantern light flickered on dirt walls, worn nearly smooth through time. I sat on a wooden keg of some sort. Others like it were stacked in the corner. That was it. Nothing else to see. Nothing to help me get out of this mess. My chances of surviving the night weren't looking too promising. Once Spencer was convinced I hadn't told anyone else about the bag of money, I'd find myself in the Savannah River, added to the body count. My job was to convince him. I absolutely, positively could *not* let him know that Cleo and Jonas knew. Not a hint, no clue…nothing. No matter what.

What time was it? There was no way of knowing down here. It could be the middle of the brightest day of the year, and you'd never know it. Stygian darkness pressed in toward the lantern, pulsing. It seemed almost alive…probably *was*…with ghosts.

I'd no sooner thought that final word, when Raymond stood before me. I gasped, practically swallowing my tongue, and jumped to my feet. I scrambled over the keg, trying to put something between me and…

Raymond?

I stopped and slowly turned around, heart thumping with both fear and sadness when I realized what I was seeing.

Raymond was standing in front of me, or maybe I

should say he was *floating* in front of me, since his feet were about six inches off the ground. Though he looked pretty solid, he had a slightly transparent quality about him, and I was pretty sure I could see the dirt wall behind him when I stared at his chest. That meant...

"Oh, Raymond," I whispered. "Why'd you leave the house? You were safe there. You—" I broke off. Fussing at him wouldn't undo anything. Dead was dead, no matter how it happened, no matter whose fault it was.

He looked wet...dripping wet, though the ground below him remained dusty and dry. It must've just happened if he was this wet. Another homeless man would be showing up in the river, soon. He'd come straight here, probably to warn me.

"Miz Lily," he croaked. "I gotta tell ya. Spencer's lookin' for ya." His ghostly eyes filled with tears. "Forgive me, Miz Lily. I couldn't help it. He was hurtin' me so bad, I *had* to tell him. He knows about your hat. Ya need to get rid of that thing. If ya ain't wearing it, he can't find ya. You won't stick out none. You'll look just like any other homeless lady."

Before I could open my mouth to reply, Spencer appeared out of the darkness. "Who the hell are you talking to, old woman?"

Couldn't he see Raymond? I studied his expression. All I could see was disgust for a dirty old homeless woman. He didn't see the ghost that was standing between us. I wasn't sure if that was a good or a bad thing. I turned my attention back to my friend, ignoring Mark completely.

Raymond was staring at me with horror-filled eyes. "I'm too late? Oh, no! Miz Lily, I'm sorry. I'm so sorry."

"I'll be okay. Don't worry. Go on, now. I'll probably catch up with you later, and if you see my sister, Rose, tell her what happened."

Raymond sniffed and then nodded. He disappeared with a *puff*.

Spencer stared at me with narrowed eyes, then shuddered before turning away, and I heard him mutter, "Crazy old bat."

From the darkness around the corner, I could hear a low rumble of voices. Someone was coming! Maybe they could help me. Mark whirled, pulling his gun. He was poised and waiting. I had to warn them...whoever it was.

"Look out! He has a gun!"

Spencer's hit men burst around the corner, with their guns drawn too. He relaxed as soon as he saw them. "Done?"

"Yeah, boss. Went without a hitch. Same as usual. Where'd you find her?"

"Wandering the streets. She was wearing that hat, just like he said. Kind of hard to miss," he chuckled, then he pointed his gun at my forehead, and growled, "You do anything stupid like that again, you're a dead woman." He turned away, muttering, "God, I wish I had some duct tape!" then, "I'm starving. One of you guys needs to go get us something to eat." He reached in his wallet, and pulled out a hundred dollar bill, grinning. "Here, use this. Might as well work it into the local economy."

Chapter Twenty-Four

Cleo

I gnawed another fingernail and stared at the dark restaurant across the street. Arguing with myself hadn't done anything, but given me several mangled nails. I glanced at the clock. Seven minutes had passed. Seven minutes that seemed like seven days since Jonas had disappeared into the darkness. I'd actually started across the street, three different times, but ran back each time. Jonas had asked me to wait...he said, *please.* He doesn't play fair.

I'd told his boss everything, stressing that we couldn't call the police since they were involved. He'd assured me that he'd take care of it, but what did that mean? How? Who in the world could he contact that would have authority to actually do something about this? We were dealing with a bad cop. Who could help us in a situation like this?

I'd long since tuned out Ellie's noise from the back seat, but a loud spitting sound caught my attention. Uh-oh. She'd somehow managed to remove the gag, and was wiggling into a sitting position. The streetlight on the other side of the road provided enough light for me to see her expression. Enough angry sparks shot from her eyes to ignite the interior of the car.

"Untie me...*now!*" she demanded.

I ignored her as best I could.

She changed tactics. "He's been gone a long time, hasn't he? I hope he's okay."

Now she was harder to ignore. I gnawed another fingernail.

"They must be down in the tunnel. I looked everywhere except there before showing up in that alley. I know he has meetings down there sometimes. I would've checked here earlier, but I'm kind of afraid. I've heard that tunnel is haunted, and I don't wanna mess with any ghosts. We could go together. I know if I could just talk to Mark…make him see reason, he'd stop all this craziness before it goes any further, before something happens to Jonas. It's gotten out of hand, and he's not thinking clearly. He's got plenty of money. We could get away…head to Brazil or someplace else with no extradition laws."

I couldn't believe she still wanted to be with that creep. "Do you hear yourself, Ellie? Think about what you're saying, please. The man is a murderer!"

"No, he's not! He never pulled the trigger."

I couldn't believe she was so gullible. She'd never seemed that way before. He had her under some kind of spell. That had to be it; otherwise she wouldn't have swallowed all the lies…her own, included. "Listen…just because someone else did his dirty work doesn't make him any less guilty. Besides…he *did* pull the trigger one of the times."

"He did not! How can you say that?"

"Because it's true! There was an eyewitness."

"I don't believe you."

"Well, it's the truth. I wouldn't lie about something like that."

"Who? Who is this alleged eyewitness? Why haven't they come forward?"

"Because Mark's a cop and they knew it wouldn't do any good."

"Well, I don't care. It doesn't matter. I love him…and he loves me, too. No, don't look at me like that. He *told* me! We'll probably get married, but we have to wait until after his divorce is final. His wife is dragging her feet, throwing up all kind of roadblocks, trying to make things as difficult as possible for him."

I shook my head sadly. Mark Spencer's wife probably couldn't wait for her escape, likely counting the days until she was finally free. I doubted Ellie would be taking her place either, but it would do no good to tell her that. She'd never believe me.

I eyed the clock again. Ten minutes. What was happening down there? This waiting was killing me. That's all I'd been doing all day long! First, I had to wait for Jonas to pick me up tonight. Then I had to wait in the alley. Mmm…okay, that was different…I *liked* that kind of waiting. But then I had to wait in the truck stop parking, and now here I sat again! Wait, wait, wait! I was ready to *do* something. I couldn't just sit here any longer.

I turned to Ellie. "You know the way down there?"

Her expression brightened. "To the tunnel? Yeah."

"You'll help me with Jonas if he's in trouble?"

"Of course I will. And maybe it won't seem so scary with two of us."

"All right then, let's get you untied."

****

Ellie was right. It *was* scary, and we weren't even *in* the tunnel yet. We'd already scaled a wrought iron gate into a tiny courtyard where the entrance to the tunnel was hidden. We now stood at the top of the steepest, most rickety wooden stairs I'd ever seen. The flashlight beam wouldn't even reach the bottom of the darn things. I worried that they'd collapse under our combined weight, then thought about Spencer's beefy hit men and relaxed a bit. If these stairs had managed to handle that pair of oxen, I was certain they'd hold us. Well...*almost* certain.

I wasn't sure what the tunnel's original purpose was, but besides pirates smuggling rum, I'd heard it'd been used during the Underground Railroad back in the days of slavery. Then in 1876, Savannah had another terrible yellow fever epidemic and they'd used the tunnel as storage for dead victims. According to the history books, they'd waited until after dark, then they'd loaded the corpses up on wagons and hauled them down to a marshy area for burial. The reason they did it at night, was supposedly to keep prying eyes from seeing just how many people had died. It sounded like drastic measures, but that had been their third huge outbreak in a little over fifty years and people were starting to panic. Added together, those three episodes claimed nearly 4,000 people, and droves of folks fled for their lives. I could see why the city officials had gone to such great lengths to hide the actual numbers; if everyone flew the coop, there'd be no tax base.

It was cold down here, that creepy kind of cold that sort of seeps into your bones, making you shiver from the inside out. The air venting through the chamber was damp and musty, the scent of mildew swirled with the unmistakable smell of decomposition. It was that last bit that worried me. I hoped it was just the history of the place, and not from something more recent. It was bad enough that it felt like the ghosts of every one of those fever victims were down here in the tunnel with us. I wasn't sure *what* I'd do if I came across a dead body.

Part of me was beginning to wish I'd listened to Jonas and stayed in the car. The sword of yellow light that had beamed so strongly from the flashlight I'd found in the glove box was looking decidedly weaker the longer we walked, but I tried not to think about it. Of course, I had a flashlight option on my phone, but I didn't want to want to use the battery up, in case I needed to make a call. I wished now, that I hadn't left Jonas' phone in the car.

We'd come to a thick wooden door, with forged iron hinges and latch, standing slightly ajar. I stopped Ellie from pushing it open.

"Wait! Listen."

I could hear a low, unintelligible murmur, then a hard slap.

Oh no! Who was on the receiving end of that?

"Tell me! Tell me who else knows!" A voice snarled, then another slap.

The few fingernails that I had left after my gnawing episode in the car, dug into my palms. I swallowed back a wave of nausea.

"That's him!" Ellie's whisper actually sounded buoyed with excitement. "That's Mark! I recognize his voice!"

Before I could say anything, another voice rang out, "Why don't you just leave her alone. She told you no one else knows! Why would she lie?"

Jonas! Oh, God! Spencer has him. What can I do?

What can I do? Wait…he said *she*…Does that mean…?

"Common sense is like deodorant; the people who need it the most, are the ones who never use it." The voice rang low, but clear.

I gasped. "Lily!"

Ellie whirled to face me. "That's the name!" Her whisper was frantic. "That's the name I heard them say! They have her! No! I'll make Mark listen this time. No one else can get hurt!"

"Ellie, don't…" I grabbed her arm, but she shook me off, turned, and burst through the door.

I waited in horrified silence for what would happen next. It wasn't a long wait. I heard Ellie scream, "Mark! Please!"

An immediate clamor of exclamations exploded, but Spencer's roar overpowered them all. "What the hell are you doing here, Elle?"

A sound of scuffling, a grunt of pain, another slap. Ellie's scream echoed down the tunnel, but it was cut short by a loud *thunk*.

The silence that followed was so complete, I thought I'd suddenly gone deaf.

Chapter Twenty-Five

Jonas

I dashed through the shadows toward the darker hulk of the restaurant, thankful for my dark clothes. In them, I was virtually invisible, able to blend right in to the blackness surrounding me. Darting alongside the building, I crackled, face-first, through a spider web.

Ugh! What was that thing doing here at this time of year? It was *December*, for crying out loud. I shuddered, picking ineffectually at the sticky threads that clung to my skin and hair. I hated it when that happened. It reminded me of hiking in the woods with my brothers. I'd never wondered why they'd let me lead, and had always jumped at the chance. It was a rare thing for me to be first in anything with that many siblings older than me. I'd always felt like a big shot on those hikes. It wasn't until I was much older that I figured out their strategy. I went first in order to clear the path of spider webs. I always managed to find them with my face. Gave different meaning to the term, webmaster. I just hoped the owner of *this* particular web wasn't too ticked off at me for messing up his or her handiwork. Now wasn't a good time to have a confrontation with an angry spider.

I pressed against the building, hidden in the shadow of an enormous bush, waiting for my eyes to adjust to yet another level of darkness, an activity I'd been doing for most of the night, it seemed. This darkness was cold...not like in the alley with Cleo. That had been anything *but* cold. A vision of her decked out in that hot little cat suit flashed through my mind, but I shook the memory away. No time for that now. I needed all my senses present and accounted for. Anything less than that could get me hurt...or worse.

My ears strained as I listened for any sound that didn't belong, something out of place. At the same time, I tried my best not to breathe loud and give my position away. I waited in tense anticipation for several long minutes.

Nothing.

Now what? I knew you could get to the tunnel from inside the restaurant, but it was closed now. Was there a way in from the outside? There must be. Either that, or Spencer and his men had their own key, which was possible, but not likely. Maybe I needed to creep around the perimeter and investigate, check for broken branches on these bushes, footprints in any loose dirt, flattened grass or a discarded cigarette...anything that might help me determine what to do next.

I took steps and froze, sniffing the air like a bloodhound. Hmm. Smelled like fast food. That unmistakable scent of grease and onions. Before I could move, something cold and hard pressed against the back of my neck. There was an ominous *click* and I froze.

A rough hand flung me around. A blinding light flashed in my face. A voice growled, "You! What are you doing here?"

"It's almost midnight," I answered, taking a

chance. What did I have to lose? "I'm nothing if not punctual."

"Punctual?"

The flashlight still had me blinded so I couldn't see a thing, but the voice sounded confused. Spencer obviously hired his men for their brawn and not their brains. "Yeah…it means "on time."" Probably not the smartest move for me to taunt him like that—him having a gun and all—but the words sort of popped out, and then I couldn't take them back.

"I know what the word means, wise guy. And I also know this wasn't where we were supposed to meet. C'mon…Boss is gonna want to talk to you."

****

The decrepit stairs that led down to the tunnel were definitely not coded to withstand the weight of two full grown men, one nearly twice the size of the other, and the creaking and groaning were scaring me worse than the gun pointed at the back of my head. Each step seemed in danger of being our last. The whole shebang trembled and swayed like a house of cards every time we moved. Thank goodness it was just Tweedle Dee and me—not Tweedle Dum, too—creeping down these stairs. I doubted this ancient carpentry could handle anything more. Then again, maybe it would be better for them to go ahead and collapse. I think I'd rather die that way, instead of being shot and dumped in the river.

I wished for my phone again. Spencer's guy had been too dumb to frisk me, so chances are, I'd still have it, if I hadn't left it with Cleo. I was certain she'd called my boss by now, and I hoped help was on the way. I knew he had connections, but how far away were they? How long would it take for them to get here? And would it be in time?

Don't think like that! I ordered myself. *Think positively. Good thoughts, only.*

At least I didn't have to worry about Cleo, and could rest in the fact that she was safe and sound, in my car.

You dummy! What in the world makes you think she stayed in the car?

The thought was so startling that I literally froze; my foot hung in space, wavering several inches above the next shaky tread, unable to move. The hulk, behind me, was oblivious to my dilemma, not noticing until he slammed into my back, which nearly pitched me off into space. I managed to grab the thick rope that served as a sort of handrail running along the wall beside the stairs. My heart thudded at the close call.

"Try that again, buddy, and you'll save yourself the worry of talking to the boss." An angry voice snapped behind me, then he prodded me with the gun barrel. "Now move it!"

I had no choice, but to obey him. He had the upper hand, in the form of a gun, not to mention liberal amounts of steroid enhanced strength. I was sure he wouldn't hesitate to use either or both, if necessary. I was just as sure that I'd been fooling myself about Cleo...sedating my concern with wishful thinking. There was *no way* she would stay in the car.

I should've tied her up, too.

At the bottom of the stairs, I pushed open a heavy wooden door. A faint light glowed around a corner ahead. A rumbled echo of low voices sounded almost like the growling of large cats...a veritable den of lions.

My heart sank when I rounded the corner. I'd

expected Spencer and his other goon. They were there, of course, but so was someone else…the reason for my sinking heart.

Lily.

She was perched on a small keg, her comical hat askew on her head. A line of blood spooled from the side of her mouth, her lip already bruised and puffy. Her hands were pulled behind her, and she was staring daggers at Spencer.

The scene made my blood boil. What kind of animal would do that to an old woman? I already knew the answer to that. The same kind that would use the homeless as disposable pawns in his game.

The instant we stepped into the room, Mark Spencer's head jerked to attention, instantly suspicious. "Who's this?" he demanded.

Lily was staring at me now. I sent her a warning look, hoping she'd not give me away. She narrowed her eyes and pressed her lips together, clearly not happy that I was there, but she gave me a small nod.

My captor answered, "The new guy I was telling you about, boss. Problem is…I found him poking around outside here, not at the place we were supposed to meet."

Spencer's eyes skewered me. "What's your name?"

My thoughts raced. Should I tell him? I was sure he read the paper, but would he recognize it? Put two and two together? Doubtful, but possible, and it would seal my fate if he did. Better use an alias…at least the last name. Maybe it would buy some time. "Jonas Knight."

"Well, Jonas Knight, maybe you better explain why you're nosing around."

"I, uh…I was anxious to get started on my new

job."

"Anxious, huh?" His eyes narrowed. "Why'd you show up here?"

Uh-oh. A trickle of sweat slid down my back. "I heard this was where you had meetings, sometimes."

Mark's eyebrows shot up. "You heard? From who?"

I shrugged. "Nobody in particular. You know…just word on the street."

He nodded, still eyeing me shrewdly, while he reached into his shirt pocket for a pack of cigarettes, shaking one out, grabbing it with his lips. A hand went into his pants pocket to retrieve a lighter. His face glowed, twin flares in his eyes as he sucked the flame into the end of the cigarette. He inhaled deeply, his cheeks caving with the effort, then the lighter snapped shut and he shoved it back into his pocket. Tendrils of smoke streamed from his nostrils as he stared at me. A fire-breathing dragon.

I saw something flicker in his eyes, before he replied, "The "street" knows better than to talk about me." Then he turned and barked at his man, "Tie him up until I figure out what to do with him."

The goon with the tattoo on his neck spun me around and slammed me up against the wall with enough force to knock the breath out of me. I felt my nose crunch on impact, and immediately tasted blood. Rough rope fibers bit into my wrists, tight enough to cut off circulation. Giving a satisfied grunt when he was done, he yanked me away from the wall and whipped me back around. I could feel blood streaming from my destroyed nose, into my open mouth, dripping off my chin. I ran my tongue across my teeth. At least they were okay, not that maintaining the two years of work by my orthodontist mattered much at this point. I didn't see myself walking out of this one.

A glance at Lily turned into a double-take. Why was she smiling? This was *not* the time or place for it. Had her mind snapped? Didn't she realize the danger we were in?

Then her voice rang out, echoing down the tunnel. "Smile...it will either warm their heart or piss them off, either way, you win!"

I groaned. Not one of her stupid quotes...not *now!* She was pouring gasoline on a fire that would burn us both.

Mark whirled and stalked up to her, pointing an angry finger in her face, almost touching her nose. He trembled with barely suppressed rage. "This is the last time I'm warning you, old woman," he ground out between clenched teeth. "Shut up! Or next time, I'll break your scrawny neck!" He took a deep breath, exhaled slowly as if trying to calm himself, then forced a tight smile. "Now, then...where were we? Ah, yes, you were about to tell me who else knows about the bag. Who'd you tell?"

I stared at Lily with dread, watched her stand up, then lean forward to spit out a mouthful of blood. It landed dangerously close to the toe of Spencer's Italian leather shoes.

"Tell me!" Spencer roared. "Tell me who else knows!"

"Asked and answered," she whispered defiantly, her expression daring him not to believe her. "No one else knows." Then she sort of sucked in her cheeks, almost making a fish-face. What on earth was she doing? Spencer looked just at mystified.

We didn't have to wonder long.

It wasn't until she leaned forward again that I figured out her plan, but by then it was too late. Taking careful aim, she spit out the mouthful of blood she'd worked to accumulate, hitting her intended target...dead on.

Everything in the room seemed to freeze. Spencer's expression morphed through several expressions, from astonishment to fury laced with disgust. I groaned. Spencer gazed at the toe of his shoe, now coated with a juicy red splat, while rage painted his face a bright shade of magenta.

THWACK!

There'd been no warning...no opportunity for her to even take a step back, to possibly avoid the strike. There'd been a blur of movement, then the horrifying impact of his hand against her face, so hard that it caused her hat to sail off and land on the floor. She collapsed in a heap, her ragged clothing made her look like a pile of dirty rags.

I bit my lip to keep from calling out her name, twisting and yanking my hands against the rope until my wrists were raw, but all my struggling seemed to do was pull the knots tighter. I couldn't get loose. Oh, God! She wasn't moving. Had he killed her? She was *old*, for God's sake! She couldn't take that kind of abuse. Old people's bones are fragile. Everybody knew that. I snarled in frustration, "Why don't you just leave her alone. She told you, no else knows. Why would she lie?"

I cast a silent appeal to first one, and then the other of Spencer's henchmen. They wouldn't just stand there and watch their boss beat an old woman to death, would they?

Apparently so. They stood like large, wooden Indians, their thick arms folded across even thicker chests, faces hard and expressionless, eyes hooded and cold. There'd be no help from them.

My attention went back to Lily, searching...praying for some sign of life. There! She moved! Oh, thank God...she was alive. He must've just knocked her out.

She looked up, shook her head as if shaking cobwebs away, then...uh-oh, I knew that look...she was smiling again; fresh blood coated her teeth giving her a ghoulish appearance. *No! Not another quote. Please, Lily...* I begged her with my eyes. *Don't!*

"Common sense is like deodorant, the people who need it most, are the ones who never use it."

Before the magnitude of what she'd done fully penetrated my senses, there was a flurry of movement around the corner, then Ellie burst into the room, crying, "Mark! Please!"

Ellie? Oh, no! How'd she get loose? If she *was down here, then—*

Spencer looked thunderstruck. "What the hell are you doing here, Elle?"

She grabbed his arm, fingernails digging in for dear life, trying to keep him from reaching for Lily. At first, he tried to shake her off, and when that didn't work, he tried prying. They scuffled around in a violent dance of intricate steps. He grunted in pain when one of her flailing knees made contact with his groin, then he clutched a fistful of her hair, pulling her head back, slapping her hard. Ellie screamed as he flung her away from him, but the scream was abruptly cut off when her head *thunked* against the tunnel wall.

Again, the room seemed to freeze in place. An icy silence wove its way throughout the scene.

Chapter Twenty-Six

Cleo

As soon as Ellie rounded the corner, I switched off the flashlight and dropped to the floor. Inky darkness immediately pressed against my spine, and my panic ballooned. The lack of light felt solid...thick and smothering, giving me the feeling of being deep underwater, disoriented, blind. I wanted to move forward, but suddenly couldn't remember which way that was.

As soon as my eyes adjusted, I realized the darkness wasn't quite as heavy as I'd first thought. I could see the faintest of faint glows ahead of me, coming from around a corner. I crawled toward it as quickly as I could, a moth to a flame.

I was thankful for the bedlam that I could clearly hear. It allowed me to move much more quickly than I'd have dared without its camouflaging noise. I jumped violently when Ellie screamed, and barely kept from echoing it with my own. The silence that followed chilled me to my core.

I had no plan when I peeked around the corner; I only knew I had to do *something*. The first person I saw was Jonas, hands tied behind him. I clapped a hand over my gasp, not wanting to give myself away. They'd hurt him! Blood was dripping from his nose and off his chin, making dark, wet stains on his shirt. He was staring directly at me, almost as if he knew I'd be at this exact place, at this exact moment. A flicker of some emotion I didn't recognize flitted across his face, then he smiled. It was only one side of his mouth and only the corner tilted up, but I saw it, and my heart swelled.

Then I saw Ellie. She was lying in a puddle of blood that grew while I watched. Her eyes were open. Was she dead? No, that was a blink. She was alive, but not for long if she kept losing blood like that. The jagged gash at her temple drooled a steady stream of red. Just beyond her, Lily was struggling to get to her feet, hampered by the fact that her hands were tied behind her.

Spencer barked, "Clean this up! I want this over...*now!*"

His words triggered everything happening at once.

Spencer's henchmen drew their guns. One took a step toward Lily and the other toward Jonas.

I scrambled forward on all fours, screaming bloody murder at the exact moment I saw a flash of fiery red in front of me. Lily finally lurched to her feet and shrieked, "Rose!"

Immediately, Spencer's men looked as if they'd been hit by an unseen linebacker. They soared through the air like muscle-bound marionettes pulled by invisible strings, crashing violently into the dirt wall of the tunnel, and then collapsing into an unconscious heap, their guns thudding to the dirt floor. One of those guns skidded across the floor toward me as if kicked by an unseen foot. I snatched it up at the same moment Mark pulled his weapon.

Then all action stopped.

Four people still stood: Lily, Jonas, Mark Spencer, and me. Or was it five? In my periphery, I kept seeing that same flash of red, but when I turned my head, there was no one there. I couldn't allow myself to dwell on it. The situation was too tense. We all stood there, out of breath, and staring warily at each other. Now what?

I'd never shot a gun before, never even *held* one, but I was pretty sure from watching TV, that a point and click method would do the trick. There was just one problem with that plan, and it was a big one. While I was aiming my gun at Mark Spencer, *he* was aiming his, not at *me*, but at *Jonas!* How did he know? How could he possibly know that Jonas was important to me? I couldn't breathe and my hand started shaking so badly, I was afraid that if I tried taking a shot, I'd end up hitting *anything* but my intended target.

Spencer studied me like a specimen under a microscope, then laughed, but his eyes were cold and hard...deadly. "Didn't your daddy ever teach you that children shouldn't play with guns?" His folksy drawl was mocking. "Maybe you better put that thing down before you hurt yourself, little girl."

His words stiffened my spine, steadied my hands. Little girl? I'd show him! "Who said I was playing?" It would've been the perfect comeback if my voice hadn't cracked on the last syllable.

His smile faded, face hardened. "Put it down, girl, or I'll shoot him."

"Don't do it, Cleo," Jonas warned. "He's going to shoot me anyway. He's going to shoot all of us. There are never witnesses. You know that."

"Shut up, Holmes!" Spencer snapped, then smirked at Jonas' surprised expression. "Yeah, I know your last name's not Knight. You write for the paper. I didn't get to where I am today by being an idiot."

Tears stung my eyes, but I impatiently blinked them away. I flicked a glance at Jonas. "I did what you said." My eyes went back to Mark, and added. "It's all taken care of."

Mark narrowed his eyes. "What's taken care of?"

I gave him a tight-lipped smile. "You. Even if you kill us all, you're *still* going down."

"Do not regret growing older. It's a privilege denied to many." Lily's announcement might've seemed funny if this hadn't been a life and death situation. Even so, I felt the strangest urge to giggle, but fought it back. Now wasn't the time for hysterics.

Spencer's jaw clenched. I could see the muscle working back and forth. I'd definitely gotten him thinking, looking for a way out. When he spoke, his voice was low and cold…like death.

"Well, *he* won't be writing the story!"

His words set everything into a blur of motion, but to my eyes, the scene moved at half-speed, like a movie played at half-speed, frame by frame.

Mark and I fired our guns simultaneously. Of course I missed, and my quaking legs collapsed, dropping me to my knees.

At the moment the guns fired, Lily lunged in front of Jonas and they both fell to the ground like lead weights.

The exact instant he pulled the trigger, Mark Spencer screamed in agony as his arm jerked up and out like someone hit it with an invisible bat. His weapon sailed back over his head and into the tunnel; a soft thump sounded somewhere in the darkness; his arm dropped and dangled helplessly at his side,

A half a second later, there was a muffled pop that came from my right; then a surprised expression spread across Mark's face as he gazed down at the small red dot staining the front of his shirt, as if not understanding what he was seeing.

My gun thudded to the floor, and I followed it.

When I opened my eyes, the first thing I noticed was sunshine. Stripes of warm yellow painted the bedspread, my arms. I was in my own bedroom.

I shuddered. What a dream! No...what a *nightmare!* I stared at the dust motes floating in the beams of light, quietly urging that brightness to chase away the shadows in my mind.

I frowned. But it had seemed so real...could I have imagined darkness that oppressive? The cold sneer on Mark Spencer's face? The pool of blood growing around Ellie's still form? Jonas and Lily falling to the ground?

I gasped and sat straight up in bed, horrified, my heart pounding. It hadn't been a dream! It had really happened! Oh, God! Jonas! Lily! Were they all right? Were they—

Just then, my bedroom door swung open, and I jumped so violently, I felt like I cleared the mattress by at least a couple of inches. Jonas walked in, carrying a tray. Relief and something else flashed in his eyes as soon as he saw me. He hurried across the room, setting the tray down on the bedside table before taking a seat on the bed, facing me. One hand grabbed mine; the other tucked a strand of hair behind my ear, and then tilted up my chin, searing my skin. He studied me carefully. "How do you feel?" he asked.

"I'm fine. Are you okay?" My eyes flicked to the white gauze taped at his hair-line, to the tape across his swollen nose. My fingers gently touched his head. "What happened?"

"One of Spencer's shots grazed me. Oh, and this…" he pointed at his nose. "Turns out, noses don't fare very well when they're smashed against a wall."

My heart squeezed inside me. "What?"

He shook his head slightly. "It's okay. I'm fine. It could've been worse. I don't know how he missed. It was an easy shot."

A vision of Mark's arm being violently whacked by something unseen, just as he was firing the gun, filled my mind. "It was Rose."

His eyebrows shot up and he winced at the movement. "Huh?"

"Rose knocked Spencer's arm so he'd miss."

"Who's Rose?"

"Lily's sister."

Something in his eyes flickered at the mention of Lily name. "Baby, there was no one else down there."

"Rose is a ghost," I managed to whisper around my heart that was suddenly wedged in my throat. "Where's Lily?"

Jonas' face grew a little paler. "Her sister is a ghost?"

"I'll explain that part later, Jonas…where's Lily?"

His eyes were grave. "She's all right, but she's at St. Joe's. She's been shot. The bullet that Mark intended for me got her, instead."

A million questions exploded in my brain, as I scrambled out of bed and headed to my closet for clothes, but they'd have to wait. I needed to get to the hospital. "I'll be ready in a minute."

****

"Okay, now take up where you left off," I demanded as soon as we were in his car and on our way. "How did Lily get shot when Mark was aiming at you?"

"She dove right in front of me just as Mark squeezed off two quick shots. One of them hit her in the shoulder, the other grazed my head. We're both fine," he added quickly when my mouth popped open. "She lost a lot of blood, both from the gunshot and the beating Mark gave her, but thankfully, no bones were broken, and the doctors were able to remove the bullet. They're "cautiously optimistic," which I think means she's going to be fine."

"Oh, thank God," I breathed a prayer of thanks, then something in my brain clicked. "Wait a minute! Did you say *two* shots? Seriously? He fired *twice*, hitting two different people in spite of having his arm knocked out of the way? And I couldn't hit him *once?* At nearly point blank range? Jeez, I'm pathetic."

"I didn't see anybody knock his arm," he pointed out.

"I told you. It was Rose; Lily's sister."

"Oh, right. The ghost." He flashed me a questioning look. "You said you'd explain about that."

"I will. Tell me the rest, first."

I could tell by the look on his face that he didn't want to let me off the hook that easy, but he finally continued, "You don't have to worry about your shot missing Mark. Ellie took care of it for you. In all the melee, a gun landed near her. She picked it up and managed to shoot him…right in the chest. He died on the way to the hospital."

Dead? Mark was dead? How was I supposed to feel about that? Yes, he was a slimy, underhanded creep who deserved to be punished for what he'd done, but this... I swallowed hard, having a hard time wrapping my head around the permanence of it all.

"What about his men?" I finally asked

"One of them is in a coma. He suffered a severe head injury when he crashed against the wall." He glanced at me and asked, "Rose, again?"

I nodded, and he drew a deep breath before continuing, "The other one is also in the hospital— under police surveillance—but he's recovering well. He's already copped a plea with the FBI agents who flew to Savannah from Charleston after my boss called them. The guy's already told them everything they wanted to know about the counterfeiting operation and all the murders. Of course, he's pinned everything on Mark and the other guy. It'll be interesting to see what the unconscious one will have to say, if he ever wakes up."

"I guess it's all's well that ends well, then, but I can't help feeling sorry for Ellie. That must've been a hard thing for her to do; shooting Mark like that. I think she was actually in love with him. Maybe for the first time ever. But...maybe it taught her a lesson, and when she recovers, she'll choose future boyfriends a little more wisely."

When Jonas made no reply, I glanced his direction. The muscles in his jaw were working; his expression was tense; his knuckles white where they gripped the steering wheel.

"What?" I asked. "What is it? What's wrong?"

"Cleo…Ellie didn't make it, either."

His voice was so quiet that I wasn't sure I heard him right, but his whispered, "I'm sorry," told me I had.

I blinked the sting from my eyes, but more tears blurred my vision, and more. I couldn't seem to stop them. I leaned my head back against the headrest and let them flow. Ellie was dead? My one-time friend and now nemesis was gone?

Jonas was trying to explain, "When Mark flung her away from him, her head *whacked*—really hard—against the wall. I saw it. She dropped like a sack of sand and there was blood everywhere. I don't know if it was losing all that blood or if she injured her brain with that hard hit, but the paramedics were never able to get a pulse." He reached over and squeezed my hand. "I'm sorry," he said again, and then was quiet, giving me time to grieve.

Why was I crying? Ellie had been nothing but a thorn in my side for years. I should feel relieved, but as hard as I tried at that moment, I couldn't remember any of the bad stuff, only the good…when she used to be my friend.

After a minute or two, I used my sleeve to dry my eyes, and sat up.

I quietly explained to Jonas all about Rose, and the flash of fiery red that I'd seen right when Lily had yelled out her sister's name, but I don't think he believed me. I don't know what kind of explanation he was telling himself about Spencer's men flying through the air, and crashing into the wall like they had, or how Mark's shooting arm had ended up dangling uselessly at his side, but I'd let him work it out.

I stared out the window, smiling sadly when Jonas

squeezed my hand. The scenery whizzing past the window didn't interest me. I had too much to think about.

To say that finding Lily had changed my life would be a major understatement. There wasn't a doubt in my mind that I'd still be the painfully introverted, terminally shy, and extremely lonely girl I'd been if it hadn't been for that fateful day in Forsyth Park. God had definitely been smiling on me, and I would never stop thanking Him. Lily had opened my eyes to the fact that I'd just been watching life go by. Somehow, she'd gently—or maybe not so gently—led me along, enabling me to jump on for the ride. Had it been all those quirky sayings? Her outlandish appearance? Her attempt to make ghosts happy with a bag full of glitter? Whatever it was, I knew I could never thank her enough, but I'd try.

****

I pushed open her hospital room door and stepped in, then smiled in relief.

Lily was awake. She was hooked to several beeping, whirring machines. I could see where her shoulder was bandaged, an unnatural lump under the pale blue hospital gown. She had a clear tube attached under her nose, piping in oxygen, I supposed. Another tube was taped to the back of her left hand; its other end led up to a hanging bag, which dripped in regular intervals. Her hair was a mess, and dark bruises marred her pale skin along the left side of her face where Mark had slapped her, but I'd never seen her look more beautiful.

And she wasn't alone.

A handsome, distinguished, silver-haired man

turned around as soon as we entered, smiling a welcome. He wore a doctor's white jacket and had a stethoscope hanging around his neck. The chair he sat in was pulled up close to the bed, and he was holding Lily's right hand.

Lily beamed when she saw us. "Cleo! Jonas! I'm so glad you're here. I'd like you to meet Michael."

****

We stepped out into the hallway and I breathed a sigh of relief. All seemed right with my world. Christmas was just a couple of days away and I'd been granted the best gift ever. I smiled up at Jonas, happier than I ever remember being. He squeezed my hand, sending me a warm smile in return.

"Jonas!" a voice called from behind us.

His eyes changed in an instant, from melted to frozen chocolate, tension radiated from him in waves. I heard him groan, "Oh, no," just before he turned toward the voice, his face painted with a thick layer of dread. Who in the world would cause *this* type of reaction? I turned around to see for myself.

The blonde woman beamed at us—correction…she was beaming at *Jonas*, not me—as she hurried down the hallway. She was one of those long-legged beauties men tended to go ga-ga over, not the gangly, coltish kind. No, no, she was runway model tall, regal, slim— well, except for some significant surgically enhanced curves that had me suddenly feeling very inadequate. I fought the urge to cross my arms over my chest, staring at the miles of suntanned perfection that made my hackles rise until I was sure I resembled a porcupine. Who was she?

The woman was breathless by the time she reached

us. A delicate wave of expensive perfume caught me in its wake. "Jonas! It's so good to see you again!"

"What are you doing here, Jill?" he asked in a dead-sounding voice.

Jill?

"I don't see you for three years and that's the response I get?" Her light laughter held a hint of reproach, then she glanced at me. "You must be Cleo."

Hold on! I blinked in surprise. She knew my name? How could she know my name, and I not know a thing about her? Who *was* this woman? I narrowed my eyes at Jonas. "Aren't you going to introduce us?" I asked him.

I watched the muscles work in his jaw before he spoke. "Cleo...meet Jill Parker. Jill...this is Cleo Davis."

So...this was Jill. I remembered the night at Moon River when I'd seen her name on his phone and my heart sank. The sophisticated, obviously professional woman standing in front of me made me feel like the gauche school girl that I was, and threatened to drag the old Cleo back from where I'd banished her. What was this woman doing here? Was she a doctor? Did she work here? Visiting someone? What?

Jill acknowledged the introduction with the briefest flicker of a smile in my general direction before turning her attention back to Jonas. Her laughter trilled. "Oh, Jonas, surely you can do better than that, darling." One of her finely plucked eyebrows rose, and she rested her well-manicured left hand on his arm in a very he's-mine-so-don't-get-any-ideas kind of way, giving it a gentle squeeze. "After all, I *am* your fiancée."

Time stopped. The earth tilted a little further on its

axis, before everything sort of...crashed. I caught a flash of a diamond ring on the hand clutching Jonas' arm, and a brief glimpse of his stricken expression, before I spun around and dashed toward the elevators. My eyes were so full of tears, I didn't know how I kept from bowling over the orderly pushing the meal cart, but somehow I managed to zigzag around him. As I skidded to a stop in front of the bank of elevators, I thought I heard Jonas shout my name, but by that time I was sobbing so hard that I might've imagined it. One set of doors were just sliding shut, and without knowing whether the elevator was going up or down, I slipped in.

The doors shut in Jonas' anguished face.

Chapter Twenty-Seven

Cleo

I looked at the grade on the evaluation sheet and tried to smile. Dr. Hudson had given me an "A," and even added "Exceptional work" in the comment section. Everybody knew he didn't hand out that sort of praise. I should be happy, but that emotion was something I hadn't felt in a while. Three months, ten days to be exact. I refused to look at my watch to figure the hours. I could probably even figure the minutes and seconds. Pitiful, I know.

In addition to the good grade, my paintings of Lily had been chosen, with two other students' work, for a celebrated "Faces of Savannah" exhibit in Morris Hall at school. As soon as I'd found out, I'd called Lily up in Mt. Pleasant where she lived now with Michael. They'd gotten married soon after she'd been released from the hospital and he'd moved her to his house there, where he could take care of her. Who better for the job? With him being a surgeon at St. Francis, she couldn't be in better hands.

Though I missed her terribly, I was so glad for her. If anybody deserved a fairytale ending, it was that amazing lady. What I still had a hard time believing was that her sister had made it all possible. If it hadn't been for Rose, those two love birds would've probably never found each other again. Even now, I couldn't believe how it had all worked out.

The morning after the show-down in the tunnel, when I'd gone into the bathroom to get dressed before rushing to the hospital, I'd been greeted with a mirror full of graffiti.

My first thought had been that Minnie had scrawled an angry message for me. Upon further examination, I realized it was a name and phone number, scrawled in lipstick—which is something I didn't wear and neither did Minnie. I'm strictly a gloss kind of girl.

But it was definitely lipstick, and it was red...*bright* red...the exact color of the flash I'd seen in the tunnel the night before when Lily had screamed her sister's name. In that moment I knew the message—big crimson letters scribbled across the mirror—was from Rose; a long-overdue attempt to undo a wrong.

Dr. Michael Weston, widower, followed by a phone number.

Michael? Could this possibly be the same Michael from Lily's past? There was only one way to find out. Without giving myself time to talk myself out of it, I had pressed the numbers and then, SEND; waited for someone to pick up on the other end.

"Hello?" It was only one word, but it seemed to exude strength and confidence.

"Dr. Weston? Dr. Michael Weston?"

"Speaking."

"My name is Cleo Davis. You don't know me, but I'm hoping you know a friend of mine...Lily. Lily Telfair-Gordon. Is this the right Michael?"

The long, crackly silence stretched for such a long

time that I glanced at the screen of my phone to make sure I hadn't lost the call.

"What's this all about, young lady?" he finally asked, his voice gruff, now

"I don't have time to go into everything, so listen fast and don't ask questions. Lily has been shot." I heard him gasp and hurried on. "She's okay, but she's at St. Joseph's here in Savannah. I'm on my way there now. I just thought you should know. Gotta run. Bye."

****

In retrospect, I felt sort of bad about dropping a bombshell like that, and then hanging up. He was pretty old, too. I could've given the poor man a heart attack. I found out later that he'd basically commandeered the St. Francis hospital helicopter in Charleston, ordering an emergency flight to Savannah. That's how he'd arrived before us.

Rose's penance for the terrible wrong she'd done to her sister all those years ago, had worked out beautifully, but she'd also done something to help *me* heal.

I hadn't known it, but Lily had asked her sister to locate Aunt Patricia and find out why she'd hated me so much. Believe it or not, Rose had been able to do just that. I now knew the whole story: my mother's willful defiance against her aunt, her eloping with her tutor, my father...the same man poor Aunt Patricia had fallen for; the betrayal she'd never gotten over.

When I'd arrived in Savannah, looking almost exactly like my mother, all of Aunt Patricia's bottled-up bitterness came boiling out. She'd transferred all those hurts and negative feelings to me, since my mother was no longer around for her to blame. I'd been the scapegoat; the one who had to pay for my mother's "sin." No, it wasn't fair—a lot of things in life aren't—but at least now, I understood.

It took me a while, but I'd finally managed to forgive Aunt Patricia. I mean, if Lily could forgive Rose for the awful things she'd done, then who was I not to forgive this? The relief that came with releasing that load made me as if someone had pumped me full of helium.

Something else I'd learned was that the building where Lily had lived in that tiny fifth-floor room with the red curtains, actually *belonged* to Lily. For years, she'd had her attorney handle renting out each floor, putting the money into a bank account for her. That money had grown to quite a sizeable sum after so many years. Of course, it had been a cruel twist of fate that Mark Spencer had used the basement of that house to operate his counterfeiting scheme. She was trying to atone for that now, though, by using some of the accrued monies to transform the entire house into a homeless shelter, much to her snooty neighbors' dismay. The identity she'd kept for all those years had given her a first-hand look at the plight of folks like her. She wanted to provide a warm meal and a safe, clean environment for those less fortunate, as well as offering training programs and job placements so they could stay off the streets. The shelter was named, "The Garden," after her and her sister…two flowers, Calla Lily and Rose.

Though I hadn't seen or talked to him since that terrible day at the hospital, I'd heard that Jonas' newspaper series was huge! The Tribune covered it for several days with photos and interviews galore. The

Associated Press even got hold of it. The buzz it created was so great, that when he queried the idea to a big New York publisher, they offered him a book deal with a healthy advance. I was sure the writing was keeping him busy, and I was happy for him in a bittersweet sort of way. He'd worked hard. He deserved it. I tried not to think about him too much. Maybe it wouldn't hurt too badly one day, but right now, the pain of loving and losing him was still raw.

****

I was sitting in one of the playground swings in Forsyth Park, watching Mr. Waltham walk his dogs. To anyone who frequented this park, he was a common sight, one that's not easily forgotten. A short, bald man trying to successfully manage the leashes of not one, not two, but *three* Great Danes, was a sight to behold.

"Has his hands full, doesn't he?"

My battered heart thudded to a stop, before surging into a break-neck gallop.

Jonas' low, sexy voice still made my heart misbehave. Little shivers went up my spine. *Run!* I told myself. *Make a break for it. Escape while you still can!* It was good advice…advice I should take, but I couldn't get my feet to move. My foolish heart was in command, overriding my brain, taking control. I knew myself well enough to know that I'd endure whatever torture was necessary, just to exist in his presence again for a short while. Besides, I knew I would have to face him eventually. It was inevitable. Savannah wasn't that big of a town. I took a deep breath, steeling myself before twisting the swing to face him. This was going to hurt me, and I knew it. I must be masochistic.

"Hello, Jonas."

He'd been running. He was breathing hard, and his t-shirt was damp with sweat, clinging to the rise and fall of his chest. His eyes hadn't changed. They were still melted chocolate, staring at me hungrily, making me quiver inside. He shouldn't be looking at me like that. He was engaged to someone else! He might even be married already.

He took a step toward me and paused, watching me carefully before taking another step. What was he doing? Gauging my reaction? Checking to make sure I wouldn't dart away like I was a wild pony that he didn't want to spook? Did I look that fragile? I hoped not.

After a few more cautious steps forward, he squatted in front of me so we were eye level. "You've been avoiding me, Cleo."

My heart flip-flopped. I loved the way he said my name. I had to swallow the lump that was lodged in my throat before I could reply. "So?"

He nodded once, accepting my answer as an admission that he'd been right. "I think we have some unresolved issues to discuss."

I snorted. "Is that what you're calling it? Unresolved issues? Not telling me that you were engaged? Letting me fall for—" I broke off, blinking back tears, then continued, "There's nothing more to say, Jonas." I stood quickly, hoping my quivering legs would hold me up. I needed to get out of here...to escape.

He jumped to his feet, reaching a hand to grab my shoulder. I caught my breath at the jolt of electricity that zinged through my body.

"Cleo...please, wait," he begged. His hand slid down my arm, and he twined his fingers through mine.

They still fit perfectly. "Walk with me?"

My resolve fell in crumbles at my feet. "Fine. Let's walk."

****

We strolled along the wide sidewalk under massive live-oak trees. Though only early March, the air was already getting sticky, hinting at the oppressive heat that summer would soon bring. Flowers were already blooming everywhere, perfuming the morning breeze. A variety of sounds filled the air: laughter, a child squealing, an occasional barking dog, warped, tinny music from an ice cream truck a couple of blocks away…all the familiar sounds of springtime. Sunlight spilled through the canopy of leaves overhead splatting blobs of warm yellow onto the sidewalk all around us.

Jonas cleared his throat. "I was engaged."

Pain stabbed through my heart like a knife. "I think we've already covered that base, Jonas."

"Was."

"I'm sorry, what?"

"I *was* engaged. Past tense. It ended a long time ago…three years, to be exact."

I couldn't help it. A tiny balloon of hope swelled…just a little. "But Jill said—"

"She lied," he raked an angry hand through his hair. "One of the plethora of her talents, I'm afraid."

"Did you just say, *plethora?*" I bit my lip, squelching a smile.

He nodded, his eyes sparkling. "Yep."

Now, my smile refused to be squelched. "Sounds like somebody's been spending too much time with a thesaurus."

He threw back his head and laughed, "Yeah, well,

it's not been by choice." Then he sobered. "Cleo, what did you start to say earlier?"

I knew exactly what he was talking about, but I wasn't ready to go there, yet. "Tell me what happened."

He sighed, but the look he gave me promised that this was just a delay, that we'd be returning to the subject later. "Okay…a little over three years ago, when Jill and I were on our way to our rehearsal dinner, we broke up."

I waited for him to continue, until I realized that he thought he was done. The key word being, "thought." "And…?" I prompted.

"And, *nothing*. End of story."

Yeah, right. Nice try, big boy! "Okay, let's put it this way. *Why* did you break up?"

Silence.

Had he heard me? I studied his expression, his furrowed brow, the set of his jaw. Oh, he'd heard me, all right, and he was thinking hard about something. Okay. I could wait.

After a while, I rethought that, "I could wait" policy. Jeez! Was he going to tell me, or not? What had happened? Was it bad? It *must* be, if it was taking him this long to tell me. How bad could it be? My mind started creating all sorts of imagined scenarios, each worse than the other, until he finally blurted, "Jill didn't really love me…not *me*. She was in love with my money."

What? I hadn't seen *that* coming, and it was so far removed from anything I'd been thinking, I almost laughed. Was he kidding? He didn't *have* any money! "Was she on drugs, or something? You work for the *Trib*, Jonas. How could she be in love with your money?"

"Maybe I should've said she was in love with the Holmes' money. *I'm* not rich, but my *family* is." He was watching me carefully while I processed this. It was a lot to take in, and I was still confused.

"So?"

"So, it's a lot of money."

"So?" I repeated with more force.

"So...I've never been able to have a relationship in which that didn't play a major role. Jill's betrayal was really a wakeup call. I knew the only way I could ever be sure that someone loved me and not the Holmes cash and clout, was to live like I didn't have it. So I left. I moved down here, got an apartment. Well, I call it an apartment...my mother calls it a slightly oversized dumpster. Anyway, it was a place to live. Then I found a job, not flipping hamburgers like my brothers thought. And by the way, I've got five of them."

"Jobs?"

He laughed. "No. Brothers. Peter, Phillip, Paul, Barnabas, and Andrew. Can you tell my Mom was hung up on Bible names during her childbearing years? Except for Sam. Sam broke the mold."

"Sam? Oh, right...your *sister.* You told me about her, just not the others. So, there are *seven* of you?" I was shocked, as well as slightly jealous. I'd always wanted a sibling.

"Yeah, that contributed to me leaving Charleston, too. I was tired of being a number. Anyway, I got my job at the Trib...a legitimate writing job. Sure, I wasn't making much, but it was enough to get by and I knew it wouldn't be that way forever. I had goals. I'd get my own column someday, and things would get better, but

I had to prove my worth to my boss, first. The homeless story was supposed to be that proof. Then I met you and everything changed."

The look he gave me nearly singed my eyebrows. My throat went dry and I couldn't say a word.

Our walk had made a big loop, dumping us back at the swings. He led me over to them and sat me down in one. Putting his hands to my back, he gave me a gentle push, swinging me forward. Two little girls, who were playing in the sand near us, pointed at me. I could hear them giggling. I shook my head and smiled. I might look like a kid, but each time Jonas' hands touched my back, giving me another push, it caused some very grown-up feelings...feelings which I hadn't been sure I'd ever experience again. My world felt right.

"Hey, Cleo!" he shouted, giving me a huge push, actually running under me and ending up in front.

"What?" I squealed, laughing.

"You know what I love?"

"No, Jonas. What do you love?"

"I love the fact that it doesn't seem to matter to you whether or not I have money."

I laughed, flinging my head back and swinging myself higher.

He stood there, wearing a huge grin, and the balloon of hope inside me swelled. I'd felt dead during our months apart, and now I was coming back to life. It couldn't get any better than this.

"Hey, Cleo!" he shouted again.

"What?" I giggled.

"You know what else I love?"

"What?"

"You!" he called out, his face suddenly serious.

The truth of the statement was there, shining for the world to see.

I gasped. He'd never said those words to me before. My legs dangled; I was too stunned to pump them back and forth, and the swing slowed while I stared at him in open-mouthed shock. I was wrong...it *could* get better!

Before I could say anything, though, he dropped to one knee in the sand and my heart nearly stopped beating.

"I was wondering..." he reached into his pocket and pulled out a small black box, opening it and holding it out with one hand. "...if you'd marry me, please?"

Extending my feet, I dragged them to an abrupt stop. I put my hand to my mouth, happy tears blurring my vision. I impatiently blinked them away, not wanting to miss anything. Then I jumped to my feet and stumbled over to him, dropping to my knees, flinging my arms around his neck, and nearly knocking us both over.

"Whoa, baby!" He wrapped his arms around me, holding me tightly. "Does this mean, yes?"

I leaned my head back so I could see his face. "Rich or poor, it doesn't matter. I love you, Jonas Holmes. Being your wife would make me the happiest girl in the world. Yes!"

His laugh sounded triumphant. "Well, I better get this ring on you then!"

He slipped it on my finger, kissing it into place. His hands went to either side of my face. "Thank you," he whispered fervently before giving me a tender kiss.

Yes...it could get much, much better!

****

Later...*a lot* later, I sat up and smoothed my hair back from my flushed cheeks. "Let's go tell Minnie. I know she'll be glad not to have me moping around the house anymore."

"Uh..." he made a face. "I think she might already know."

"What? How?" I demanded.

He looked sheepish. "Um...she's how I found you."

I cocked an eyebrow at him. "I think you better explain."

"Well, when I woke up this morning, I made the decision that we were going to talk this out, come hell or high water, so I drove to your house, sweet-talked my way inside, then explained everything to Minnie. She told me you were over here. I already had your ring, but it was back at my apartment. It used to be my grandmother's, and I've had it ever since Christmas...which, by the way, was when I'd originally planned to ask you to marry me."

My mouth dropped open. *Christmas! You mean I spent all this time sinking in a sea of despair, when—* He interrupted my thoughts with another kiss.

"I'm curious," I said as soon as I could think coherently. "How were *you* able to get your grandmother's ring? I mean, after all, there *are* seven of you. Why were you the lucky one?"

He grinned and whispered. "I was always Grammy's favorite." Then his grin faded. "And just so you know...this *wasn't* the ring I gave to Jill."

"Why? I mean, don't get me wrong. I'm glad, but why didn't you give it to her?"

"I'm not sure. It just never felt *right* for her to have it. I guess that should've been a clue for me, huh?"

"Does it feel right now?"

"No."

"What?"

He cupped his hand alongside my cheek and smiled. "It feels perfect."

****

"Anyway," he continued after several more otherwise occupied minutes. "I wanted to have your ring with me before I talked to you—just in case—so, I drove back to my apartment, grabbed the ring, and ran back here to the park." He wrinkled his nose, looking adorable. "I hope you don't mind that Minnie already knows. I haven't told my family, so we can tell them together. My mom's dying to meet you, by the way."

I tried to look stern, but I guess my giggle sort of gave me away. "Well, since you put it like that, I guess it's okay, especially since Minnie hasn't seen the ring, yet, but *I* want to be the one to tell Lily."

Minnie's Garlic Lime Chicken

Seasoning:
1 tsp. salt
¼ tsp pepper
¼ tsp cayenne pepper
¼ tsp paprika
1 tsp garlic powder
½ tsp onion powder
½ tsp thyme

Mix together and place in a gallon sized ziplock bag. Drop 4 boneless, skinless chicken breasts into bag, one at a time, and shake until coated.

In large skillet, combine:
2 T butter
2 T olive oil

Heat over med/high heat. Sauté chicken until golden brown (about 5 minutes on each side.)

Remove chicken. Add:
4 T lime juice
½ cup chicken broth

Whisk together, making sure to scrape browned bits off the bottom of the pan. Keep cooking until thickened slightly. Add chicken back to the pan and coat thoroughly before serving.

Minnie's Lasagna

1 lb. ground beef
¾ c. chopped onion
1 clove garlic, minced
1 can tomatoes
2 (6 oz.) cans of tomato paste
2 c. water
1 T chopped parsley
2 tsp salt
1 tsp sugar
½ tsp pepper
½ tsp oregano
8 oz. lasagna noodles
1 lb. ricotta or cottage cheese
8 oz. shredded Mozzarella cheese
1 c. grated Parmesan cheese

Brown ground beef, onion, and garlic. Drain.

Add tomatoes, paste, water, parsley, salt, sugar, pepper, and oregano; simmer uncovered, stirring occasionally about 30 minutes.

Cook lasagna noodles as per package instructions.

In greased 13x9 pan, spread 1 c. sauce, then alternate layers of noodles, sauce, ricotta, Mozzarella, and Parmesan. Bake at 350º for 40-50 minutes. Allow to stand 15 minutes before serving.

Minnie's Home-Made Granola Bars

4 c. dry quick oats
½ c. brown sugar
1 ½ c. chopped walnuts
1 tsp. salt
1 c. semi sweet chocolate chips
1 c. flaked coconut
1 ½ sticks melted butter
½ c. peanut butter
1 tsp. vanilla
½ c. honey

Combine first 6 ingredients in a bowl.

In separate bowl, combine next 4 ingredients. When smooth, stir into dry ingredients.

Press mixture into greased 10x15 baking dish.

Bake 10-15 minutes at 375° until golden.

When partially cooled, cut into bars.

Allow to cool completely before removing from pan.

Wrap individually in plastic wrap and store in airtight container in fridge.

A word about the author...

Leanna Sain earned her BA from the University of South Carolina and now lives in the mountains of western NC with her husband. Her first novel, *Gate to Nowhere*, won *Foreword Magazine*'s Book-of-the-Year award in fiction. The sequel, *Return to Nowhere*, was nominated for the Thomas Wolfe Memorial Literary Award. *Magnolia Blossoms*, the thrilling conclusion to this time-travel trilogy, was nominated for the Global Ebook Award. All three of the Gate Trilogy books won the Clark Cox Historical Fiction Award from the North Carolina Society of Historians. Sain's fourth novel, *Wish*, is a stand-alone, YA crossover that is a change from her usual Southern romantic suspense or "grit-lit," but fans will still get the strong, sometimes-snarky characters, gripping dialogue, and vivid descriptions that they've come to expect from her novels. Three additional GRITS novels are awaiting publication.

Sain has skillfully created her own character-supported, plot-driven style that successfully rolls Mary Kay Andrews, Nicholas Sparks, and Jan Karon all into one. Regional fiction lovers and readers who enjoy suspense with a magical twist will want these books.

She loves leading discussion groups and book clubs. For more information or to contact her, visit: www.LeannaSain.com